P9-COP-178

**Murder always comes with
strings attached. . . .**

Ariadne straightened, both relieved and dismayed. "I'm in here, Aunt Laura."

"What happened? Was it a robbery?" Laura Sheehan, eyes sharp, her trim athletic body tense, rushed toward Ariadne. "There's no sign of a break-in—oh." She looked down in disbelief at the body behind the counter. "Edith? Edith Perry?"

Ari leaned against the door frame. "Laura, what are you doing here?"

"I heard the call on my police radio. They didn't say anything about a body."

"And you decided to come here?"

"You might have been in danger. I did take that self-defense class. I must say, this is a bit of a sticky wicket, isn't it?"

Ari let out a breath. "You've been reading English mysteries again."

"This could be a good cozy mystery, though. *The Body in the Yarn Shop.*"

"Laura, please."

Laura's bemused expression faded. "I'm sorry." She stood beside her niece. "Poor Edith," she said, and then slung her arm around Ari's shoulders. "And poor you."

Ari closed her eyes, suddenly tired. "I know. Oh—the police." She crossed to the door as an officer rapped sharply against the glass, and opened it for him.

Much later, she would think that finding the body was the easy part. . . .

Also by Mary Kruger

KNIT FAST, DIE YOUNG

DIED IN THE WOOL

DIED IN THE WOOL

A Knitting Mystery

MARY KRUGER

Pocket Books
New York   Toronto   London   Sydney

If you purchased this book without a cover you should be aware that this book is stolen property. It was reported as "unsold and destroyed" to the publisher and neither the author nor the publisher has received any payment for this "stripped book."

 POCKET BOOKS, a division of Simon & Schuster Inc.
1230 Avenue of the Americas, New York, NY 10020

This book is a work of fiction. Names, characters, places and incidents are products of the author's imagination or are used fictitiously. Any resemblance to actual events or locales or persons, living or dead, is entirely coincidental.

Copyright © 2005 by Mary Kruger

All rights reserved, including the right to reproduce this book or portions thereof in any form whatsoever. For information address Pocket Books, 1230 Avenue of the Americas, New York, NY 10020

ISBN-13: 978-1-4165-4465-4
ISBN-10: 1-4165-4465-8

This Pocket Books paperback edition August 2007

10 9 8 7 6 5 4 3 2 1

POCKET and colophon are registered trademarks of Simon & Schuster Inc.

Cover illustration by Mary Ann Lasher

Manufactured in the United States of America

For information regarding special discounts for bulk purchases, please contact Simon & Schuster Special Sales at 1-800-456-6798 or business@simonandschuster.com.

In loving memory of my mother,
Madelyn Sweeney Kruger,
who always believed in me and who was always there.
You and me against the world, Mom. Forever.

CHAPTER 1

Later, Ariadne would be appalled that her first reaction at seeing Edith Perry's body sprawled on the floor of her shop, a tangle of yarn around her throat, was that Edith had finally chosen good yarn. She would be horrified that she had wished the yarn wasn't one of her favorites. It was shock, she knew: finding a dead body always had that effect.

After her initial reaction she stood, shocked in place, then kneeled beside the counter. "Omigod. Omigod," she gasped. A purple wool homespun yarn was tangled about Edith's neck and tied in back to two sticks in a crude, but effective, garrote. "Omigod, Edith, wake up." She took the woman's wrist in her hand, hoping, praying that she might be alive. There was no pulse. Instead, Edith's hand was limp and cool. "No, Edith, not in my shop," Ari said, hearing herself for the first time. *Dear God.* There was a dead body in her shop.

It couldn't be real. Until this moment her morning had been unremarkable. She'd yawned over the newspaper, tussled with her young daughter, Megan, about what to wear to school, and fielded a call from her friend Diane, who rose before the birds. Ari was a night person who moved in slow motion in the mornings. It was only as she took her usual brisk walk from home through the center of Freeport to her shop that she came fully awake. Only then did she become excited about the day ahead, her mind teeming with ideas for new sweaters, scarves, hats. Finding someone murdered in her shop changed all that.

She looked up. The shop itself seemed normal. The plate glass windows on the front and side of her building still filtered the bright September sun through the gray coating designed to keep the light from fading the yarn. The high shelves on the inside wall still held diamond-shaped bins filled with various yarns: Heilo yarn from Norway; Lopi, made from the wool of Icelandic sheep; fisherman yarn from Ireland. So did the low shelves under the side windows; so did the waist-high counter in the middle of the shop, with its colorful knitted goods displayed on top. Soothed as she always was by the sight of her yarns and the possibilities they presented, she looked back down. Edith's body was still there, between the counter and the wall, sprawled in the careless abandon of death.

Calm, Ari, she told herself as she rose. Odd how her mind seemed to have separated from the rest of her, viewing what was happening with detachment. Again she looked at her yarn, and suddenly stopped, counting. One ball of the purple yarn was missing. Only a small amount was twined around Edith's neck. The murderer had, at some point, taken one of the balls of yarn.

Ari stumbled as she crossed the room to the phone. She had to call 911. After she reported the murder and the police assured her they would arrive shortly, she sat at the old wooden desk in her office, elbows resting on the tidy surface, and put her fisted hands to her eyes, trying to control her shaking.

"Ariadne," a voice called from the shop's front door, sharp and concerned. "Ari! Where are you?"

Ariadne straightened, both relieved and dismayed, and rose to leave her sanctuary. "Here, Aunt Laura."

"What happened? Was it a robbery?" Laura Sheehan, eyes sharp, her trim, athletic body tense, rushed toward her. Her polo shirt wasn't quite tucked into her jeans, which was unusual for Laura. "There's no sign of a break-in—oh." She looked down in disbelief at the body behind the counter. "Edith? Edith Perry?"

Ari leaned her head against the door frame. "Laura, what are you doing here?"

"I heard the call on my police radio. They didn't say anything about a body."

"And you decided to come here?"

"You might have been in danger."

"For God's sake."

"I did take that self-defense class. I must say, this is a bit of a sticky wicket, isn't it?"

Ari let out a breath. "You've been reading English mysteries again."

"No, Ed McBain. This could be a good cozy mystery, though. *The Body in the Yarn Shop.*" She shook her head. "No. Not a good title."

"Laura, please."

Laura's bemused expression faded. "I'm sorry." She stood beside her niece. "Poor Edith," she said, and then slung her arm around Ari's shoulders. "And poor you."

Ari closed her eyes, suddenly tired. "I know. Oh—the police." She crossed to the door as an officer rapped sharply against the glass, and opened it for him.

Much later, she would think that finding the body was the easy part.

✂

Joshua Pierce, only recently hired as detective on Freeport's small police force, stared down at the body in the shop. *Well.* This was different. In Boston he'd handled drive-by shootings and the occasional domestic murder, but never anything like this. He knew where to start, he thought, glancing over at the shop's owner, who was perched on a high stool behind a counter for the cash register. Mrs. Evans was going to come in for some close questioning.

Hands tucked into the pockets of his chinos, he studied the body impassively. It wasn't that the sight of death didn't bother him; it did. He'd learned long ago to tuck his emotions away. He felt nothing but professional interest now as he went about his work. The victim had been a woman somewhere in her sixties, or perhaps early seventies. It was hard to tell because in spite of her short white hair, her face was relatively unlined and her body was compact and firm. Being new to Freeport, he knew nothing about her, but that was an advantage. He'd come to the investigation without any preconceptions.

Around him, the crime scene investigators were at work. The medical examiner had come and gone, the district attorney was near the door with the chief of police, and the crime scene technicians were at work, dusting for fingerprints and packing up the remainder of the yarn used for the murder in paper evidence bags. Other technicians were vacuuming the floor for fibers and other evidence. The police photographer had taken many pictures, and Josh himself had drawn a careful sketch of the scene. This part of his investigation was done. It was time to move on to the next phase.

"Mrs. Evans?" He held out his hand. "Joshua Pierce."

"I didn't kill her," she said swiftly.

"I didn't say you did, ma'am." Interesting that she'd say that right away, he thought. "Is there somewhere we can talk?"

She stared at him for a moment, then climbed down from the stool. "The back room's the best place," she said, leading him through a doorway at the back of the retail area and into a long, narrow room with a bolted door in the far wall. The back entrance, he assumed, making a careful note of it. They still didn't know how the victim, or the murderer, had gotten into the shop.

"Would you like coffee?" Mrs. Evans went on,

crossing to a counter against the wall. "I just made it. I was thinking of sending out for doughnuts—oh." She scrunched her eyes shut. "Tell me I didn't say that."

"A cop's usual snack?" He smiled slightly. "No, don't bother on my account. Coffee's fine."

She nodded and poured coffee into two mugs, giving him a chance to study her. In spite of what had had happened, she looked cool and neat, in tan linen pants and a crisp white blouse. Her hair, a light blondish brown, was long and held back from her face with clips. Only her eyes betrayed her agitation, he thought as she brought the cups over to the old green Formica-topped table. Rather nice hazel eyes, he noted.

"Now, Mrs. Evans," he began.

"Ms."

He looked up from his notebook. "Ms.? Okay."

"I'm divorced," she added defiantly.

He flipped his pen back and forth between his index and middle fingers. "Then Evans is your maiden name?"

"No. Jorgensen. Ariadne Jorgensen. A mouthful, isn't it?"

He frowned. "I thought Arachne was the goddess of spinning."

She blinked. "Well, yes, but my father vetoed that name, thank God. Ariadne was a compromise. She's the one who spun a thread to lead Theseus out of the labyrinth, in Greek mythology. It sort of fits for the shop."

"Mmm-hmm." He glanced down at his notebook,

though he didn't need to refresh his memory. "Could you tell me how you found the body?"

"I already answered that."

"I'd like to go over it again."

She looked at him warily. "All right. I looked on the floor, and there she was."

"Just like that?"

"Well, no. She looked the same as she does now, except that I felt for a pulse. I realize I tampered with a crime scene."

"Mrs. Evans—"

"Ms."

"Ms. Evans, did you want to see if she was still alive?"

She thought about that for a moment. "No, I think I knew she was dead right away. But I still wanted to see if I could help her. Even if I didn't like her."

He gave her a long look. "Why not?"

She bit her lip. "It wasn't personal. No one liked her very much. It's not that she's a terrible person—was a terrible person. Like doing mean things to people, the way victims on TV mysteries do."

"Real crimes aren't usually like TV crimes."

"No." Ms. Evans glanced away, into her shop. "The only person I know for certain she had problems with was her son. They fought about something, so she cut him out of her will. Other than that, I don't think she ever did anything terrible. She just liked getting her own way."

He leaned back in his chair. "You don't know what they fought about?"

"No one does. So far as I know, she hasn't talked to him since. He lives in Amherst and doesn't have a key to this place. How could he have done it?"

"Why didn't you like her?"

Ms. Evans took a deep breath. "No real reason. She just wasn't a very pleasant person. She never smiled and didn't talk much, and, oh, she was always trying to get things cheap."

That made him look up. "Such as your stock?"

She nodded. "And my designs. Of course, she never did. If she'd been nicer I might have given her a discount now and then, but she was usually rude about it."

"And that bothered you?"

"Of course it did, but not enough for me to kill her."

He nodded. "Tell me how you found her," he said again.

"Well." Her hands rubbed together. "I came in early to do paperwork. I wish I had some knitting," she added.

It was his turn to be surprised. "Why?"

"Because when I get nervous it soothes me."

Nervousness could be a sign of innocence, he thought, especially in a case like this. It could also be a sign of an amateur's guilt. Whoever had killed Edith had to have known her well. Strangling, especially in such a way, was an intimate crime. "Can't help you there. Go on."

"Well. It was—is—a beautiful morning. Most mornings I walk."

"Where do you live?"

"Walnut Street. A few blocks away." She gestured vaguely. "I was thinking how much I like this time of year."

"All right. I'll ask," he said when she paused. "Because of the weather?"

"Oh, no. Well, yes, I do like the colors. A little like you."

"What?" he said, startled.

"N-nothing." She looked hastily away. "This time of year—yes, I like the colors, and the air, and—I'm babbling." She took another deep breath and then went on, more composed. "This time of year, people start to think of making sweaters, so they come in."

"Good for business, then."

"Yes. In the summer, people want cottons or light yarns, but most crafters switch to cross-stitch or something cooler. In a couple of months, people will want supplies for afghans, and when we get the January freeze, we'll do a good business in wool hats and mittens. Well. You don't care about that." She took a sip of her coffee. "I have paperwork to do. Bills to pay, stock to order, things like that. Do you know what I mean?"

Josh only nodded, and so she went on. "I love early mornings here, when I'm alone and I know I won't be interrupted. I like to switch on the lights and just look at everything." She smiled. "Ted—my ex—complained when I put in the Ott lights—"

"The what?"

"Oh, of course you wouldn't know. Full-spectrum

lamps, like daylight. They're expensive, but they're worth it for matching colors and shades. I just like to look at my yarns. All the skeins and twists and colors, and all the patterns and notions and needles. I love everything in my shop. There's just so much possibility here."

"So that's what you did this morning?"

Her enthusiasm faded. "Not at first. I was really thinking about everything I have to do today when I went around the counter and found Edith."

"So you were alone?" he said.

"Yes. We don't open until ten."

"But you came in early."

"Yes." Her hands rubbed together again. "I do, sometimes."

"What time did you leave last night?"

"I'm not open on Mondays." She paused. "When did she die?"

"We don't know yet," he said, though the medical examiner had given him a rough idea. Early morning, he'd said, somewhere between five and eight. Ms. Evans was definitely in contention as the culprit. "When were you in the shop last?"

"Saturday. I close at two. I stayed until around two-thirty to count the day's receipts, clean up a little."

"What kind?"

"Dusting and vacuuming."

So any fingerprints and trace evidence would be new, he thought, and more likely to belong to the murderer. That was a break. "What about your employees?"

"Yes, one was supposed to come in at ten."

"And she is?"

"Summer Foley. She's worked here since I opened."

"Does she have a key?"

"Yes. Oh, but she couldn't have had anything to do with this."

"How well did she know Mrs. Perry?"

Ms. Evans looked surprised. "Summer? I don't know. She's only a college student, Detective. She works part-time around her class schedule."

That didn't necessarily mean anything, but the age difference made it unlikely that the Foley girl had known the victim well. "Any idea where she might have been?"

"With her boyfriend, I imagine. They live together."

"What about any other employees?"

"There's one other girl, Kaitlyn Silveira. She used to be a student at RISD, so I hired her only for Saturdays."

"The Rhode Island School of Design? Why isn't she there anymore?"

"Money problems. She transferred to UMass Dartmouth," she added.

"RISD is an expensive school."

"Yes. It's where I went. I wanted to—never mind."

He sat back. "What?"

"It doesn't matter, does it?"

"At this point, anything could."

"That I wanted to be a designer in New York? How could that help?"

"I don't know yet."

She frowned at him. "How can you be so calm?"

"What do you mean?"

"Calm, cool, expressionless. How am I supposed to know what you're thinking?"

He smiled. "You're not. So you only have two employees?"

"Well, there's my aunt Laura, but she doesn't count."

He consulted his notebook. "Laura Sheehan? She was here with you this morning, wasn't she?"

"Yes."

"Why doesn't she count?"

"Because she wouldn't do anything to hurt me."

He gave her that level look again. "Does she have a key?"

"Laura? No. I know better than that."

"Why?"

"Because then she'd be here at all hours."

It was his turn to sigh. "I think you'd better explain."

"Didn't I? Oh, no, I didn't. Laura loves yarn, you see. The shop is like a plaything to her."

"I see. Who else has a key?" he asked,

"Only my mother. Detective Pierce, neither of them could have killed Edith Perry. I'd swear to that," she said, and as she did so apparently realized the implications of all that she'd said. "Omigod. I'm a suspect, aren't I?"

"It's early for that."

"Is it?" Something in her face changed. "I don't think I want to answer any more questions," she said, rising.

He stayed seated. "If you haven't done anything, you don't have anything to fear."

"You know better than that," she chided him, and rose. "I'm calling my ex-husband."

"Why?"

"He's an attorney."

Josh looked at her and got up at last. "All right," he said finally, and shut his notebook. "This should be enough to start with. I'll want to talk with you again."

She nodded. "With Ted along," she said, her fingers gripping the edge of the table.

Count on it, Josh thought as he left the back room. Whether she had her lawyer with her or not, Ms. Evans had some questions to answer. At the moment she was his prime, and only, suspect.

✂

"Yes, I know this is a crime scene," an irritated voice said from outside sometime later. "I'm Mrs. Evans's attorney."

Ari rolled her eyes and got up from the office chair, where she'd been slumped for nearly an hour. *Mrs. Evans, just as though they were still married,* she thought. "Ted," she said from the office doorway.

Her ex-husband stood just outside the door of the shop, glaring pugnaciously at the policeman who was guarding it. "Ari, what the hell have you gotten yourself into now?"

"He's my lawyer," she said quietly to Detective Pierce, who was looking at Ted with the same level look he'd used on her.

Ted and this detective were so different, she thought. It wasn't just that Ted was short, in comparison to the taller and rangier detective. It wasn't anything about his appearance, though his suit, made by an Italian designer, was a contrast to Detective Pierce's off-the-rack tweed sport coat. The real difference was attitude: It was Ted's belligerence, stemming from his lack of stature, among other things, that stood out against Detective Pierce's laid-back watchfulness. Yet right now Ted was the person she wanted on her side.

"Ariadne," Ted said as he strode past the policeman to her. "Are you all right?"

"Of course I am." She stepped out of the office, making a wide circle past the point where Edith's body, now removed from the shop, had lain. The surfaces of the counter were coated with the dreaded black fingerprint powder. "I'm glad you're here."

Ted looked past her, and she realized he was frowning at Josh. "Is she free to go?" he demanded.

"Yes." By contrast, Detective Pierce's voice was calm. "We're not holding her."

"Did you read her her rights?"

"No. She's not under arrest."

Ted glared at him, so obviously ready to erupt that Ari stepped in. "Please let me know when you're done here," she said.

Detective Pierce nodded. "You'll be hearing from us, Ms. Evans."

"You'll be hearing from me," Ted retorted.

"Sure. Ms. Evans, I'll need your key."

Ari stared at him in blank dismay as she took her

key ring out of her pocketbook. "My house key's on it," she said, "and my Shaw's discount card."

"For God's sake, Ariadne, you won't be going to the supermarket today," Ted said impatiently.

"They have a special on chicken—no, I won't be, will I?"

"Damn straight. Just give him the key to the shop." He turned to the detective. "Can we go?"

"Sure," Detective Pierce said again. "Just stay somewhere where we can reach you, Ms. Evans."

"You have my cell phone number," she said, as Ted pulled her toward the door. "Be careful with my yarn!"

"Your yarn," Ted grumbled, and pushed his way out of the shop, leaving Ari to trail behind him, and abandoning her to the questions of curious bystanders and reporters alike. Without looking at her, he strode toward the parking lot across the street and wrenched open the door of his BMW, all the time muttering to himself. Ari knew better than to ask him what he was saying.

He had not, of course, been thoughtful enough to hold the passenger door open for her. Ari glanced at him as she climbed in, feeling her own temper rising. It had been a trying day, to put it mildly. "Would you drive by Marty's first?" she asked, naming a local convenience store, as he roared out of the lot.

"Why?"

"I need some chocolate."

"Chocolate!" he exploded. "You're suspected of murder and you want candy?"

"Why not?" she shot back. "It's better than drinking."

That stopped him, as she'd known it would. Only for a moment, though. "What the *hell* have you gotten yourself into this time, Ariadne?"

"I didn't get myself into anything," she retorted. "I walked in and there she was."

"Do you realize you're the prime suspect right now?"

"I'm not stupid, Ted."

"What did you say to him before you called me?"

"I'll have to think about it to remember. Ted, it's been an awful morning."

"It'll get worse if you get arrested."

"Well, I don't think I said anything damaging." She paused. "I told him a lot of people didn't like her."

"Oh, great. Like you?"

"Well, yes."

"Damn it, Ariadne!" He slammed his hand on the steering wheel. "Don't you realize what you admitted?"

"He doesn't know Edith was going to buy my building," she shot back.

"He will soon."

"He'll find things out about Herb Perry and Eric, too."

"They don't have keys to the store."

"They could have got in some other way."

"How? And why?"

"I don't know!"

"You've got a hell of a motive, Ari."

"That Edith was going to raise my rent? Really, Ted."

"It'll interest them. So will the Drift Road development," he went on. "But I forgot. That's not something you'd want to think about, not with what it means for your friend."

"Other people are affected by that, too."

"No one else you care about."

"Diane doesn't have a key."

"If it's not you, it has to be someone." He jolted to a stop in the small parking lot in front of the store. "Don't take long."

Without a word, Ari climbed out and disappeared into the store. A few minutes later she emerged carrying a large bag of M&M's. She didn't get back in the car right away, though, not with Ted in his current mood. For a moment she looked diagonally across the small nearby bridge that spanned the inlet from the bay. Everything appeared so normal, it was almost unreal. Already it looked like fall. The leaves of the maple trees that shaded the street were just a little crisp around the edges, and the sky was the electric blue peculiar to September. Too warm to be sweater weather yet, she thought, and shivered. After what had happened today, she wondered if it would ever be sweater weather again at Ariadne's Web.

That afternoon, Diane Camacho looked around in blank horror at the disaster that once had been Ariadne's Web. "My God, you should call the EPA to clean this place up."

"I know." Ari smiled wearily at Diane, who had been her friend since high school. "I'd read that fingerprint powder was hard to get off, but I never knew how hard." She brushed a strand of hair off her face. "It clings to everything. I don't know how I'll get the shop clean."

"We'll work together. You've got some on your face."

She grimaced. "Do I? Damn."

Diane frowned, her hands on her hips. "All your beautiful yarn, Ari. Will insurance cover it?"

"The police were good about that. They put on rubber gloves and put it all in paper bags before they started fingerprinting." *Almost all,* she amended to herself. It was going to be hard to tell Diane that one bin, particularly one section of the yarn, had received special treatment.

"We'll need some big aprons before we get started. Does anyone sell them anymore?"

"Laura told me she had some smocks."

"They should do." She frowned. "All this because of Edith Perry. Why her?"

Ari picked up a damp cloth and ran it across a countertop. "I don't know. A lot of people didn't like her."

"That's the trouble. She sure spread it around equally, didn't she? Ari?"

Ari turned. "What?"

"Have you thought that maybe you're the real target?"

"What? Why?"

"Because of where she was killed. Maybe someone wants to frame you."

"Oh, get real. No one hates me that much. Not even Ted."

"Ted likes you too much."

"He's crazy, Di, but not like this." Now she frowned. "Of course, I've wondered why it happened here."

"You've got to admit there are a lot of weapons in a knitting shop."

Ari stiffened. The cause of death was common knowledge. What wasn't, was which yarn had been used, or exactly how. "Such as?"

Diane grinned, the unholy smile that Ari had learned long ago meant trouble. "The killer had to be pretty sharp."

"What?"

"It's the best place to needle someone."

"That's not funny, Di."

Her grin broadened, in spite of, or maybe because of, Ari's reaction. "Yeah, but you got the point."

"Di—"

"I hope the police do, or they'll get all tangled up."

"You and I both are tangled up," Ari snapped.

Diane had been looking around as if in search of another source of puns, but at that she looked at Ari. "What do you mean? I had nothing to do with it."

"I'm afraid you did." Ari took a deep breath. "She was strangled with your yarn."

CHAPTER 2

Diane stared at her blankly. "Which color?"

"The purple heather."

"Damn, that was my favorite." She began to pace. "Joe is going to freak when he hears about this. He doesn't like me keeping sheep as it is."

"I know, but they make a nice sideline for your farm."

"Yeah, but tell Joe that. He thinks they take up too much land, and that I should spend more time at bookkeeping and stuff instead of spinning wool."

"And carding it, and then using natural dyes—what are we doing?" Ari's eyes met Diane's. "A woman is dead and we're talking about yarn."

"So? What was your first reaction?"

"Never mind that," Ari said crisply. "We should be thinking of Edith and her family."

"I know," Diane said after a minute. "My God. *My* yarn." She went white, the horror of the situation striking her for the first time. "Where did you find her?"

"Near one of the counters." Ari deliberately didn't meet Diane's eyes. The police wanted certain facts held back that only they and the murderer—and Ari—knew. The location of the body was one. Precisely how she had died was another. People somehow had learned about the yarn, but no one knew about the garrote. The thought of that still made Ari sick.

"I wonder how the yarn got around her neck. I don't see Edith standing still while someone strangled her."

"Diane, I don't know," Ari said, suddenly annoyed with her friend. "I don't seem to know anything at the moment."

"I'm sorry." Diane laid a hand on her arm. "I didn't mean to give you a hard time, but it's my yarn."

Ari nodded. "Di?" she said after a moment.

"What?"

"You realize what the police will think once they find out, don't you?"

"I'll be a suspect. You, too. You had a reason."

"I wouldn't kill for it, though."

"Well, neither would I, but it could look like it." Diane suddenly grinned. "It won't be the first time we've been in trouble."

Ari closed her mouth against hysterical, inappropriate laughter. "It's not funny, Di."

"No." Diane's smile faded. "It isn't, is it?"

"No." The two friends looked at each other, serious now. "You'd better get a lawyer."

"Yeah. You should, too."

"I have."

Diane eyed her with dismay. "Not Ted."

"Yes, for now."

"Ari, he's a tax lawyer!"

"Who knows better how to avoid jail?"

"It's not a joke."

"If anything happens, he'll find me someone else." She gazed around the shop, grimy with fingerprint powder, colorless without yarn filling the bins. "I don't know what will happen here. If people think I killed Edith, I'm sunk."

"That won't happen. Listen. Let's start cleaning, and we'll both feel better. Do you have anything we can use?"

Ari nodded and moved toward the back room, where she had left some cleaning supplies. Even the cash register had been dusted for fingerprints, she noticed as she passed it. Did the police think the killer had rung up a sale while she was there?

She frowned at that. Funny, how she automatically assumed that the killer was female. Or, maybe not. There were certainly men who did needlework, but the vast majority of her customers were women. It was hard to imagine anyone she knew doing such a thing, and yet likely that was the answer. Why else had her shop been chosen?

She and Diane were about to get started when a sharp rap on the door made both her and Diane jump. For a moment they stared at each other, and then Ari strode across to the door. This was her shop. She wasn't going to cower inside it. Still, she peered around the old-fashioned shade she'd pulled over the plate glass window of the door. She was besieged by both the curious and the press—print and electronic. Reporters from the New Bedford *Standard-Times* and the Providence *Journal* vied for the story, along with those from the two Boston papers. Huge broadcasting trucks from all the local stations jockeyed for space on the narrow streets, while reporters stood at the bandstand on the town green near the harbor and beamed their stories back to their stations. Ari wasn't up for more of their attempts at an interview, though she knew she'd inevitably have to give one.

"It's Kaitlyn," she said in surprise, and opened the door. "Kait, why aren't you in school—oh! Susan. You and Kaitlyn look too much alike," she said, stepping back to let Kaitlyn's mother come in.

Susan Silveira ignored the implied compliment. "Kaitlyn's in school. The police fingerprinted her," she said indignantly. "Ari, what's going on?"

"They fingerprinted me, too, and Laura."

"Why?" Susan's aggressiveness lessened.

"To rule out anyone who has a legitimate reason to be here. Detective Pierce explained it to me."

A deep frown furrowing her face, Susan looked around the shop and ran a hand over her short, expertly highlighted hair. "What a hell of a thing, Ari."

Ari looked around, too, more helplessly. There was so much to do to get things back into shape. "I know."

"Is Kaitlyn in danger?"

Ari blinked. "I don't know why she would be."

"Edith was killed here in your shop."

"Kaitlyn was home at the time, wasn't she? So was I, and Summer was with her boyfriend. Why would someone want to kill us, anyway?"

"I don't want to take any chances."

"Of course not."

"I'm surprised you weren't here earlier, if that's the case," Diane put in.

"I had a tee time in Marion this morning."

"You couldn't miss it?"

"My friend Beth invited me. Kittansett's an exclusive course. It's impossible to get a membership there. I only played nine holes," she added, sounding defensive.

Ari nodded as if she knew what Susan was talking about. As a real estate agent, Susan had to socialize to do her job. Golf, however, seemed supremely unimportant compared to what had happened this morning. "I have my work cut out for me here," she said, with a sweep of the hand indicating the chaos in the shop.

"Did the police confiscate your yarn?" Susan asked.

"No. They bagged it and took it away, but I'll be getting it back."

"I'll help you clean up."

"Why, thank you, Susan. That's generous of you."

"We could use the help," Diane said. "Here's an extra smock."

Susan looked with distaste at the loose, colorful garment, and then pulled it on over her immaculate polo shirt and golf shorts. "Thank you."

"Let's get moving, then," Diane said. "If you don't open for business, you'll be in real trouble."

"I know." Suspect or not, betrayed by someone she knew or not, Ari did have more immediate concerns. "Let's get to it."

"By the way, Kaitlyn said she's been working on your web page," Susan said as she took the sponge Ari handed her. "She said you'll be able to sell your designs online soon. I don't understand it myself."

"I do, but . . ." In Ari's mind she saw her shop restocked, with colorful yarn and samples. Selling over the Internet would help, but it wouldn't be enough. "Thank her for me. And thank you for coming today."

Susan glanced around again. "It's the least I can do, since you've been so good to Kaitlyn. If Ariadne's Web goes under, Kaitlyn will lose her job."

Diane gave her a look. "She won't. Right, Ari?"

"No, of course not," Ari said. "We'll get things straightened out. Hopefully I can reopen tomorrow."

"Bet on it," Diane said. "Now, let's get going."

Josh walked out of the chief's office, pulling on his tie to loosen it, and at the same time blowing out a silent whistle. The meetings with the chief, and with the district attorney, had been intense. "Well?" Paul Bouchard, his sometime partner, said.

"They want to bring Ms. Evans in." Josh sprawled in the ancient swivel chair behind his metal desk. "As a material witness, anyway."

"You gotta admit, Josh, she looks good for it. No one else could get into the shop."

Josh shrugged. The fingerprint evidence was inconclusive, since Ari had cleaned her shop before she closed it Saturday afternoon. What prints there were either belonged to Ari, her aunt Laura, her employees, Kaitlyn and Summer, or they were smudged. Nor was there any good fiber evidence—mainly because of all the yarn fibers collected. That didn't mean, though, that someone else hadn't been there.

Once again, he looked at the preliminary autopsy report. Edith Perry had indeed died of strangulation, but the surprise was that she had been hit on the head first, probably by something long and round in shape. No wonder the perp had been able to kill Edith in such a close-up, intimate way. By all accounts, Edith, though nearing seventy, had been feisty. She would have fought her attacker, whoever it was.

The report on the weapon disclosed that the yarn, one of the strangest murder weapons Josh had ever seen, had been hand-spun and -dyed. The other part of the weapon, the two pieces of wood, were at the state police lab in Framingham being analyzed. They were unfamiliar to Josh: narrow and thin, rough on one side and painted white on the other, with one long edge having a tongue designed to fit into some groove.

"What's a window stop?" Josh asked, looking up from the report.

"What?" Paul said.

"A window stop."

"Never heard of it. Why?"

"The report says it was used to make the garrote."

Paul frowned. "Oh, yeah, I know what that is. It's used to cover the space in a sash window."

Josh must have looked confused, because Paul went on. "You know, the old windows that work with pulleys and rope and sash weights. The window stop—never knew it was called that—covers the space where the rope is."

"Where would someone find one of those?"

Paul grinned. "Are you kidding? Have you noticed how many old houses there are around here?"

Josh flipped a pencil back and forth between his index and middle fingers. "So it could have come from anywhere?"

"Yeah, even Perry's house." Paul looked across at him. "Ari's house is old, too."

"How old?"

"Don't know. Over a hundred years, anyway."

So she'd had access to a weapon, Josh thought, returning his attention to the autopsy report and the time of death. The best estimate the medical examiner could give was between five and eight in the morning, a good span of time. Josh leaned toward the earlier time. Edith's stomach had been nearly empty, indicating that she hadn't eaten in some time. She certainly hadn't had breakfast before going out to meet her attacker, in one of the most unlikely places Josh could imagine.

"I don't think Ms. Evans has told us all she knows about who had access to the shop," he said.

Paul looked up. "Then get her in for more questioning."

"Yeah." Josh stared into space. He didn't know why he was so reluctant to suspect Ariadne. God knew he'd seen his share of homicides when he'd worked in Boston. God knew she was, as Paul said, the best suspect, and that the obvious answer was usually the right one. For some reason, though, he doubted that Ariadne had done it. It seemed too pat. "I don't know," he said slowly. "Seems to me she cares too much about that shop to hurt it."

"Hurt it?" Paul stared at him. "What the hell does that mean?"

"I can't see her ruining her business. She talks about yarn as if it's alive," he said mildly. If the facts warranted it, he'd be the first to pull Ariadne in. *If.* "Is she as ditzy as she seems?"

Paul shrugged. "Not according to what I've heard so far. From all accounts she's made a go of that store."

"So why would she jeopardize it? No. I don't see it yet." Evidence aside, there was such a thing as a person fitting the crime. "I can see her killing Perry— maybe—but not there. There's something behind this we don't know yet."

"Such as?"

"I don't know. It was a private kill. Our perp *chose* Perry."

"You ever had one of those in Boston?" Paul asked curiously.

"Once or twice, but not like this. Listen. You've lived here a long time. What do you know about Perry?"

"Not that much, really," Paul said after a moment.

Josh grunted in surprise. In the past, he'd found that Paul's knowledge of the town was encyclopedic. He needed that information now. "Any family?"

"Husband and son. Anyone else—let me see what I can find out." He spun in his chair, then punched in some numbers on his desk phone. "Yeah, hi—yes," he said, a pained expression crossing his face. "No, Ma, I'm fine. Yeah, I know everyone was sick at the party, but . . . No, Jennifer's fine, too. Listen, Ma, this is business." He made a desperate face at Josh, who made no attempt to hide his grin. "About Edith Perry . . . yeah, it's awful, yeah, but look, Ma." This time he closed his eyes and held the receiver away from his ear, letting out a rush of tinny monologue. "Listen, if I could talk a minute. Thanks. Who were Edith's friends?"

The pause was considerably briefer this time. "Yeah, I remember now. Anyone who didn't like her? No, forget that one. . . . Well, I have to ask, Ma. It's my job. What's that?" Paul suddenly looked intent. "No, I didn't know that," he said finally, glancing over at Josh. "No. When did this happen? . . . Mmm. Yeah, that helps a lot. Thanks. What?" He swiveled his chair away from Josh. "Yeah, Jennifer and I are still coming for supper tomorrow. Yeah . . . Uh, Ma? I'm supposed to be working. Okay, yeah, see you then. . . . You, too."

With that he cradled the receiver with a softness far more eloquent than banging it down would have been. "One of your informants?" Josh said, still grinning.

"She knows everyone in town," Paul said defensively, color slashing across his cheekbones. "I figured if anyone knew about Edith, she would. God, that woman can talk."

"Except when you asked about Perry's friends."

"You noticed that? Yeah, just as I said." He stretched out, arms crossed on his chest, legs crossed at his ankles. "She was friendly with Helen Sullivan, but Helen moved to Chicago a few years ago to live with her daughter."

"So she'd have nothing to do with it. Okay. Enemies?"

"No more than anyone else. At least, almost anyone else," Paul amended.

"Meaning?"

"Meaning that all of us have people who don't like us. But, look." He leaned forward. "Usually it's personal, right?"

"So?"

"From what I gather, Perry never got close enough to anyone to have that kind of enemy."

"So who didn't like her?"

Paul shrugged again. "Well, the thing is, she was active in town affairs."

"In what way?"

"You're from Rehoboth," he said, naming a town northwest of Freeport. "You know what small towns are like. There's always someone who's into everything. Town meetings, of course, and finance committee meetings, not to mention selectmen's meetings. Here." He swiveled in his chair and picked up a thin newspaper. "Last week's *Courier*. Bet you anything she's in there somewhere."

Josh laid the paper aside for the moment. "I understand she was outspoken."

"Putting it mildly. Any time the town wanted to spend her money—"

"Her money?"

"Taxpayers' money. She led the opposition. She voted against everything, practically. School expansions, a new library building, that kind of thing."

"So a lot of people had reason to dislike her in general?"

"Yeah, but a lot admired her, too." He grew serious. "The thing is, it's changing around here. Freeport's becoming a bedroom community for Boston."

"Like Rehoboth."

"Yeah, and it'll get worse if New Bedford ever gets commuter rail from Boston. That means new people moving in, building houses, having kids. They want all the services they're used to. But people like Perry, and others who own a lot of land—"

"Did she own land?" Josh interrupted.

"The old Robeson farm out on Drift Road, and some two- and three-family houses. She didn't want her property taxes raised."

"Land rich, cash poor," Josh mused.

"Not so's I've heard. Yeah, I know how she looked when we found her. Old slacks, old blouse, old sweater. I'd think those houses she owns—"

"With her husband?"

"Yeah, I guess. She and her first one started buying up property. It's all got to be worth a lot. That land on Drift Road will be worth a fortune if it's developed."

Josh frowned. Money was so often at the root of crime. "Was Perry going to develop it?"

"Yeah, I heard she filed a plan. Yeah, but listen. Want to hear the best?"

"What?"

"Edith was going to buy Ari's building."

"What?"

"Yeah. She'd put in an offer for it and it was accepted. Word is, she was going to raise the tenants' rents."

"Hmm. What would that have done to the yarn shop?"

"Don't know, but it would hurt."

"Mmm-hmm." So Ms. Evans had a motive, after all. Maybe she wouldn't risk ruining her business by committing murder, but would she kill to save it? "Who inherits, do you know?"

"Don't know yet, but my bet's on her husband. The son, Eric—I went to school with him—moved out to Amherst a few years ago. He teaches at UMass Amherst."

"Ariadne mentioned they'd quarreled."

"Ariadne?"

"Oh, hell, Ms. Evans."

"Yeah." Paul smirked for a moment. "Yeah, Eric would be worth a look if he was in town yesterday."

"Which we don't know. If the husband inherits, will he still buy the building?"

"Don't know that, but he wasn't as big as Edith in real estate. He's more a construction-type guy. Retired now, of course. He has to be in his early seventies, like Edith."

"Mmm. So maybe Ms. Evans is our perp. But here's a question. If she's not, how did our murderer get into the yarn shop? There was no sign of tampering on the lock."

"Who has keys?"

"From what Ariadne told me, only she does, and her mother and one of her employees."

"Mrs. Jorgensen wouldn't hurt a fly." Paul grinned. "Not even Edith Perry."

"Why?" Josh's attention sharpened. "Was there a problem there?"

"Yeah, but years ago. I don't remember what happened."

"Ha."

"Hey, even my memory's not perfect," he said good-naturedly. "I'll find out. Whatever it was, they didn't speak. More Edith's doing than Mrs. J.'s, I think."

Josh flipped his pencil back and forth again. "We can't rule anyone out yet."

"Yeah, we've got some work to do." Paul's phone rang at that moment, and he swiveled back to his desk to answer it, leaving Josh alone with his thoughts.

It was going to be a bear of a case. No easy access to the yarn shop for those who might have had reason to want Perry dead; no apparent reason for those who did have access. Why that particular place, he wondered again. Why that particular way, making a garrote out of yarn? It was bizarre. But then, the whole thing was bizarre.

Paul was obviously talking about some other, unrelated police work on the phone. Josh rose and, hooking a finger under the collar of his sport coat, lifted it off his chair. He liked to talk things out when he was working a case, as he and Paul had done just now. He not only learned the facts, but he got them straight in his head. The picture he had was incomplete, though. They'd find out who benefited from Perry's death soon enough. What he really needed to do, Josh thought as he shrugged into his coat and left the office, was to find out just who could have gotten into the shop.

The yarn, Ari's precious yarn, had been returned by the police and restored to its bins. Her sample items were again displayed properly, and every trace of fingerprint powder was gone. The day after the murder, Ariadne's Web was open again, and it was crowded.

"Murder's good for business," Laura muttered as Ariadne rang up another sale, this time, ironically enough, of Diane's homespun.

"Oh, Laura, stop," Ariadne said irritably, mostly because she'd had the same thought. She'd had more than a few inappropriate thoughts since she'd found Edith's body. She knew that was likely due to the shock—she didn't find dead bodies every day, after all—but she also guessed that no one currently in the shop had liked Edith very much. Few people mourned her loss, and that, Ari thought, was sad.

"I can't believe what you've sold," Laura went on, pulling out more yarn from the skein on the counter. The fuzzy scarf she'd started just this morning had already grown on the needles she held in her quick, competent fingers. "Five skeins of that silk yarn! That's over one hundred dollars."

"This will all die down soon enough." She winced at her choice of words. "The thing is," she said, as the customer left the counter and they were briefly alone, "why here? That's what I can't figure out."

"Maybe Edith saw someone stealing the homespun."

"Oh, come on, Laura. You don't believe that."

"Of course I don't. She'd have been right in there helping herself, too."

"Laura! That's not true. Can I help you?" She smiled at the customer who had brought a pattern up to the counter, and for the moment forgot about everything except answering the customer's question. When she'd rung up that sale and there was again a lull in business, she turned back to Laura. "The thing is, why here?"

"You asked that already."

"What? Oh. Yes, I did." She put her hand to her forehead. "This whole thing's got me discombobulated."

"I can't imagine why," Laura said dryly. "Ari, have you thought that maybe you're a target, too?"

"Diane said something similar. But, why? I haven't done anything to anyone."

"Well, dear, we won't know that until we know who did it."

"We have to know the motive to figure that out," Ari said, irritated again. "You know they always do in mystery novels. Means, motive, and opportunity."

"Books, dear," Laura chided. "This isn't like a TV mystery where there are all sorts of people with grudges against the victim."

"It'd better not be an Agatha Christie, with the least likely suspect."

"Agatha was rarely so obvious, dear. Still, I can't help thinking this was aimed against you for some reason."

Ari glanced around at the shop and its customers. All were obviously trying to listen, and just as obviously trying to hide that fact. "I think Edith was the victim, Laura. Getting at me might have been a side benefit." She smiled at a woman who had laid her purchases on the counter. "Or it might not have anything to do with me at all."

"If you say so, dear," Laura said, and turned to take care of customers herself.

It's all well and good for Laura to say, Ari thought. She tried harder to focus, but only a small part of her mind was busy with the work that usually consumed her. She was, she knew, still a suspect, though she hadn't yet been charged, or even questioned again. Sooner or later, though, someone from the police would show up. *Detective Pierce, maybe,* she thought, then frowned. She shouldn't be taking a feminine interest in a man who might arrest her. She remembered quite clearly how he had looked in her shop, as autumnal as the weather in pressed chinos, a blue shirt that she suspected was Egyptian cotton, and a good tweed sport coat. His reddish brown hair was thick, but neat. A precise man, the detective, and Ari, precise herself, found that appealing.

It was foolishness, she reminded herself sharply. No matter how attractive he might be, she had nothing to gain by talking to him, and everything to lose. She hadn't needed Ted to tell her that. In the books she read, it always seemed that the character who declared she had nothing to hide, as Ari herself had, was the first one arrested. Wrongly, of course. That went without saying.

The bells over the door jangled, and she looked up. "Speak of the devil," Laura said in a stage whisper.

"What? We weren't."

"We would have been. Good afternoon, Detective."

"Afternoon." Detective Pierce nodded at them both, his face so pleasantly bland that Ari was immediately on guard. At the same time, she wondered if he really did suspect her. He was a hard man to read, which was likely a secret to his success.

"Has there been any progress?" she asked, aware that her one remaining customer was listening openly. It was Ruth Taylor, and that meant that the news of this would soon be all over town.

"Some," he said vaguely. "I see you've gotten right back into business."

"Yes." Ari gazed thoughtfully at him. As long as he didn't arrest her, she might be in a position to help him. Or he, her. "A lot of it is just curiosity."

"Ariadne, are you going to introduce me to this handsome young man?" Ruth's voice gushed.

Ari turned. "Of course," she said, and made the introductions. "Did you find all you need?"

"What?" Ruth looked away from Detective Pierce, a little flustered. To Ari's amusement, she was patting at her tightly permed gray curls. "Oh. Yes, I did."

"I'm so glad. Laura?"

Her aunt turned from where she had been straightening a bin of yarn. "Yes?"

"Could you lock the door and flip the Closed sign? Thanks, Mrs. Taylor." She handed the woman her package. "Please come back if you have any questions."

Ruth looked from the detective to Laura, who waited by the door, her hand on the bolt. "Is there anything I can help you with?"

Ari smiled. "Thank you, but no, not now."

"Here, Ruth, I'll get the door for you," Laura said. Ruth had no choice but to leave, casting an avid glance back at them as she did so.

"Whew!" Laura walked back to the counter. "That'll get around town fast."

"Mrs. Taylor talks a lot," Ari explained to the detective.

"Does she?" He glanced at the door, and once again she had the feeling that he was sharper than he let himself appear. "Do you mind if I ask you a question?"

She eyed him warily. "Will I need my lawyer?"

"Don't mind Ari," Laura put in. "She reads too many mysteries."

Ari glared at her. "And I might get in trouble if I talk too much."

"Oh, no, dear. I'm sure this nice young man won't ask anything that serious."

That "nice young man" was looking away, but Ari could see a smile lurking on his lips. She nudged Laura, hard, and then turned to Josh. "I'll answer what I can, if you'll answer something."

"Maybe." He looked wary.

"What time did Edith die?"

He looked at her for a moment, obviously debating about answering her. "Where were you yesterday between five and eight in the morning?"

"Was that your question?" she asked, satisfied that he'd answered her.

"No, actually, though I'd like to know."

"At home, of course."

"Mmm-hmm." Resting his forearms on the counter, Detective Pierce gazed around the shop. "Things look back to normal here."

"Oh, we've been doing very well all day," Laura said. "Everyone's wanted to see what they can."

"Anyone out of the ordinary?"

"Some people who surprised me."

Ari gritted her teeth. So much for that nudge,

though there didn't seem to be any harm in Laura's answering that particular question. "Yes, some people who never showed any interest in knitting before," Ari said. "Is there some reason you ask?"

"You never know," he said vaguely. "Anyone show any interest in what happened?"

"Everyone did." Ari looked up suddenly. "Do you mean any *particular* interest?"

"You don't think the murderer came here today, do you?" Laura asked.

"You never know," he said again, shrugging.

"So they *do* return to the scene of the crime?"

"Laura," Ari said, though her admonition was automatic.

"Oh, it's all right, Ari, I just said we read mysteries." She beamed at Pierce. "Which is where we get our ideas, of course. Do criminals return to the scene of the crime?"

Still smiling blandly, he shrugged. "What's been puzzling me is how whoever killed Perry—Mrs. Perry—got in."

"That's why you suspect me," Ari said, before Laura could.

"Now, Ari, what a thing to say," Laura chided her.

He nodded, the smile gone from his face. "There was no sign of tampering with the locks, front door or back. Seems to me someone would have had to have a key."

Ari nodded reluctantly. "I know. I've thought of that."

"Have you thought of anyone else who might have one?"

"Of course I've thought of it, but there are only the people I've told you about."

"Ari, dear," Laura said.

Ari wanted to close her eyes. Now what? "What?"

"How do you think I got in here the other morning?"

"What?" Ari stared at her. "You don't mean . . ."

"Yes, dear." Laura nodded. "I have a key."

CHAPTER 3

"You have a key?" Josh said sharply, abandoning his pretense of casualness.

"Since when?" Ariadne said at the same time.

"Since the beginning, dear. After all, I'm your partner."

"No, you're not."

Josh wondered if Ariadne were grinding her teeth, her jaw was clenched so tightly. "I thought you weren't actually employed here, Mrs. Sheehan."

Ariadne barely glanced at him. "Laura loaned me money to open the shop. Who else?" she demanded, staring at her aunt.

"Let's see," Laura said calmly, as if she were unaware of the tension in the shop. "Ariadne, her employee Summer, and her mother, Eileen, as she said." She counted them on her fingers. "Ted."

"Ted!"

"Ted." Another finger. "Diane—"

"Why Ted?" Ariadne demanded. "And, for God's sake, why Diane?"

"Well, dear, your mother thought it would be a good idea for Ted to have a key. Just in case, you know. Then he gave me one."

"Why?"

"I asked."

Ariadne groaned. "So you could get in whenever you wanted."

Laura's eyes were flinty, changing her from dotty to formidable. "Do you think I killed Edith?"

"Of course I don't." Ariadne rested her head on her hands. "I didn't mean that the way it came out. But I do know that you think of this place as a playground sometimes."

"Well, of course, dear. Didn't I teach you how to knit?"

"Yes, so I could make padded coat hangers for you."

Laura nodded. "True. I will admit, there have been times I've wanted to come in to straighten the bins, or rearrange the samples. I don't think, for example, that the Aran sweater over there is shown to advantage. But I never have done so, dear."

Ariadne sighed. "No, I know. I also don't think she came in with Edith the other morning," she said to Josh.

He nodded noncommittally. "Mrs. Sheehan, you say that Ted Evans has a key?"

"Yes. Now, Ariadne, don't look at me that way. It was your mother's idea, after all. You know how she feels about you running a business."

"Yes, but—"

"How does she feel about it?" Josh interrupted her, though he usually preferred to allow people who were involved in a case to talk freely. He often got more information than they realized.

"She thinks I'll fail," Ariadne said, giving him an annoyed look, as if she thought he agreed. "Why she thought giving Ted a key was a good idea, I don't know. And Diane." She rounded on her aunt. "Why her?"

"Well, dear, she is your friend."

"I don't have a key to her house," Ariadne retorted, "just because she spins yarn for me."

"Does she?" Josh said, keeping his voice neutral.

"Yes. Her yarn is popular. People like the homespun—oh."

Ariadne's look of horror gave Josh the clue. "Was it her yarn that was used?"

"Yes," Ariadne said reluctantly. "Oh, but you can't think she had anything to do with it! Diane would never abuse her yarn in that way."

"No, especially not the purple heather," Laura put in. "She was proud of that."

Josh scratched behind his ear and looked away, bemused. They talked about yarn as if it were alive, and ran the shop with single-minded devotion. As he'd said earlier, that seemed to him reason enough to doubt Ariadne's guilt. Now, though, he wondered. If for some reason something threatened her precious shop, how would Ariadne react?

One thing was definite: He didn't know enough

about any of the people involved. Being a newcomer to the town was a disadvantage. Only his instincts told him that he might have good reason not to suspect Ariadne. What he needed to do was a lot more investigating. "Where does your friend Diane . . ."

"Camacho," Ariadne filled in for him.

"Thanks. Where does she live?"

"She and her husband have a dairy farm out on Acushnet Road. She has sheep, as well."

"Near Drift Road?" he said, as casually as he could.

"Yes." Ariadne looked at him sharply. "Why do you ask?"

"I'm not familiar enough with the town yet." He straightened. "Is there anyone in your family who doesn't have a key?"

"I don't know," she said, sounding exasperated. "Maybe Megan."

"Megan?"

"My daughter. And no, I'm not serious. The most she has to do with my keys is find them when I lose them."

His attention sharpened. "Any time in particular?"

She looked startled. "I don't know. Everyone loses keys now and then."

"There was that time a few months ago when you couldn't find them for a couple of days," Laura reminded her.

"That's right. I'd forgotten."

"When was this?" Josh asked.

"I don't know. June? July? Sometime around then. Megan, by the way, is only seven."

"Where did the keys show up?"

"In the house somewhere. Actually, I think in my pocketbook." She laughed a little sheepishly. "It wasn't the first place I looked."

"Could someone have used them in that time?"

"What?" Ariadne looked startled. "Oh, no, I doubt it. I don't carry my bag all the time. When I walk to work, I have my keys in my pocket."

"You did have to use your mother's key to get in," Laura said. "Isn't it just as well I have an extra one?"

Ariadne shot her a look. "Yes, isn't it."

"Could someone have taken your keys without you knowing?" Josh asked.

"I doubt it." Ariadne frowned. "At least, I don't think so. Lord." She stared at him. "Are you thinking that's how someone got in?"

"Too soon to tell yet." He rotated his shoulders. The case was only just beginning, and already he felt tension in his back. "If you find out anything, call me."

"Yes," Ariadne said as she walked him to the door. "But I really don't think I'll remember anything more from that far back."

"Good enough," he said, and, after Ariadne had unlocked the door, went out.

From inside the store Ari watched the detective walk away. Several of her customers stood outside. Though one or two of them signaled that they wanted to come in, Ariadne shook her head, pulled the shade on the door, and turned away. The last thing she wanted to deal with now was people's curiosity.

"I'm sorry about the key," Laura said quietly as Ari walked back to the counter.

"What? Oh, that. It's really not that bad an idea. I just wish I'd known." She set her elbows on the counter and rested her chin squarely on her hands. "I'm up to my neck in it, aren't I?"

"At least he's good-looking."

"That's beside the point."

"A good-looking man is never beside the point."

Ari smiled unwillingly. "He is if he's trying to put you in prison. All those keys." She put her fingers to her eyes. "All my friends and family for him to suspect."

"Unless someone did take your keys when you missed them."

"No. They were at home, where I left them. I had a senior moment, that's all." She frowned. "Diane has a key."

Laura's face was troubled. "He mentioned Drift Road."

"I know."

"If he doesn't already know, he will soon."

"I know," Ari repeated, and reached for the phone. "I'd better warn her."

"You need to tell Ted, too."

Ari set the receiver down. "Oh, Lord, I suppose I do. Thank God." She shuddered. "I had the lock changed first thing this morning. I hate the idea of someone out there with a key who could get in at any time."

"Whoever it is, is probably done with it."

"I hope so." She picked up the phone again. The shock of finding Edith's body was beginning to wear off, and she was thinking clearly again. She didn't know why Edith had been killed, or by whom. All she knew was that people close to her were being threatened, and so was her livelihood, her long-cherished dream. She wasn't going to let that continue. It was just another job to Detective Pierce, but it was her life. She couldn't trust anyone else with it. Someone had to find out what was going on. Why not she herself? She probably knew enough about investigating from her reading to try it. And putting together clues would likely be—well, like putting the pieces of a new pattern together.

She smiled grimly at the thought as she dialed Diane's number at last. She'd untangle the clues, she thought, and then she'd knit them together properly.

Ari slammed her keys onto the counter just inside the entrance from the mudroom of her house, looked at them in distaste for a moment, and then walked into the kitchen, shrugging off her sweater. That counter inevitably became the repository of various items, from keys to mail to notepads and pens. The room beyond it was spacious and neat, however. It was lightened by white walls, while the light pine cabinets and deep red countertops gave it warmth. When Ari and Ted had moved back to Freeport, they hadn't planned to buy a huge white Greek Revival house built in the mid-1800s.

The rooms were small, the clapboarding needed frequent and expensive painting, and only the kitchen and bathrooms had been modernized. Altogether it was an inconvenient house, and she loved it.

Ari had made one change, knocking down the wall between the kitchen and an adjoining room to form a nook where her drafting table and stool stood. At the moment Megan, her seven-year-old daughter, was sitting at it, drawing.

"Hey, kiddo," she said. "What are you doing using my markers?"

"Hi, Mom," Megan looked up. "Want to see my drawing?"

"Yes, let me see." She crossed the room and picked up the drawing of several improbably colored mermaids swimming in a sea populated by equally colorful fish, plants, and shells. Ari's expensive markers lay scattered on the table. At least Megan had inherited her artistic skills, Ari thought, even if she tolerated yarn only because of its many variations of color. "I like it," she said, automatically putting the markers back in their holder. "The eyelashes on the mermaids are new."

"I figured them out," Megan said proudly.

"Good for you." Ari bent to kiss her daughter's head. "I suppose you left the covers off your markers again."

Megan again bent to her drawing. "Sorry, Mom."

"How many times do I have to tell you . . ." Ari began, and then stopped herself. That age-old motherly reproach never worked. "Did Nana say she'd buy you more?"

"Uh-uh. But she said she'd take me to the Dollar Tree so I can buy another box myself."

"Ariadne?" a voice called from the other room.

"Yes, Mom," Ari called back. "I just got in."

"I thought I heard the door." Eileen Jorgensen walked in through the family room, worry lines etched between her brows and her hands clutched together. Eileen, tall and spare in her classic shirtwaist dress, always looked like a nervous wreck. Yet she ruled her high school literature classes with a will of iron. "Was it very bad today?"

"No, we actually did pretty well." Ari looked into the freezer and frowned. "I don't know what we're going to have for supper."

"Pizza!" Megan chipped in.

"I should have defrosted the hamburger today." She shut the freezer door. "I guess my mind was on other things."

Eileen sat at the counter. "Have you heard anything more about Edith?"

"No." She'd already decided not to say anything about the problem of the keys, or about Diane's possible involvement. Her mother worried enough as it was.

"I heard that detective came by today."

Ari opened the refrigerator, hesitated for a moment, and then pulled out a half-empty bottle of wine and poured herself a glass. "Where did you hear that?"

"I met Mrs. Taylor at Shaw's."

"I should have known." She sat across the counter from her mother, idly turning her wineglass by its stem. "Mom, what do you know about Edith?"

"Probably what everyone knows. Why?"

"What do you know about her husband, or Eric?"

"Her son? Why?"

"I wish you'd just answer my questions for once. We all know she had money," she went on, before Eileen could protest. "Do you have any idea who gets it?"

"Eric is in town, you know."

"Is he? Of course, he would be. I haven't seen him."

"I haven't either, and I haven't seen Herbert since it happened," she said, referring to Edith's widower.

"I guess I can't blame them for keeping a low profile." Again she went to the refrigerator, this time to take out some cheese, then she arranged it on a plate with some crackers. Megan, briefly distracted from her drawing, jumped down, took a slice, and then returned to the drafting table. "Mr. Perry must be a suspect, too." If money were involved, he'd have had more motive than anyone. The problem was, how could he have possibly gotten into her shop? And why? "If anyplace, I'd think if he did it, he'd have left her body at Town Hall."

Eileen laughed unexpectedly. "Just the place for her," she agreed, "since she practically lived there."

"Will he inherit, do you know?"

"Probably." Eileen sliced a piece of cheese and put it on a water cracker. "She cut Eric out years ago."

"Yes, I know." Ari frowned. "I wonder if Mr. Perry will go ahead with the Drift Road project."

"I don't see why not. He'll make more money doing that than leaving the land empty."

"More McMansions," Ari said gloomily.

"I'd be more concerned about his buying your building."

"Believe me, I am." She propped her chin on her hand. "Mom, did he and Edith get along okay?"

"So far as I know. Though whoever knew with Edith."

"Is that the lady who was in your shop?" Megan asked unexpectedly.

Ari turned to look at her. "How do you know that?"

"Jacob was talking about it in school today."

She sighed. It was too much to hope that Megan wouldn't hear something. "Yes, she was. Don't worry about it, Meg."

"I'm not," Megan said, and returned to her drawing.

Ari watched her for a minute and then turned back to see her mother watching her, those lines of worry deep again. "What?"

"Why are you asking about Edith?"

"All things considered, Mom, why shouldn't I?"

"You really should leave these things to Ted."

"Ted is a tax attorney."

"He called today, by the way. He's found someone to represent you, just in case.

Ari looked down at her glass, both annoyed and apprehensive. Annoyed because Ted was being high-handed as usual, apprehensive because he had good reason to be. "I suppose he had to. Megan?"

"What?" Megan said after a moment.

"Do you remember when I lost my keys?"

"No."

"In the summer. You found them for me."

"Uh-huh."

"Megan," she said sharply. "Pay attention to me."

Megan at last looked up from her drawing. "What, Mom?"

"Think. You wanted to go to the beach."

"Yeah." Resentment tinged Megan's voice. "You said you couldn't take me."

"I had to work," she said patiently, and then memory struck. "Omigod."

"What?" Eileen asked.

"Nothing." Ari automatically fell into the old habit of avoiding a subject that would make her mother fret. *But, omigod.* They'd found her keys in the shop, not at home as she'd said. She'd forgotten that. "Mom, why did you . . ."

"Why did I what?" Eileen said, when Ari didn't go on.

"Nothing." Again she decided against bringing up the subject of the keys, or why Ted had one. "Do you think I should call Mr. Perry?"

"About your building? Ari, do you think this is the time?"

"No, not that. I want to give him my condolences. I'm not sure I should go to the funeral." She opened the refrigerator again, this time taking out the remains of the chicken she'd cooked the other night. "If I make potatoes with this and some broccoli, it should be enough."

"Yuck," Megan said without looking around.

"Why shouldn't you?" Eileen asked.

"After what happened, he might not want me there."

"Oh, dear." Eileen had gotten up, too. "I wish you weren't involved in this."

"So do I." She put a pot of water on the stove for the potatoes. "With luck the police will find out who did it soon, and it'll all be over. Do you want to stay for supper?"

"Yes. Oh, Ari, what a mess this is."

"I know." Ari began to peel the potatoes. *I know,* she added to herself. It was only likely to get worse. The task she'd set herself was daunting, but she couldn't think of another way out. She was already involved. "Go get washed, Megan."

"Awww." Megan managed to stretch the protest into five syllables.

"Now. One, two——"

"Okay!" Megan jumped down from the stool before Ari reached the magic number of three, at which point she'd have a time out. "Jeez."

"What?" Startled, Ari stared after her daughter as she scuttled toward the small bathroom tucked under the front stairs. Then, smiling, she turned back to her task and let the commonplaces of her life enfold her.

On Thursday Josh spent the morning in the chief's office, discussing the various implications of the case: the problem posed by the number of keys to Ariadne's

Web, the probability that Ari was their culprit, and the new fact that the yarn used as a weapon had been made locally. There was also the question of what had been used to hit Edith on the head. In searching the shop that first morning, neither he nor any of the others had found anything to match the description. Whatever it was must somehow tie the murderer to the crime, or it would probably have been left behind.

Its disappearance didn't point to anyone in particular, and yet Josh thought it might work to Ariadne's advantage, if in a small and circumstantial way. Edith had been murdered in Ariadne's shop, with yarns she owned, implicating her in the crime already. Why, then, would she have removed whatever had been used as the first weapon? It didn't make sense. Add that to the fact that no one he'd talked to had anything bad to say about her, and he was coming to believe in her innocence more and more.

With all that in mind, he left the office and went to Town Hall to try to learn about Edith's involvement with the town. It didn't take him long to discover that the property Edith Perry had owned was valuable. She had paid her fair share of taxes on it, though she had asked for abatements for both the tax and for water usage, claiming her age as a reason. More important, she had filed plans to develop the property on Drift Road. Though those plans hadn't yet been approved by the town, what he'd learned from them was significant. He thought he might have one more piece of the puzzle in place. Once he learned who her beneficiaries were, he'd have more.

Josh emerged into the bright, warm sunshine of an early fall day with the realization that it was noon. Since he planned to spend more time at Town Hall this afternoon looking at minutes of selectmen's meetings, he drove to Marty's and went to the deli section. When he'd first moved to Freeport, Marty's had been a surprise to him: part market, part deli and sandwich shop, part gourmet food shop. Now, with a paper bag in hand, he walked out again, and nearly collided with a woman near the door.

"Why, Detective Pierce," she said, before he could apologize. "This is a surprise."

Josh's memory brought up her name almost immediately. "Mrs. Taylor, isn't it?"

"Why, yes." Ruth Taylor beamed at him. "We met at Ariadne's Web yesterday."

"Yes, I remember." Nodding politely, he began to edge past her.

"What happened was terrible, wasn't it?" she said, following him to the parking lot.

"Yes." Josh paused in the act of reaching for his car door. Mrs. Taylor was a gossip, Ariadne had said yesterday. "Could I buy you lunch, Mrs. Taylor? Or," he went quickly on, as she gave his bag a dubious look, "a cup of coffee?"

"Coffee would be nice," she allowed, nodding graciously.

"Good. I'll get it for you."

A few minutes later, they settled at one of the picnic tables on the narrow strip of lawn between the store and the inlet. Beyond them the marsh grass swayed golden in the breeze, and the sun glinted so brightly on the bay that it almost hurt to look at it. In such a tranquil setting, so different from Boston's busy streets, it could be hard to remember that he was dealing with a murder.

"We've never had anything like this happen here before," Ruth said brightly. "It's stunned just everyone. Of course, there are always problems. Riffraff, you know. I never go near the waterfront if I can help it."

Josh finished unwrapping the deli paper from his sub sandwich and spilled some potato chips onto it, thinking. As with any working port, Freeport had its problems, but the majority of fishermen he'd met were hardworking and decent. "Why?"

"Oh, you probably know that better than I. And kids, too." Her laugh was artificial. "Always up to something."

"Do you have any children, Mrs. Taylor?" he asked, after taking a drink from his can of soda.

"Oh, yes. Four. Two here and the others in Chicago. And five grandchildren." She reached for her wallet. "Would you like to see some pictures?"

"Sure." Josh patiently admired the snapshots. She had some reason for bringing up the subject of young people; he'd seen the gleam in her eyes. "Nice-looking kids."

"Oh, yes, and so well behaved. Not like many I could tell you about."

"Such as?"

"I suppose I shouldn't have been surprised to see you at Ariadne's yesterday."

"Mmm."

"Such a terrible thing to happen to her, and in her shop. Of course, we all thought she was crazy to open up a yarn shop, what with all the department stores and that big craft store out in Dartmouth. But she seems to be doing well enough."

"Mmm-hmm."

"She's a nice girl. She's had her share of problems, but then, who hasn't?"

"Oh?"

"Oh, yes. She was arrested, you know."

That brought his head up. "When?" he snapped.

"A long time ago. Vandalism. But I'm sure you'd know more about that than I would, with your job."

He chose to ignore her implication. "What did she vandalize?"

"School property. Oh, and some cars," she said, the gleam in her eyes more pronounced.

People could still surprise him. He'd rarely met an informant who showed such relish for her task, especially since what she'd told him didn't sound at all like the Ariadne he'd met. "I'll look into it. Now—"

"Of course, she was young. As I said before, kids." She smiled. "Not that it means she deserves what happened to her, oh, no."

"From what I've heard about Mrs. Perry, I'm surprised she had any interest in knitting," he said, deciding to change the subject. He'd check Ariadne's record later, though he doubted he'd find anything serious.

"Edith? Oh, yes, she was always a champion knitter. And I do mean a champion. One of her sweaters won an award at a county fair."

Josh looked up from his sandwich. "I didn't know there were awards for such things," he said.

"Oh, yes. Edith was a country girl. She appreciated good quality, Detective. She liked homespun yarn."

He looked up sharply at that, but she gave no indication that she knew she'd said something of significance. The type of yarn that had been used in the murder was a closely guarded secret. "And didn't mind paying for it?"

"Oh, no, I wouldn't say that. It's not as if she was poor, you know, not even when she was young. But she knew the value of a dollar, not like the young people today."

"Did she buy things at Ariadne's Web?"

"Yarn, I believe, but not the patterns. I can't say I blame her."

"Why not?"

"Oh, they're much too expensive. I don't know why Ariadne prices them so high. After all, any experienced knitter can design things. But she won't come down on the prices."

"Do you knit, Mrs. Taylor?"

"Not in the summertime," she said with a bit of pride. "I'd rather walk or swim."

"I see," Josh said.

"Of course, I keep active in the winter, too," she continued. "I use the walking track at the YMCA and the pool. I make mittens and things for my grandchildren, but I'd rather be out and about. People are so much more interesting. Don't you find that?"

Too interesting, sometimes. "Tell me something." He picked up his soda, more to give the impression of casualness than to drink. "Did Edith buy homespun yarn from Ariadne's Web?"

"Do you mean Diane Camacho's yarn? No, she always said it was too expensive. Of course, she wouldn't have bought it recently anyway."

"Why not?"

"Because—oh, I keep forgetting you're new to Freeport. You wouldn't know what's been going on."

After his research at Town Hall, Josh had a good idea what she was talking about. "No, what?"

Mrs. Taylor eyed him shrewdly. "Did you know that the old Robeson farm, the property Edith owned, abuts the Camacho farm?"

"Yes. Did it cause trouble?"

"Trouble!" Mrs. Taylor leaned back and laughed. "Oh, my, yes, to put it mildly. The last thing the Camachos want is a big housing development next to their farm."

"I don't blame them," he said, more to draw Mrs. Taylor out than to express his own opinion. "There are a lot of newcomers in the town, I understand."

Again her look was shrewd. "You really don't understand, do you?"

He frowned. "No. What?"

"There's no town water out there, or sewage. Well water and septic systems." She sat back. "It wouldn't be the first time the Camachos had trouble with neighbors over water. And a development of that size . . ."

Josh was from the country, too. "There'd be problems with the water table," he said.

"Yes, and runoff. All those new roads to be sanded and salted in the wintertime, you know. Well, you can imagine what would happen to the ground water."

He went very still. "It would be contaminated."

She sat back with a satisfied air. "Exactly."

His mind was working swiftly. "How did the Camachos feel about it?"

"Oh, they fought it, of course. They're one of the reasons the development plans haven't been approved yet."

Good God. Mrs. Taylor didn't know it, but she'd just helped him slot another puzzle piece into place. If the underground water level was lowered, the Camachos would either have to drill a new well, an expensive proposition, or have less water for their livestock. The impact of that, along with possible contamination, would be devastating to a dairy farm.

Means, motive, and opportunity. Until a few moments ago, he'd thought Diane had only two of the three, and that she was an unlikely suspect. Now he knew differently. Diane Camacho, it seemed, had one hell of a motive.

CHAPTER 4

"You didn't tell me Ariadne has a record," Josh said to his partner accusingly as he folded himself into his desk chair later that afternoon.

Paul Bouchard looked blank. "Who told you she does?"

"Ruth Taylor. Something about vandalism and destruction of school property."

Paul scratched behind his ear. "Are we talking high school?" he asked, and then began to grin. "Oh, that."

"What?"

"Not much, actually."

Josh leaned forward. "Then it's true?"

"Juvie records are sealed."

Josh waved that off impatiently. "What happened?"

"Maybe you'd better ask her."

"Listen, Bouchard—"

"Listen, yourself. Do you think a high school prank

means she's a murderer? Though she looks good for it," he added.

Damn it, Ariadne still was a likely suspect. He couldn't see her progressing from vandalism to murder, though. If she'd vandalized anything. If she'd committed murder. "What about Diane Camacho?"

Paul's grin widened. "Ask her," he said again.

Josh gave him a sour look. "I will," he said, and opened his case file, thinking again about the time of Edith's death. He suspected that the murder had been committed at the early end of the range, nearer to five o'clock than eight. Surely at eight someone would have seen something at the shop. Certainly the police patrols would have. Yet no one had.

He pursed his lips. So far he hadn't found out where Ariadne had been at the time. He needed to establish her whereabouts as best he could. As the mother of a young child, she had probably been at home, as she claimed. He had no corroborating evidence, however. High time he went looking, even if finding what he needed was probably going to be impossible.

✂

Ari was grumbling over the shop's quarterly tax forms when the phone rang the next morning. Absently, she picked up the receiver. "Ariadne's Web."

A voice spoke briskly at the other end. "Josh Pierce."

She sat up, taxes forgotten. "Yes, Detective. Can I do something for you?"

"Actually, yes. Could you have lunch with me?"

That made her pull the receiver away from her ear and stare at it for a moment. "Are you allowed to socialize with a suspect?"

"This isn't exactly social. I'm not talking anything formal, Ms. Evans," he added quickly. "I need to ask you some things. You won't need a lawyer."

"All right," she said after a moment. "At noon?"

"Sure. What kind of sandwich do you like?"

She resisted the impulse to stare at the phone again. "Chicken salad."

"Good enough. I'll see you then."

"All right," she said, and hung up, mystified.

"You're going to have lunch with him?" Laura said, grinning knowingly.

Ari turned to Laura, who was sitting in one of the comfortable rocking chairs Ari had placed in the back corner to encourage customers to relax, or to try out different patterns. The sweater Laura was working on had grown nearly to chest level now. The teal, rose, and cream-colored yarns she was knitting in the classic horizontal zig-zag of an Icelandic sweater were unusual, but they worked well together.

"It's not like that," Ari said.

"Like what, dear?"

Ari glared at her, but decided against a direct answer. "We'll be talking about the case."

"The case?" Laura continued to grin, and Ari's annoyance grew. She was grateful to Laura for all her help, but it was beginning to grate on her. Laura, for all her active social life and involvement in various groups and organizations, hadn't missed a day in the shop since Edith's death. Ari wasn't sure whether she was lending her support, or if she simply wanted to know everything that was going on. "Ted will be jealous."

"That's silly."

"You do need Ted on your side, dear."

"To do my taxes?" Ari said, in spite of her earlier defense of Ted's competence.

"To keep you from going inside. Up the river. The slammer. The big house. Gaol," she added. "The old cell block. The—"

"Ash Street Jail," Ari broke in. "Walpole."

"It's called Cedar Junction now," Laura said, correcting her on the name of the maximum security prison. "Not a place you'd like, dear. I don't imagine they allow knitting needles there."

"No, only knives. I didn't kill Edith, Laura. You know that."

"Of course I do. But do the police?"

Ari frowned. "Do you know, I'm not sure? I can't understand why Josh invited me to lunch. Detective Pierce," she said hastily, but too late. Laura was grinning again. "Really, Laura. He's a cop."

"A good-looking man, too," Laura said, and deliberately turned her back.

They did their work in silence until the bells over the door jangled.

"Well, well," murmured Laura.

Ari took a deep breath as Josh came in, cooler in hand. "Detective," she said.

"Hi." He walked farther into the shop. "Am I early?"

From outside, Ari heard the Town Hall clock striking twelve. "No, you're right on time. Summer?" She turned. "I should be back in an hour or so."

Summer, Ari's official employee, had been putting away a new shipment of yarn, but now she looked at Josh with frank interest. "Sure. Take your time."

Ari barely refrained from grimacing at the arch tone in Summer's voice, and the equally arch look on Laura's face. Protesting that this lunch didn't mean what they thought it did wouldn't do her any good. Of course she was innocent of Edith's murder. What her family and friends didn't seem to realize, though, was that she was still under suspicion. This wasn't by any means a friendly lunch. "In an hour," she said again, and, draping her favorite pink cable-stitch sweater over her shoulders, went out. Josh, she noted, held the door for her. But this wasn't a date, she reminded herself.

"I thought we could eat at the bandstand," he said, turning right outside the shop and heading toward the waterfront. "If you'd like."

"That's fine. It's a beautiful day." The sky was richly blue and the sun was warm, but there was just enough of an autumn tang in the air to make her suspect she'd need her sweater by the water. "I don't quite understand why you wanted to meet me this way."

"I just want some background information. Remember, I'm new here."

"Didn't Mrs. Taylor tell you enough yesterday?" she said dryly.

He gave her a quick look. "So you heard about that."

"It's a small town, Detective."

"Call me Josh," he interrupted her.

Ari blinked. First the invitation for lunch, and now this. Surely he wouldn't treat a suspect in such a way, would he? "Okay. I'm Ari. People in small towns are nosy," she went on.

"True. Everyone knows everyone else's business."

"Something like that. I'll bet they even know what kind of sandwiches are in there," she said, indicating the cooler.

"I doubt that."

"They're not from Marty's?"

"Nope."

"You made them?"

"Sure. Why not?"

"Then you cook," she said inanely. "Your wife must appreciate that."

He gave her an amused look. "Subtle."

"I didn't mean . . ." she began, flustered, and then gave it up. "Well, yes, I suppose I did."

"You wouldn't make a good detective."

Ari looked sharply up at him. He couldn't know her ideas about him, unformed though they were, could he? "So are you married?"

He didn't exactly smile, but the corners of his mouth drew in and his eyes looked amused. "No. Not divorced, either," he went on, before she could ask.

"You never married?"

"Nope." He sounded cheerful. "Never met anyone I cared enough about."

Oh, crumb, she thought. Just what she needed, a man who couldn't commit to anyone. Not that that mattered, she told herself hastily.

"The thing is," he went on, as they skirted the bandstand to its opening facing the harbor, "a cop's life is hard on his family. We see too many things we don't want touching them." He set the cooler on the bandstand's floor as they sat on the sun-baked concrete steps. "Then after a while we only talk to other cops, because they're the only ones who understand."

"So let's not give the wife a chance," she said.

"Unfair," he said as he opened the cooler. "Would you want to know about your husband's work if he was a cop?"

"Ex," she reminded him. "I never wanted to know about his work. He's a tax attorney."

"Can't say I blame you." He reached into the cooler, bringing out paper cups and cans of soda. "I'd've brought wine at another time—"

"Wine!"

"But as I said, this isn't social."

"Soda's fine. No, I'll drink from the can." She popped the top of the Diet Coke and took a long swallow. As she'd expected, it was cool by the water. The light cotton yarn of the sweater was perfect for such a day.

Josh was studying her. "Did you make that sweater?"

"Of course." She bloused it out over her hips and adjusted the collar of her white Oxford shirt neatly inside the cabled neckline. "I make all my own sweaters."

He unwrapped a sandwich, placed it on a paper plate, and handed it to her. "Design them, too?"

She looked at him with eyebrows raised. "Of course," she said again. "This design is one of the first I ever did."

"How did you get into it?"

She frowned a little. "Why are you interested?" she asked, taking the bag of potato chips he handed her.

"This case." He took some chips himself. "I've got a feeling it's tied up with knitting somehow."

Ari laughed. "You sound like Diane, with her puns."

"Have you and she been friends long?"

"Since freshman year in high school. This is good," she said in surprise, looking at her sandwich. The bread was seven-grain, and the filling was made up of chunks of light and dark chicken, mixed with walnuts and something familiar, which she couldn't quite identify. "Is there bacon in this?"

"Mmm-hmm."

"It's good. And here Ruth Taylor said you had ham and cheese from Marty's."

"Ham and—no." He grinned. "Prosciutto and Swiss, with white-wine Dijon."

"You do like food."

"Mrs. Taylor likes to talk."

"Yes." Ari grew serious. She hadn't spoken to Ruth herself. Laura had had that dubious pleasure. Still, she knew that Ruth and Josh had talked about more than Marty's selection of sandwiches.

"I heard something interesting about you," he said, looking off toward the harbor, where a fishing boat was heading out to sea.

"Oh?"

"Is it true you have a juvenile record?"

Ari blinked. "What?"

"Something about destruction of school property." She burst out laughing. "Not quite."

He was looking at her. "What was it, then?"

Ari nonchalantly took a bite of her sandwich before answering. "I got up to some pranks in high school."

"Nothing more?"

"No."

"Then, the charges against you?"

"Technically accurate. It was our senior dare, you see."

"Your what?"

"Senior dare. The sort of silly thing you do when school's almost out and you can't wait to graduate." Her smile grew. "It landed us in court, but it was worth it."

"But you have a record," he pointed out.

"Not really. Do you know that the school mascot is a Viking? Because there are so many Norwegians who live in the area."

"No, I didn't."

"Senior year, we decided to do something special for homecoming. We made a statue of a Viking. Well, not a statue, really, just a flat piece of wood painted and shaped like one. We raised the money for the materials with car washes and bake sales, and our class adviser managed to get the woodworking teacher at the vocational school to take it on as a project for his students."

"And?"

"It came out great. Twenty feet high, and so fierce-looking you'd swear it was real. It was a big hit. The school took it out for every football game."

He frowned a little. "I haven't seen it."

"No, it got put away after what happened."

"Which was?"

"I'm getting to it. A few weeks before school ended, some of us who hung out together started talking. One thing led to another, and before long we had a dare." She grinned at him. "My group dared the other one to steal the Viking."

He stared at her. "My God. How much did it weigh?"

"I don't know, but a few strong guys got together and it came down."

"How did you get away with it?"

"Oh, we didn't. One of the guys lived on a farm and sort of borrowed a flatbed truck for it, but can you imagine going around in a town of this size with a twenty-foot Viking on a truck? The guys got caught right away."

"What about you?"

"Diane and I T.P.'d the principal's car."

He was startled into laughter. "You got arrested because you toilet-papered someone's car?"

"Yes. Oh, ordinarily Mr. Morris wouldn't have prosecuted for something like that, but he was so mad about the Viking that he called the police. Anyway," she went on, "afterwards, I was charged with the theft, too."

"Because your group made the dare?"

"Well, that, too." She smiled down at the ground. "It was my idea."

He let out a laugh, and then grew serious. "You got a record because of it."

"Well, no. We could've argued that the Viking belonged to the senior class, because we paid for it, but it was such a silly thing that the case was continued without finding. The record was wiped clean when I turned twenty-one." She grinned at him. "So that's my life of crime. Masterminding the stealing of a Viking. Not exactly the background of a dangerous criminal, is it?"

Josh looked suspiciously at a seagull that was standing nearby and eyeing their food. "No."

"Don't encourage it," Ari advised him, following his gaze. "Gulls are scavengers."

"I know. There's something else."

Something in his voice made Ari look up. "What?"

"Is it true Edith Perry was going to buy your building?"

She sighed. "I wondered when you'd ask me that. Yes, she was."

"What would that have done to your business?"

"It depends on how much she would have raised the rent. I might have had to move, and I don't know where I'd find another shop that size for the price."

She put down her sandwich. "I have a motive. That puts me in trouble."

"Yes, except for one thing."

"What?"

"Your alibi stood up. You're in the clear, since this morning. Provisionally, anyway. It's one of the things I wanted to talk to you about."

"What happened?" she asked.

"I talked with some of your neighbors."

Instantly she understood. "Ronnie Dean."

"Yep. She confirmed what you told us."

"I should have guessed. I swear that woman knows what's going on in my head sometimes."

"On the day Edith Perry died, Mrs. Dean saw you open your door at five A.M. to get your newspaper. She said you were in your robe and your hair needed combing."

Ari's hand flew to her head. "I hadn't taken my shower yet."

"You remember that day?"

"Of course I do. I've gone over it and over it in my mind. Besides, it's what I do every day. Nearly every day," she amended. "Sundays, I sleep in if I can."

"Morning person?"

"No, not really." Frowning, she took the last bite of her sandwich. "When did Edith die?"

"The best estimate is somewhere between five and eight A.M."

"Then I'm not totally out of it, am I?"

"The D.A. could throw doubt on it," he agreed.

"And you?"

"No." He stacked her empty paper plate with his. "I don't think you did it, although your neighbor can't swear you weren't out at the wrong time. The right time, depending on how you look at it."

"You don't know Ronnie," she said dryly. "If there's something to see in that neighborhood, she sees it. She sits by her window with the lights out and watches everything. I don't know when she sleeps."

"Hmm. It might not stand up in court."

"Do you think it will come to that?"

"It might. You did have a motive, and the opportunity."

"I didn't do anything," she protested.

"Mmm-hmm."

Ari looked at him suspiciously. There it was again, that subtle indication in his manner that perhaps meant that he *didn't* suspect her. "What did you mean when you said you think Edith's death is connected with knitting?"

He shrugged. "Because of where it happened. Why in your shop? Why in that way?"

"Laura thinks the killer might have been after me as well as Edith."

It was his turn to regard her. "Is there anyone who dislikes you that much?"

"No, not that I know of. Those who don't like me tend to be backstabbers. I mean, they act behind my back."

"Did she come into your shop often?"

"Edith? Once in a while. She liked to knit, but she usually didn't buy anything from me."

"Why not?"

"She thought I charged too much. Well, I have to," she said defensively. "My stock is expensive, and I sell original designs. Plus, I have to pay my bills."

"You seem to be doing well enough," he commented.

"Oh, a lot of that's curiosity. It'll die out—oops."

"So you're not doing a good business?"

"What does that have to do with anything?" she asked suspiciously.

"Maybe nothing. You never know what's going to be important in a case."

"Well, I didn't kill Edith to bring customers in. Generally I do well enough without having to do something like that. Knitting's popular right now. A lot of young people are into it, and so are some celebrities."

"Mostly women?"

"Yes, though there are men involved, too. Why? Are you thinking a man did it?"

"You never know," he said vaguely.

So he wasn't going to give information away, she thought, unless she kept prying. "I keep thinking of a woman doing it."

"Why?" he asked, interested.

"Because of my clientele. What bothers me about that, though, is the way she was killed. Do women usually choose weapons like that?"

He looked at her. "What made you think of that?"

"It took strength. Was Edith hit on the head first?"

That seemed to throw him off balance, if the look on his face were any indicator. "Why do you ask?"

"Edith would have struggled when she felt the yarn around her neck. The killer would have had to be strong. Were any fibers found under her fingernails?"

He sighed. "You read too many mysteries."

"Well?"

"No," he said reluctantly.

"Then she didn't struggle. It makes sense that she was knocked out first."

"You're forgetting something," he said, neither denying nor confirming her suspicion. "How did the perp—the killer—"

"I know what 'perp' means."

"Yeah, of course you do. So how did he, or she, get into your shop?"

"I don't know. I'm working on that."

"What do you mean?"

"Oh, I've just been doing some thinking."

He eyed her suspiciously. "You haven't been asking anyone questions, have you?"

"Why would I do that?"

"I don't know. You tell me."

The social aspect of the day, what there had been of it, was gone. Josh was a policeman again. She'd do well to remember that he probably always was, Ari thought. "It's my business that's been affected, and my life."

"Yes. Your life. Maybe in ways you don't know."

"Are you saying I'm in danger?"

"If you ask the wrong person something, you might be."

She looked out at the harbor. "There's a way we could prevent that."

The suspicion on his face deepened. " 'We'?"

"Yes." She smiled brightly at him. "If we team up."

CHAPTER 5

J osh burst out laughing. "You're kidding."

"No, I'm not," Ari said, a little surprised by his reaction. "I think it's a good idea."

"No," he said, still grinning.

"You're already asking me for information," she argued. "Why not share what we know?"

"Because you're a civilian." His voice was patient,
but humor still lurked in his eyes.

"You need me, Detective."

"How?"

"I know this town. You don't."

"I know it well enough to know that people will
think we're seeing each other."

That left her gaping. "Heaven forbid!"

"Yeah. It is a ridiculous idea."

"It's not that," she protested.

"Yeah, it is, but that's beside the point," he said after

a moment. "I can't let you get involved in an investigation."

"I'm already involved."

"It's dangerous. It's unethical." Josh pulled at his ear, his habit when he was either deep in thought or perplexed. She certainly had him at a loss now. "I'd be under investigation myself if I permitted it."

"I don't want that, but I have no choice." She turned toward him. "I think I was a target."

He wasn't about to tell her that he was beginning to think so, too. "All the more reason for you to stay out of it."

"I'm still a suspect," she said urgently. "My life's been affected in every way. I've got to keep at it, whether I do so officially or not."

He pulled at his ear again. "Jeez, Ari."

"I don't see how you can stop me."

"I could put you into protective custody." Of all the things he'd thought might come out of this lunch, this was the very last he'd expected.

She stared at him. "You wouldn't."

"Try me."

"Under what pretext?" she demanded. "Can you show there's a threat to me?"

"Look, Ari. You just said there might be."

"Don't use my logic against me!"

That made him laugh. "Look, you have to see it won't work. This isn't one of your mystery stories. I won't put you into custody—"

"Good, because I have an ex who's an attorney."

"A tax attorney," he shot back.

"He serves the purpose," she answered just as sharply, and for a moment there was silence.

Josh passed his hand over his hair, his anger under control again. Funny. He seldom lost his temper. "Look," he said finally. "I really can't let you get involved in this."

"You need me." She leaned forward urgently. "You really don't know the town the way I do, and you don't know a knitting knobby from a bobbin."

"What?"

"You said yourself knitting's involved in this. And it's almost certain that I know the person who killed Edith."

"What happens if you say the wrong thing to that person? She's killed once already. If you get in her way, she might do it again. A threat," he added.

"Do you think that's what happened with Edith? Did she get in someone's way?"

He almost decided not to answer that, though there was no real reason not to. "Maybe. She seems to have had enemies."

"Yes," Ari said tonelessly.

He sent her a quick glance. Her face was set and stony. There was no way around it. She had had a grudge against Edith. So had her friend Diane. "Money could have something to do with it, too," he said, letting her off the hook.

"Yes, I've thought of that." Her shoulders relaxed; she seemed as relieved as he to change the subject. "She had a lot of property. Do you know about her will yet?"

"No, but we should soon." He rose. "I have to be getting back."

"So do I." She stood up, too, dusting off her beige linen slacks. "I doubt she left anything to her son."

Josh picked up the cooler. "I can't tell you if she did."

Ari waved her hand in dismissal. "I'll find out, anyway. And, no, I won't have to ask any questions. This *is* a small town."

He glanced at her as they walked back toward her shop. It was going to be impossible to keep her out of the case. "How did you get into your business?" he asked, to distract her.

The look she gave him said clearly that she knew what he was doing. "Through Laura, of course. It was her idea."

"Not yours?"

"No. I think Laura wanted a yarn shop, but without the work. She has a way of getting what she wants."

"What do you mean?"

"Well, take knitting, for example. My mother showed me the basics, but Laura's the one who really taught me."

"Oh?"

"My grandmother Jorgensen was a wonderful knitter. She made the most beautiful Scandinavian sweaters." She smiled to herself. "I used to love to watch her. I finally said I wanted to learn, but she wouldn't teach me. She said I didn't have the patience."

"She didn't really know you, then."

"What she meant was that she didn't have the patience. She never did understand it when someone didn't catch on to something as quickly as she did. Anyway, I started pestering my mother, and she finally bought me a knitting knobby."

"What is that?" he asked again.

"A knitting spool. It has four prongs on top, and you slip yarn over them to make loops. What you end up with is a long thin tube."

He frowned. "What do you use it for?"

"The only use I ever found for it was to coil it around and stitch it to make a doll's rug. Only I didn't like to sew, and it seemed pointless. There are looms now that work on the same idea, and you can do a lot with them. Anyway, Laura overheard me complaining and offered to teach me. She just happened to need padded coat hangers."

"Let me guess. Is that what she showed you how to make?"

"Yes. I told you, she manages to get what she wants. I didn't care. I wanted to learn, so I did. I can be persistent when I want to be."

Uh-oh. "So all that led to this?" he asked, indicating her shop and ignoring the challenge in her voice.

"Yes, eventually, with a few stops along the way. Well." She stopped at the door of her shop. "This was pleasant, Detective. Thank you."

"Josh, if you don't mind. Thank you for your help."

Ari nodded, turned to go into the shop, and then paused. "I'm really not going to stop, you know."

Damn. "You're going to get yourself into trouble."

"Not if you help me. Why can't we just exchange information? Unofficially, of course."

"In this town?" He eyed her skeptically. "You know as well as I do that people will figure out what we're doing."

"They'll think we're dating."

Josh grinned in spite of himself. "Well, we aren't."

"They'll really think it." She stared at him. "It's actually a good cover."

"I told you, I'm not letting you get involved."

"And I told you, I already am."

Hands in pockets, Josh looked away. Damned if he did, damned if he didn't. She would go on investigating, no matter what he said, but if he sanctioned it, even unofficially, they'd both be in trouble. "Damn it."

"I know," she said sweetly. "You're stuck, aren't you?"

Why had he ever thought she was ditzy? She had just out-thought him, and he was no fool. "Damn it. All right."

She beamed at him. "Oh, good!"

"But I'm not going to tell you everything I know."

"Why not?"

"Be reasonable, Ari. How can I? There may be things that will compromise the investigation if I tell them. And as far as the D.A.'s concerned, you're still a suspect. There's wiggle room in the alibi."

"You don't think so."

"I still have to keep investigating you."

She made a face. "I suppose you do," she said finally, and held out her hand. "Are we partners, then?"

Josh looked at her outstretched hand, sighed, and reached out. "I'm going to regret this."

By the time Ari closed the shop that night, so many people had come in asking about her lunch with Josh that she wanted to scream. People knew that Ronnie Dean had given her an alibi, and so there was no reason for Josh to talk to her as a suspect. Good cover or not, the idea that they might be dating was going to be inconvenient.

Well, there was nothing she could do about it now. Dismissing the idea from her mind, Ari walked across the street to where her car was parked. Supper. Now what was she to make for supper? Cooking was the last thing she wanted to do, especially with the memory of that day's lunch fresh in her mind. She could never make a sandwich to compete with that one, let alone anything more complicated. Her creativity didn't lie that way.

Pizza, she decided, and headed down the shore road to Marty's. They didn't have the best pizza in town, but they were quick and convenient, and she could pick up some much-needed supplies there. Megan would be happy, she thought, and frowned. Megan hadn't wanted to go to school that morning, pleading a stomachache as an excuse. Ari had tried that tactic too many times in her own life to let Megan get away with it, but it worried her. Megan usually loved school. Something had to be bothering her, and she didn't know what.

Her cell phone rang at that moment. Muttering to herself, Ari pulled over and dug in her purse. "What happened today?" Ted asked without preamble, after she'd finally found the phone and answered it.

She sighed. "Hello to you, too, Ted."

There was a brief silence. "Sorry, Ari." His voice was milder. "It's been a bitch of a day."

Ari's experience with Ted was that every day was a bitch of a day for him. "What is it, Ted?"

"I called the shop today and found out you were having lunch with that cop," he said, aggrieved and accusing again.

"Yes, I did." She didn't owe him an apology for that, she reminded herself.

"Christ, Ari, don't you have any sense? Say the wrong thing, you'll end up in jail. Hell, knowing you, you'll say everything wrong."

"Ted—"

"Don't you know enough not to talk to him without the defense lawyer I found for you?"

"Ted—"

"Or me, for that matter. I'm your husband, Ari."

"Ex," she shot back, angry now.

"Regardless. How do you think it will look if my wife—all right, ex-wife—gets arrested?"

"I've been cleared, Ted."

"And another thing—what?"

"I've been cleared," she said, with a certain smug satisfaction.

"Are you sure?"

"Ted," she protested. "Don't talk to me like that."

"It's only because I care."

Ari rolled her eyes, though she knew that, in his own way, he did. "I'm not going to be arrested. Ronnie Dean alibied me."

"Oh. Well, if anyone could, it's her."

"Yes." She decided not to tell him how provisional the alibi was, though.

"What did he want, anyway?"

"Background."

"On what?"

"Knitting."

"Knitting!" he exploded. "What kind of cop is he?"

"Knitting's probably connected to Edith's death somehow."

"I doubt it. You know, the sooner your friend Diane is arrested, the better."

That stunned her speechless for a moment. "That's an awful thing to say."

"Come on, Ari. We both know she did it. She had a motive."

"So do I," Ari retorted. "Diane didn't do it."

"Okay. Maybe it was Joe."

"No!"

"Ari, it's only a matter of time."

Again she fell silent. The hell of it was, he could be right. "Ted, I'm in the car," she said finally. "Can we argue about this at another time?"

"I'm not arguing."

No, Ted never argued, she thought. At least, not in his own mind. "I've got to go. Megan's waiting for me."

"Look, I'll come by tonight then, okay?"

"No! I mean, there's no need, Ted."

"I think we should talk over some strategy, just in case. What if the worst happens?"

Ari put her fingers to her temples, where a headache was beginning to form. She was doomed. "All right." She sighed. "What time?"

A few minutes later, with plans made with Ted, Ari drove off. She'd taken the time to call ahead to Marty's, so that she wouldn't have to wait too long. Running into people she knew and talking with them about recent events would be inevitable, but she would keep the encounters as short as she could.

As it happened, Ari worried for nothing. Though she did, indeed, encounter acquaintances and a few friends, none seemed to want to talk. It was as busy a time of day for them as for her. She was thinking she was going to get off scot-free when she turned from the pizza counter, to be presented with a vaguely familiar masculine back. It took her a few moments to recognize him, but when she did, she wanted to turn and run. Too late, though. He had already seen her.

For just a minute they stared at each other, Ari and Eric Hall, Edith's son by her first marriage. They'd dated for a little while in high school and had been friends since.

"Eric," she said. Suddenly released from her paralysis, she moved forward to give him an awkward hug.

He returned the embrace as awkwardly as she. "Hey, Ari. I'm glad to see you."

She pulled back, startled. "Are you, Eric?"

"Yeah." He glanced around the store, and she became aware that people were likely watching them. "You got a few minutes? I'd like to talk to you."

"I'm waiting for a pizza. Five minutes or so?"

"Okay. Let's go outside."

Ari followed Eric out to the bridge spanning the inlet. It was the second time today she'd been by the water with a good-looking man, she thought. If circumstances were different, she'd say her social life was looking up.

Eric's sandy blond hair was a little too long, and his light denim shirt was rumpled, but he still moved with the loose-limbed casualness that had always appealed to her. She found it hard to reconcile his present appearance with that of the long-haired goof she'd known when she was young.

"I can't believe you're a professor at UMass," she said.

"Believe it, baby." He squinted, held up his index finger and thumb as if pointing a gun, and made a clicking noise. It struck her as an odd gesture, under the circumstances. "Damn good one, too."

Ari didn't doubt it. Eric had never had to work hard to earn good grades in high school, in spite of his goofy behavior. She wondered what his students would think if they knew he'd been involved in the infamous Theft of the Viking. Probably they wouldn't be too surprised. "Are you happy there?"

"Yeah, most of the time." He leaned on the railing overlooking the salt marsh. "So, what's been happening?"

What's happening! "Eric, for heaven's sake."

He gave her the loopy smile that had once endeared him to her, but that now only made him look silly. It was harder than ever to believe that he taught at a university. "Besides that. You seem to be doing well."

"Oh, Eric," she said. Even for him that was too much. "Do you think that matters to me right now?"

"Yeah, well, you never seemed the type to run a successful business."

"Eric." She put her hand on his arm. Someone had to put this conversation on an adult footing. "I'm so sorry about what happened."

"Yeah, well," he said again, looking away, and for the first time she noticed fine lines radiating from his eyes. For the first time she saw sadness there. He evidently wasn't as indifferent as he appeared. "Yeah, well."

"I know you were estranged from her, but still, it must be hard."

He focused on her. "We made up. Didn't you know that?"

That was a piece of information that hadn't made it onto the town grapevine. "Really? When did that happen?" she asked.

"Not long ago. Kathy and I got divorced."

"Oh, Eric, I'm sorry."

"Yeah, it had been coming for a while. Ma was right." He stared out over the inlet. "She never liked Kathy."

"But Kathy's so nice."

His look was rueful. "Yeah? Like Ted?"

"Well." *No one's ex was nice,* she thought, certainly not right after a divorce. "Of course it's none of my business, but what did your mother have against her?"

Eric shot her a look. She'd asked with the familiarity of old friendship. Perhaps it was in the same spirit that he answered. "Kathy's an environmentalist."

For a moment, the seeming non sequitur puzzled her. Then, suddenly, she got it. "You didn't want your mother to develop the Drift Road land."

"Kathy convinced me. Hell, Ari, it's a great piece of land, with that view of Buzzard's Bay. It should be baseball fields or a park. God knows Freeport needs them."

"But now you're divorced."

"Yeah, but it didn't change my mind."

"About what?"

He focused his gaze on her. "Ma left me the land. Didn't you know that?"

That staggered her more than anything else he'd told her. "I had no idea."

"No one did, but it's starting to get around."

"Are you planning to develop it, too?"

He frowned. "I don't know. Kathy thinks I should."

"You just said she's an environmentalist."

"Not when money's involved, I guess."

Kathy should have no say in anything Eric inherited after their divorce, Ari thought. "Are you going to?" she asked again.

Eric gazed out over the inlet. "Maybe—no." He

stood up straighter. "No, I want to sell it to the town as open space in perpetuity."

"Did you just decide that?"

"Yeah." He grinned. "It'll annoy the hell out of Kathy."

"Eric . . ."

"Mean to tell me you never wanted to do anything to piss Ted off?"

"Well, yes," she admitted. "But this is a big thing."

"Sure. The town'll give me less money than a developer would, but, hey, I'll have to pay most of it to Uncle Sam anyway."

"As I seem to recall, Uncle Sam and the governor pay your salary," she said dryly.

"Yeah, and then take part of it away. It's not about the money, Ari. I'm still going to make out okay."

"I wonder what your mother would think of that," she said, more to herself than to him.

"She'd go ballistic."

"Yes." Ari's mind worked furiously. In her experience, when someone said it wasn't about the money, it really was about the money. Eric might very well change his mind once he found out the difference between what the developer would pay him, and the town. The inheritance had to be a windfall for him. If he'd known he was getting the land, he had a heck of a motive. "It's too bad you didn't get to see your mom before she died."

"Yeah, but I did. I was here the day before it happened."

"What?"

"Yeah. She told me I was going to inherit, and she wanted to talk about her plans."

Oh, Lord. Eric might have had the opportunity to kill his mother, though she couldn't imagine him doing so. For the first time, Ari regretted the partnership she'd formed with Josh. He'd have to know about this. It would take police work to find out if Eric had returned to Amherst after visiting Edith, or if he had an alibi. "Eric, did you—"

"Ari!" someone called from the door to Marty's. "Your pizza's ready."

"Thank you!" she called back, though she made no immediate move to return. "I have to go."

"Yeah. Ari?" he asked, as she pushed away from the railing.

She turned. "Yes?"

"Will I see you at the funeral?"

Ari hesitated. "No. I don't think it would be a good idea. I don't want to take away attention from your mother. She deserves respect."

"I suppose she does," he said softly after a moment, and then held out his hand. "Thanks, Ari. You've always been a good friend."

Her smile was strained. "Thanks," she said, and, after saying good-bye, walked back to Marty's, arms crossed over her stomach, head bowed. All her friends were suspects. It was a depressing thought.

Ari never stayed down for long, though. As she paid for the pizza, she was already busy with plans. There were a lot of people she could talk to, and a lot of questions to be asked. For one thing, she had to find out who could have gotten into her shop, and why. For another, she had to clear Diane, if she were indeed a suspect. Head up, stride militant, she walked out of Marty's. Josh Pierce, she thought with a small smile, wouldn't know what hit him.

CHAPTER 6

Ariadne's Web was quiet the next morning, with the usual customers probably doing their Saturday morning errands. Ari took advantage of the lull to work on a new design in her office. Winter might be coming, but she had to plan for spring and summer, and for a different clientele. Her regular customers, especially the older ones, tended to be conservative in their choice of colors and styles. Warmer weather, though, demanded something different, as did the summer residents who flocked to the area from larger cities. For them she'd need something light, bright, perhaps a little clingy. The cards of sample yarns before her, which almost never failed to inspire her with their palette of colors and their range of textures, brought only the slightest wisps of design ideas. She could do a shell, she thought, fingering a silk-blend yarn that came in lovely jewel tones. A pullover with short sleeves and picot edging at the jewel neck, perhaps?

Or a sleeveless turtleneck. She would use the colors of summer, the blues of the ocean, the pinks and reds of roses. It would be attractive, she thought—and boring.

In disgust, Ari threw down her pencil and sat back, scowling. Though either style would be popular, she'd done too many similar things. Even if she knitted them in openwork stitches or a combination of patterns, they wouldn't be anything new or different.

Part of the cause of her lack of creativity was that real life had gotten in the way. Too much had happened lately, and she had a lot on her mind: the chance that Eric had something to do with his mother's death, the very real possibility that Diane would be arrested, and, always, the memory of what had happened in her shop just days ago. For all her thinking, she couldn't fathom who could have done such a thing. Thank God, Ronnie Dean had given her an alibi of sorts.

That morning, before leaving for the shop, she'd paid her neighbor a call. She didn't know what Ronnie had or hadn't seen, but one thing was definite: She owed the woman a huge debt of gratitude. Unfortunately, paying that debt involved time. At great length, and with a number of extraneous questions thrown in, Ronnie had confirmed what she'd told Josh. Her small, dark eyes were bright, her hands animated as she spoke in a rush of words that seemed nearly endless. Within a few minutes she encompassed not only Ari's alibi but also the selling price of a house several blocks away, the news that another house had been broken into, and the fact that a neighbor's teenaged son had been smoking outside his house late one night. "Did that detective talk to you?" she asked, finally winding down.

"Yes." Ari smiled at her. "Thank you for telling him what you saw. It got me out of a jam."

"Well, I said to him, that Ariadne keeps to herself. Yes, she used to get up to a lot of mischief, but she wouldn't kill anyone. That's what I told him. Did he tell you anything more about what's happening?"

"I'm glad you were looking out that morning," Ari said, ignoring the question.

"I just happened to be up to go to the bathroom, and when I saw your light I looked out."

Ari bit back a grin. She knew that Ronnie's bathroom was at the back of her house. "Well, I'm grateful to you."

"I said to myself that you'd gotten a new robe. It was early for you to be up, wasn't it?"

"Oh, I'm usually awake at that time. Didn't you know?"

"That's right, you go to bed early," Ronnie said, with no indication that she understood Ari's implication. "So when that Detective Pierce came here—what a nice man. I heard you had lunch with him."

"Yes, he had some questions."

"Do you think you'll go out with him?"

"Ronnie, were you looking out later?" Ari asked, ignoring her again.

"Why? What happened?"

"Nothing. I was just wondering."

"Not until Mr. Parsons next door left for work. He leaves at seven, you know. I saw you go out to the school bus with Megan. How does she like second grade?"

"Oh, she likes it."

"Good. Then I saw Mrs. Goodman go off with her kids—is Megan playing with the oldest girl yet?"

Now, how had Ronnie known that Megan had had a fight with her best friend? "Yes. Nothing else?"

"You went to the school bus with Megan. Why did he want to know about that time? Was that when Edith was killed?"

"Yes. So that's it?"

"No. I told him you couldn't be involved. You're too nice."

Ari blinked. "You said that?"

"It's true."

"Thank you. And thank you for what you told him." Ari smiled, but she was troubled as she continued to talk with Ronnie. Eventually, managing to elude most of her questions, she freed herself and went to work.

Now, hours later, she was still troubled. Not even Ronnie was all-seeing. There was a bit of Ari's time not accounted for, after she'd gone out for the newspaper. It would have been tight, but she could conceivably have slipped out to meet Edith at the shop, killed her, and then returned home, with no one the wiser. It bothered her that her alibi was partly built on the fact that she was a nice person. After all, many murderers had been called quiet, nice people before they killed.

No wonder the police considered her alibi to be provisional, even if Josh didn't agree.

A noise at the door made Ari look up abruptly to see Kaitlyn, her expression quizzical. "Kaitlyn? What are you doing here?"

"It's Saturday, remember?" Moving with the grace and assurance of an athlete, Kaitlyn walked in and claimed the battered wooden chair near Ari's desk. "I'm sorry I'm so late."

Ari sat back, lifting her hair back from her neck and wishing she'd pinned it up. The day was summerlike. It certainly wasn't sweater weather. "It's all right this time, but don't make a habit of it."

"My mother wanted to talk to me about something."

Ari looked at Kaitlyn, startled by the trace of anger in her voice. "Oh?" she said.

"She wants me to quit." Kaitlyn slumped against the back of the chair.

"What? Why?"

"She thinks it's not safe here."

"Oh, honestly!" Ari burst out, before she could stop herself. Sometimes Susan Silveira's protectiveness bordered on the extreme. "No one's going to hurt you here."

"That's what I told her, but she doesn't want to hear."

"Do you want me to talk to her?"

"I don't think it'd do much good. Ari, she thinks I should work at Shaw's full-time."

"As a checker?" Ari said, startled. "But the supermarket pays less than I do."

"Yeah, but I'd get more hours. It was okay when I was still at RISD and this was just a weekend job, but I'd make more there."

Ari sighed. "I can't afford to offer you or Summer any more time."

"I know that, and I don't want to stop," Kaitlyn said passionately. "I was so excited when you started this shop and then hired me."

"I know." Although she hadn't known Kaitlyn before, she'd been impressed with her knowledge of design and of knitting. "But how would you do it with your classes?"

"I don't know. Next semester I could go at night. But I don't want to," she went on fiercely. "I don't want to be a checker." Kaitlyn slumped down in the chair again, looking sullen. "Of course, she can always afford to play golf."

"The prices of real estate are taking off around here, aren't they?" Ari asked cautiously.

"Yeah." Kaitlyn ran her hand over the top of her hair, short and blond like her mother's. "And we'd've done okay, but Mrs. Perry decided to be her own broker."

"What?" Ari said, startled.

"My mom was going to be her broker with the developers."

"And Edith decided against it?"

"Yeah."

No wonder Mrs. Silveira was concerned about money. Her commission from such a sale would have been huge, and the loss of it had to be a blow. Because of the downturn in the computer industry, Kaitlyn's father had lost his job, and, being middle-aged, was finding a new one hard to get. It had affected all of them, since they'd had to move to a smaller house and Kaitlyn had had to transfer to UMass Dartmouth, which she hated. Kaitlyn's situation was rough. She badly needed this job.

Kaitlyn sat up. "Is there anything you need me to do?"

"Not right now, except for staying at the counter. Summer put the new shipment of yarn away yesterday, and it's been quiet."

"Don't worry, I'll find something to do. Maybe I can work on the web page. I brought the backup disks with me."

"That's an idea," Ari said noncommittally. She still wasn't sure about the idea of selling patterns online.

"But I wanted to show you something first." From the portfolio Kaitlyn held she drew out two papers, clipped together. One was a drawing of a striped hat-and-scarf set; the other had the directions for making it. Across the top of the first page was a large *C*, written in red.

"Oh, Kaitlyn," Ari said. "One of your designs?"

"Yes. A project I had to do for design class. It really came out nice. I don't know why I didn't get a better grade."

Ari frowned a little as she skimmed the directions. "There aren't any comments on it from the professor."

"No, but I asked him afterward about it. He didn't think the stripes work."

"Hmm." Privately Ari thought the professor had a point. The hat, a beret, was designed in vertical stripes of pink, white, and red, and looked like an oversized peppermint candy. She couldn't say that, though. "The problem with the vertical stripes is where you had to increase," Ari said, indicating the top of the hat. From the crown, Kaitlyn had added stitches to make it large enough at the edge. "They start off narrow and then grow wider, until you reach the underside and have to decrease."

"But that's why I like it," Kaitlyn said. "I think it's interesting."

That was certainly one word for it. "Why did you use sport yarn? It's too thin to be warm."

"I don't think so. It knits up tight. Anyway, I wouldn't have gotten the look I wanted if I'd used worsted. The stripes would have ended up being too wide. This way I could fit in more, too."

Oh, Lord, Ari groaned to herself. "Maybe you should try making something in bulky yarn. Or chenille. That would be a good look. Or you could add texture with different stitches. Try cables, or seed stitch."

Kaitlyn wrinkled her nose. "It wouldn't be very challenging."

"It doesn't have to be, does it? What you're looking for is good design."

"This is good design," she insisted.

Not if it made anyone who wore it look like candy. "Kaitlyn, I'm afraid it just doesn't work," she said gently.

Kaitlyn stared at her for a moment, and then

surged to her feet, flinging the design away. "I'll never get it," she said. "I'll never be any good."

"Of course you will," Ari said, startled. Did she have such dramatics to look forward to when Megan was a teenager? "I've seen the things you've made. They show promise. You're doing all right in your other classes, aren't you?"

"Yes, but I've mostly done fairly simple things." She sat down again. "When I try to be different, this is what happens."

"Simplicity's always best, Kait." Especially since the girl didn't really know what she was doing yet. That had puzzled Ari from the first. Kaitlyn obviously had originality and talent; the striped hat, though hideous, was proof of that. Yet somehow she couldn't seem to find her style, or to apply the design principles she'd learned in other subjects to her knitting work.

"That's easy for you to say. You make complex things."

"But I started off simply." It wasn't quite true; in the beginning, she'd had her share of disasters.

"Ari, I want to do this so much." Kaitlyn turned toward her. "If I don't succeed, I don't know what I'll do."

"You'll learn," Ari said. "You'll take this experience and learn from it. Someday, Kait, when you have the basics and the knowledge under your belt, you can be innovative. You'll succeed. I'm sure of it."

Kaitlyn slumped farther down in the chair. "You know, I don't understand why you did it."

"What?"

"You were getting successful. I still can't believe you were selling your designs when you were still in college. You could have gone to New York. Really." She leaned forward, brow knitted. "I think you could have gone anywhere."

Ari looked down at her desk, and the sweater design, which still refused to come to life. Kaitlyn was so young. Life was still straightforward to her, in spite of the obstacles she'd faced. "Life happened," she said finally. "I met Ted."

Kaitlyn made a face. "Ted."

"Yes, Ted. He was what I wanted at the time."

"Oh, honestly, Ari!"

"Well, he was."

"Why didn't he go to New York with you, instead of making you stay here?"

"Why should he have? Besides, he didn't make me do anything. I stayed because I wanted to."

"You can't have," Kaitlyn protested. "With such a future ahead of you?"

"I got pregnant," Ari said. "New York's no place to raise a child."

"Lots of kids grow up there."

Ari shook her head. "I didn't like the quality of living when there was an alternative. We didn't even want to stay in Providence, though it's nice enough. I like Freeport, Kait. So does Ted, so we came back here."

"Bo-ring."

"Gee, Kait, don't hold back. Tell me what you really think."

"Sorry," Kaitlyn said, but she was smiling.

"I'm happy, Kait. I've freelanced designs, and now I have this shop." Her gaze softened. "I love it here."

"Well, it's not what I want," Kaitlyn said firmly. "I want to work at a design house in New York. I don't care if I ever get my own line, as long as I can see my designs out there."

Ari stifled a smile at the naiveté of that remark. Still, Kaitlyn had the talent to succeed, and the stubbornness to keep at it. "I'll help you," she said impulsively.

Kaitlyn sat forward, face eager and hopeful. "Would you?"

"Yes."

"That would be so great." Kaitlyn glanced at the unfinished design on Ari's desk. "What's that?"

Ari made a face. "Something I can't get right. I want something different for next summer, but everything I come up with is boring."

"Could I try something?"

Ari slid the paper toward her with some apprehension. Lord only knew what Kaitlyn would come up with. "Here."

"Let's take the sleeves off." Kaitlyn erased the short, straight sleeves Ari had drawn. "Make the shoulders narrower." More erasing. "And lower the neckline, like that."

Ari frowned a bit as Kaitlyn sat back. "A tank top?"

"Why not? It will be cool, and the summer people will like it."

Just what Ari'd been thinking herself. "If I do it in cotton, with some openwork at the bottom—"

"No," Kaitlyn interrupted her. "Do it in ribbon yarn."

Ari stared at her. "You know, that might work."

"You could use a multicolored one."

"I'd have to put a lining in it if I use one with ladders in it," Ari said, thinking of the broad, thin yarns, made of rayon or nylon, that had spaces at regular intervals.

"No. Wait." Kaitlyn dashed out into the shop and came back with a yarn colored in primary shades. "This is solid. Sort of. It's thin, but can you imagine it made up? You wouldn't need to do anything fancy."

"No, maybe just a mixture of stitches to make a design," Ari said, looking at Kaitlyn with dawning respect. The yarn itself was so striking that it didn't require a complicated design. "It would be comfortable for summer, and just a little clingy. Just what I wanted, Kait."

"And the yarn's expensive enough that you'd make a bundle."

Ari laughed. "Sure." She pushed the paper back toward Kaitlyn. "You design it."

Kaitlyn's face lit up. "Are you sure?"

"It's your idea, not mine."

"Oh, thank you! Ari, you don't know what this means to me."

Ari smiled, feeling just a little smug and self-congratulatory at her generosity. "It works, Kait."

"Yeah, it does, doesn't it? Maybe I will get to New York, after all." Her smile faded at that. "I've got to, Ari. I've just got to. If I don't, I don't know what I'll do."

"You'll manage," Ari assured her. "Life has a way of working out, Kait."

"Yeah, right," Kaitlyn said, and walked out into the shop as the bells over the front door jangled.

Ari smiled after her. Maybe Kaitlyn would succeed, after all. Certainly today's ideas were good. Better than her own, she thought, looking down at her discarded sketches.

"Good morning, Ari. Isn't it such a beautiful day?"

Ari looked up to see Ruth Taylor in the office doorway. "Yes, it is, Mrs. Taylor," she said, wondering just why the older woman was here. She had a mischievous look in her eyes. "Can I help you with something?"

"Oh, no, thank you. I was taking my walk and I thought I'd stop in to see Laura. Is she here?"

"No, she's gone to Providence Place with the Red Hat group."

"Oh, I wonder if I should join that. I can't imagine wearing a purple dress with a red hat, though."

Ari smiled. A chapter of the Red Hat Society, a national organization for middle-aged women, had recently started up in Freeport and was a huge success. "Why not? It's the rule, and they seem to have fun."

"I think the colors clash."

"They do, but Laura seems to enjoy it. I'm planning a purple scarf for her," she said, indicating some fuzzy purple yarn.

"Really. Well, she always has been eccentric."

"She enjoys herself." Ari rose as the bells jangled over the door again, and went into the main part of the shop, with Ruth following. Kaitlyn was helping the customer, who had just come in to find some yarn, so Ari stood behind the sales counter.

"Have you heard any more about Edith, Ari?" Ruth asked.

"No."

"Oh. Well. I thought perhaps you might have. Eric is in town, you know."

"Yes, I do."

"That's right. You were with him at Marty's last night."

Ari sighed inwardly. "That's right."

"Do you know, I heard he was here before Edith died?"

"Oh?"

"Yes, Mrs. Joseph told me."

"Oh," Ari said again, hoping her face gave nothing away.

"I know you're friendly with Detective Pierce," she went on, an arch look on her face.

"No, not really."

"Didn't you have lunch together yesterday?"

"Mmm."

"Well? Did he tell you anything?"

"About the case, you mean?"

Ruth's face was avid. "Yes. After all, you're so involved with what's been going on."

"Not by choice."

"No, no, I didn't say that. But you and Diane . . . Well, I know you girls got up to some hijinks in high school, but I'm sure you never expected anything like this." Ruth glanced around the shop. "Diane does make beautiful yarn. Of course, you've been cleared."

Ari stacked together some papers. "Yes, I have."

"I imagine Diane hasn't."

"Oh?" Ari said, wary again. "What makes you say that?"

"Why, haven't you heard? The police are at the Camachos' right now."

CHAPTER 7

The first thing that Josh noticed when he turned into the driveway at Diane Camacho's farm was a flock of sheep grazing in the front yard near the door. Startled, he simply sat and stared. He was fast realizing he should expect the unexpected in this case.

Carefully, he opened the car door and stepped out, keeping a wary eye on the animals. They didn't look like killer sheep. In fact, they ignored him as they continued to munch on the grass. The only problem was that they were blocking the door to the house. He wasn't sure how he was going to get in.

Josh didn't have much experience with animals. He'd grown up in a rural town, but he'd lived in a development of cookie-cutter houses that looked as if they'd been dropped into place by some giant hand. This house was different. He'd seen enough old ones to know that this one, a Federal-style farmhouse, was probably at least two hundred years old. It had the twelve-over-twelve windows typical of the time, and though the front was sided with red clapboard, the other walls were covered with weathered shingles. Some long-ago farmer had sited it so that it faced south, with a carriage house behind it, and barns and a silo beyond. Farther back were pastures where cows drowsed in the warm sun, while across Acushnet Road stretched fields covered now only by yellowing stubble. They must be cornfields that had already been harvested to feed the stock, he thought, though he'd noted a small wooden structure in front, an obvious farm stand. Right now it was filled with pumpkins and gourds and various types of squash. Everything was neat, tidy, and prosperous-looking. The Camachos appeared to have made a success of their farm. What might they do if that success were threatened?

The black front door opened, and Diane stepped out onto the flagstoned stoop. "Hello," she called. "Come on around to the side door."

Josh looked dubiously at the sheep. "All right."

"Don't be sheepish, Detective. They won't bother you."

"Yeah," he said, and headed down the drive, embarrassed by Diane's grin at his predicament. Skirting the flock, he climbed the wooden stairs that led to the door. In the back, the house had been bumped out into what he suspected was a somewhat more recent addition. A pleasant veranda stretched the length of it, with pots of colorful mums hanging from the top frame. Diane let him in, and after passing through a mudroom, he found himself in a surprisingly modern kitchen. An island stood in the center of the room; it had a cooktop set into it, surrounded by gleaming granite. The same granite topped the honey oak cabinets that ran along the wall. Above those were more cabinets. One of them had a mullioned glass door, behind which he could see various types of glassware. More glasses, for different kinds of wine, hung upside down from a rack placed over the island. He noted also a huge stainless steel refrigerator, and a large sink under a broad window. This room was used for serious cooking, yet it managed to be cozy, with its ruffled curtains, rag rug, and a drop-leaf table that looked old to his unpracticed eye.

"I was just going to have tea," Diane said, taking an enameled kettle from the cooktop. "Would you like some?"

"Herbal tea?" he asked suspiciously.

"God, no! That stuff tastes like—well, I won't say that. No, I prefer regular tea. Darjeeling, today. I get my tea from High Tea," she added as she poured the water into a stoneware teapot. "You know, the tea shop in town." She set out two mismatched mugs, one of which read SPINNERS DO IT BAA-AD. "I'll let it steep for a minute. I like it strong. I have a feeling I'm going to need it." She looked at him warily. "Would you like some?"

"No, thanks."

"I've got coffee ready to brew, if you'd like that."

"Actually, I'd rather have a soda, if you have any."

"Of course. Diet Coke, or ginger ale?"

"Ginger ale." He waited while she poured some into a glass. "Thanks."

Diane picked up her mug and a plate of cookies. "We can talk in my workroom. It's sunny this time of day."

"Fine." Josh followed her down the central hallway of the house, his steps echoing on the warped, wide floorboards. To his right as they left the kitchen he saw a dining room, furnished with a pine trestle table and Windsor chairs, with a matching hutch. Only valances were at the windows, which were outlined in a painted design. "Nice," he commented.

"Thanks. I did the stenciling myself," Diane said over her shoulder.

Stenciling? Before this case Josh had known little about arts and crafts, but he was learning. "And your office?" he asked as they passed another room. The furniture, consisting of computer desk, bookcases, and filing cabinets, was utilitarian, but the rest of the decoration wasn't. Subdued burgundy-and-cream drapes were drawn at the windows, perhaps to filter out the sun, or to protect the worn, but still colorful, Oriental carpet.

"The farm office, though I keep my records there, too," she said, leading him toward the front of the house.

"Oh." A straight staircase, with a huge newel post and a banister worn smooth by the usage of years, rose to his right. The doorway to a formal-looking living room lay past it. Josh felt as if he'd had a tour of history, as well as a glimpse into quiet prosperity.

"Our bedrooms and family room are upstairs," Diane said, noting his look at the stairs. "This is my workroom."

Josh stopped in the doorway to the room, studying it unhurriedly. In contrast to the rest of the house, this room was cluttered and looked well used, with loops and cones of yarn everywhere. None of it was purple, he noticed. Across from him stood a large spinning wheel, its spindle wrapped in wool, ready to be spun. Near the window was a comfortable-looking brown leather sofa, set at right angles to a chintz armchair. "Do you spend a lot of time here?"

"Yes. I wanted it in the front of the house so I could have light from two windows."

"Natural light?" he guessed, sitting in the armchair and setting his glass on a small round table.

Diane quickly slipped a coaster under the glass, though the table was battered and scarred. "That's an antique. Yes, the natural light."

"Why does that matter?"

"It's full spectrum. Indoor light isn't, unless it's designed that way."

"I see."

She flashed him a quick grin. "You're getting an education on this case, aren't you? Do you mind if I work?"

"No, go ahead." He frowned a little as Diane sat on a ladder-back chair and pulled a wooden contraption toward her. It was about as high as her waist, and had a spoked wheel that faced out. "Is that a spinning wheel?"

"Yes. You thought I'd use that big thing?" she asked, glancing at the large spinning wheel he'd noticed when they came in.

"Yes."

"That's a high wheel. I don't know anyone who uses that type today."

"Another antique?"

"Yes. What I'm using is called a flyer wheel. Do you see this part here?" She pointed to something at the top of the spinning wheel that looked like a fork with two tines. "This is a flyer. Do you see how it's connected to the drive wheel by a band? When the drive wheel spins, the flyer turns, and that's what makes the wool into yarn. Like this." She took up some lumpy, uneven wool. "I've already started this. See how it's wound around the bobbin in the flyer? Watch."

Diane pumped a pedal at the bottom of the drive wheel. It began to spin, the flyer whirred, and the wool, which she held taut, twisted into fine yarn and wound around the bobbin. "There."

Josh sat forward, fascinated. "I've never known how that was done."

"It's easy," she said, going on with her work. "I could teach you how to do it."

He sincerely doubted that. "You like this house, don't you?"

"I love this house," she said fervently. "I grew up in a three-decker in the south end of New Bedford, before my family moved to Freeport. Even then, we lived in a development." She glanced around the room with pride on her face. "I always wanted an old house like this."

"Have you owned it long?"

"It's been in Joe's family for two hundred years. It actually came from his grandmother." She smiled. "I'm the granddaughter of Portuguese immigrants, but if I ever have a daughter she could be in the DAR."

So Diane and her husband had more reasons to protect their farm than strictly financial ones. "You must have been upset when—what was that?" he exclaimed, as a tall, oddly shaped form passed by the window.

"Probably Salvador."

"Salvador?"

"Salvador Dali Llama."

He would have groaned in response, had she not been a suspect. "Why do you have a llama?"

"To protect the sheep. Llamas keep predators away." She stopped spinning for a minute to frown at her yarn. "Not fine enough," she muttered, and went back to work. "I wanted to start keeping llamas for their wool—it's so soft and warm—but Joe put his foot down on that idea."

"Why are the sheep on the front lawn, by the way?"

"I put them there whenever I need to clean out their field. I'd like to have another field for them, but Joe needs the land for the cows."

"I see. Do you get enough wool from them for your yarn?"

"No. I still have a lot from the spring—that's when

we shear them—but I have to buy more from other producers. We've sold off lambs in the past, but next year I'm going to talk Joe into keeping some."

"Why did you sell lambs?"

Diane glanced up briefly. "Money. We sell our milk to a larger dairy for processing, but it's hard. Most dairy farms in New England are struggling these days. We can't compete with the big dairies in the Midwest."

So the farm's profit was marginal, Josh thought. Again, it was a reason for Diane to want to protect it. "What did you think of Edith Perry's plan to develop the property next to yours?"

This time Diane's eyes were hostile. "What do you think? We were furious."

"Were you?"

"Of course we were. We do as much as we can to keep down pests organically. That development would have changed everything. We'd have chemicals from road salt in winter, not to mention whatever people'd put on their grass. And let one septic system fail, and it would contaminate our ground water." The spinning wheel spun furiously as she worked. "The land at the Robeson farm is marshy in places. My guess is a developer would build it up with soil so it would pass a perk test."

Josh nodded noncommittally. He knew about perk tests, used to determine if land was dry enough for building septic systems. Building damp land up with dry fill was a common, if illegal, practice. "Did you do anything about it?"

Diane kept her eyes on the yarn winding on a spindle, her foot working the pedal vigorously. "The first we knew about it was when Edith filed the development plans. Joe tried talking to her, but all she would say was that it was her land and she could do what she wanted with it. I suppose that was true," she added grudgingly.

Josh let the silence lengthen. Most people couldn't handle silence, and usually rushed into speech to fill it. Diane didn't disappoint him.

"Joe and I went to the public hearing and spoke up against it," she said, and sat back, spinning abandoned for the moment. "I'll bet you're wondering why I'm telling you all this without a lawyer here."

"The thought crossed my mind."

"You'd find out about it anyway." She took up the wool again. "I bet you already know. It's no secret."

No, it wasn't. Did Diane realize how much she was incriminating herself, though? She had to know things didn't look good for her.

"I know I'm a suspect," she went on, as if she'd read his thoughts. "I have a key to the shop, which I've never used—not that you can tell—and I've got a humongous motive. But tell me something." She looked directly at him. "Do you really think I'd use my own yarn as a weapon?"

"I don't know."

Diane's lips firmed. "Well, I wouldn't. Do you have any idea what it takes for me to produce it?"

"No."

"We have to shear the sheep first. I have to hire

someone to do it, and that costs. Then I have to pick the fleece. That means pulling it apart, and picking out dirt or leaves or other things. After that, it has to be washed, and I'm not talking about in a washing machine. When that's done I dye it. I don't use chemicals, you know."

"No?"

"No, though I'll buy chemically dyed rovings—those are fleeces that have already been processed—and use them. My wool is dyed naturally." She turned to gesture to the yarns hanging on pegs on the wall. "See how the colors are all subdued? I tried making my own dyes, but it's too much work, so I buy them. Dyeing can take a couple of days, especially if I want to get a certain shade. I do only a limited number of colors, and even then it takes a long time for all the wool to be dyed, and to dry, before I can spin it."

"Oh."

Diane again stopped to check the yarn she had spun. Nodding in satisfaction, she set the wheel back in motion. "The yarn needs to be plied—that means spinning two or more strands together," she explained, before he could ask. "It's more work, of course, but it makes the yarn stronger and thicker. Yarn this thin is good for socks, but most people want heavier weights for sweaters."

Josh leaned forward, fascinated by the process. "I never realized there was so much involved."

She gave him a sudden smile. "Yes, but I do enjoy it."

"And then you put it into balls?"

"Yes."

"That looks like a lot of work."

"It's all a lot of work. The last thing I do is put labels on the balls, and they're ready. I charge a lot for them, but I have to. And guess what? They sell. So tell me, Detective." Her gaze was steady. "Why would I jeopardize all that work to kill someone? My God, why would I use my own yarn as a murder weapon?"

That bothered him, too. Still, stranger things had happened. "Is it profitable?"

"It's taken a while, but yes, I'm starting to turn a profit. People like what I do. If something happened to the farm, though, I couldn't support us with it."

"So it's a supplement?"

"It's what I love to do." She rested her hand on the wheel, which, judging by the lack of varnish and the darkness of the wood, was not new. "You need to understand that about us. About me. I love what I do."

Would she kill to protect it? he wondered. Somehow he couldn't see it, and yet she was the most likely suspect. "Mrs. Camacho, where were you the morning Edith Perry was killed?"

Diane gave a short laugh that held little mirth. "What are you basing your suspicions on, Detective— that my yarn was used? I already told you about that."

"You have a key to the shop."

"Had a key. Ari's changed the lock."

He looked at her steadily. After a moment, Diane looked away. "Where were you?" he asked again.

"Here." She concentrated on her spinning. "You can ask any of our workers. They'll tell you."

"What time do they start work?"

"Around six. Ask them," she repeated.

He nodded, and rose. "I will. Is now convenient?"

"No, but I suppose that doesn't matter." She rose and went into the hall, to a phone on a table there. "Pat Sylvia will be in to talk to you in a few minutes," she said, after speaking briefly into the phone.

Outside, as he waited for Sylvia to come in from wherever he was working, Josh reviewed the conversation. Diane's motive was strong. She'd had too much to lose if Edith's project had gone through: the farm, their way of life, her yarn business. Oddly enough, that last struck him most of all. She was fiercely protective of her yarn. He also had no doubt that she had an alibi. He still had to consider her a suspect.

Pat Sylvia confirmed Diane's alibi a few minutes later. He'd seen her getting ready to feed the sheep at around six o'clock, when he got to work. He was scornful of the idea that she'd kill anyone. Anyway, it was stupid to think she'd do anything to hurt the farm, or Joe. Both were too important to her.

All in all, Josh felt unsatisfied as he walked toward his car. He liked Diane. Her alibi wasn't airtight; there was a small window of time for her to get to Ari's shop and then return to the farm. Since she'd been taking care of her sheep at the time, though, he doubted it. It would take a stone-cold killer without nerves to act like that, and that didn't fit his reading of Diane's character. Motive or not, opportunity or not, he was beginning to doubt that she was his culprit.

Joe Camacho was another matter. Since the farm

had been in his family for generations, his motive was stronger than Diane's. Josh kept coming back to where Edith was killed. Why had it been in that particular place? Certainly Joe could have taken Diane's key and gotten in there, but would Edith Perry have gone along with him, or trusted him enough to let him get close enough to strangle her? It seemed doubtful. It was even more doubtful since Diane said that Joe had been there all morning. Yet Josh would have to look closely at him. There were too many connections to this farm in the case, particularly the yarn.

That left him back where he'd started, with no likely suspects and no idea what had happened. He was missing something, though, something that had been said or not said, or something that he'd seen. The question was, what?

Restless, dissatisfied, he turned, taking in the view of the farm: the old house, the barn and other outbuildings, the fields stretching in both directions. This time he looked harder at the long, low shed that extended from the back of the house, its door ajar. It was so crowded and cluttered that Josh wandered over to look in, out of sheer curiosity and amusement. It didn't seem as if the Camachos had ever thrown anything away. Crammed inside were old furniture and equipment, bits of metal he couldn't identify, an old rocking horse with rusted springs. He would never have expected to see such things, but someone obviously thought them worth saving. He pondered that as he looked past the doorway into the dimness, seeing bricks and open bags of cement mix, a trowel crusted with mortar, various and sundry tools, and a pile of wood.

That caught his attention. Scraps of wood, painted and unpainted; long, wide boards and short, narrow sticks; old laths and discarded window fittings. He now knew what he'd seen and noted without being aware of it. The solution to Edith's murder might very well be found in the shed.

CHAPTER 8

It was quiet in Ariadne's Web again on Tuesday morning, the first day in the week the shop was open. Edith's wake had been last night, and today was her funeral. Later on, customers were sure to come in to tell her about it, Ari thought, but for now she was alone. She hoped Diane would call her as well, but she doubted it. For some reason Diane was keeping very quiet about what Josh had wanted on her farm on Saturday, even to Ari. That bothered Ari more than anything that had happened after Edith's death.

Forcing her mind away from that worry, she clicked the computer's mouse to bring up a screen, and regarded it with a frown. The disk Kaitlyn had left her last weekend contained all of the work she'd done on the web page, which she'd shown Ari with great eagerness.

"See, I found a graphic with balls of yarn for the background. Isn't it great?" she'd said.

"Yes. I like the pastel shades. I like the logo, too." Ari ran the cursor over the logo on the page. It depicted a spider hanging from a web, holding a pair of knitting needles from which trailed another ball of yarn. Above the logo was the headline: "Designs by Ari," with a smaller headline below reading, "Ariadne Evans, Professional Designer."

"I do, too. The spiderweb's made of yarn. That's what makes it work." Kaitlyn smiled. "It'll make your site stand out from all the others."

Ari looked at her. "There are that many?"

"A lot of people are selling their designs on the Internet. I like the picture of you, too."

Ari looked with disfavor at the photo below the logo. In it she modeled one of her designs, an oatmeal-colored tunic with colorful autumn leaves splashed across the front of it. Knitted in seed stitch, it had a wide neck edged only with a row of single crochet stitches, and long, loose sleeves. It was one of her favorite sweaters, but seeing herself on the screen made her uncomfortable. "I still don't see the purpose of it, Kait."

"It makes everything more personal. Isn't it great that it lines up with the logo? I had to use tables to do it."

"Uh-huh," Ari said, without the slightest idea of what Kaitlyn was talking about.

"Now, look, down here is a link to the patterns." Kaitlyn clicked on the line of text, and after a moment another screen came up. This one had a background of stockinette stitch in pale gray, and on it were displayed the names of Ari's designs: "October," "Pastel Cables," "Christmas Belles." Only the caption "October" had a picture above it, the one of Ari. "I'll be adding the other photos to it soon. A customer can click on either the name or the picture to get to the pattern." As she spoke, Kaitlyn moved the cursor to the picture, and yet another screen came up, this one with a larger view of the sweater, with a description underneath. Instructions on how to buy the pattern were below that. "See? You're set up to take credit cards already, or a customer can pay by check."

"Is it safe?"

Kaitlyn stared at her. "Ari, haven't you ever bought anything online?"

"No. I don't trust it."

"It's perfectly safe. We're going to use secure technology. No one can see anyone else's personal information."

"Oh," Ari said, mystified, and watched as Kaitlyn took her through the steps of buying either a pattern or a full kit, which included yarn. There was a page for name and address, another for method of payment, still another for shipping, and then a final page, which confirmed the purchase. It seemed involved to Ari, but Kait had assured her that it would work.

"Once the order is in, the customer gets an e-mail confirming it, and you get an e-mail with the order," Kaitlyn went on.

"Which I then have to ship out."

"Yes, the charge goes through as usual, and you'll have to keep track of inventory as usual. Eventually, you should e-mail patterns as attachments."

Ari sat back. She was impressed, if a little mystified. Even though she used the computer for keeping records and for designing her projects, anything else was foreign to her. "I don't know, Kaitlyn," she said slowly. "Oh, not the website. You've done a great job with it. The design is beautiful."

Kaitlyn preened. "Thank you. I've worked hard on it."

"I appreciate it. But to sell this way, instead of helping a customer find what's right for her—I don't know."

"You'll have enough designs that people can pick what they want. It'll be almost as good as freelancing your designs. No, better, because people will know they're yours." Kaitlyn's eyes glittered. "You could have your own line. The Ariadne Evans line."

Ari laughed. Kaitlyn's ambition was not unusual, but her fervor was. "Yes, well, let's see if I get any customers before we go that far."

"You will," Kaitlyn said confidently. "Now, we should think about promotion. . . ."

Promotion, Ari thought after Kaitlyn had gone out a little while later, leaning back with her elbows on the arms of her comfortable, old-fashioned desk chair with her fingertips pressed together. *Advertisement.* There were ways to get her name out to people on the web that wouldn't cost her a penny, Kaitlyn had told her. It all sounded like a lot of work, and so foreign to what she did. Ari was resigned to the behind-the-scenes work that came with owning a business, and she'd done her fair share of promoting her work.

What she liked best, though, was design, as well as the daily contact with people who enjoyed the same things she did. Life was changing, she thought and, for some reason she couldn't fathom, she shivered.

The ringing of the phone startled her out of her reverie. *Darned thing,* she thought, and picked up. "Ariadne's Web."

"Mrs. Evans, this is Deborah Flaherty."

Ari snapped to attention. Mrs. Flaherty was the principal of Megan's school. "Is Megan all right?" she demanded.

"Yes, she's not hurt."

"Hurt!"

"Mrs. Evans, we have a problem."

Ari stood with her hand to her throat. "What kind of problem?"

"Megan has been involved in a fight."

"A fight? Megan? That doesn't sound like her."

"No, it doesn't, which is why I'm so concerned. I'd appreciate it if you could come in."

"But I don't have anyone to cover the shop," she began, and then stopped. Megan was more important. "I'll be right there," she said, and fairly flew out of the door, flipping the sign to CLOSED. Damn, of all days for her not to have taken her car, she thought as she strode toward her house. Maybe she should give up her habit of walking whenever she could.

"Ari," a voice called, and she looked sharply at the street. She had been vaguely aware that a car was cruising beside her, but hadn't paid attention to it. "Is something wrong?"

"Josh." She put her hand to her hair, looked away, and then back. "I can't talk. I have to go."

Josh leaned over and opened the passenger door. "Get in. I'll drive you."

Again Ari looked distractedly down the street, and then ran to the car. "Thanks. I'm all discombobulated," she said as she climbed in.

"Why? What happened?"

"It's Megan."

"Is she all right?" he asked, as sharply as she had a few minutes ago.

"I think so, but I have to get to the school."

"I'll drive you."

She gave him a quick, distracted smile. Who said there was never a cop around when you needed one? "No, just to my house, please, so I can get my own car. I've never been in a police car before."

"Yeah. Listen, Ari, when you have the chance, we have to talk."

"Okay," she said, pulling on the door handle as Josh stopped in front of her house. Nothing mattered now, not her shop, not whatever was happening in the murder investigation. Megan was the only important thing.

A few minutes later, Ari was sitting in the principal's office at Megan's school with Mrs. Flaherty looking gravely at her. Megan was in the outer office, and the face she'd turned up to Ari was filled with a mixture of misery and guilty defiance. Ari had time only to put her hand on her daughter's head before Mrs. Flaherty called her in.

"They won't say what started it," Mrs. Flaherty said from behind her desk. It was a position Ari had been in herself many times, but not on Megan's behalf. "What everyone does say is that Megan swung at Jacob first."

"Jacob Pina?" Ari said in disbelief. "He has to be three inches taller than she is."

"Regardless, that is what Mrs. Dyer saw."

Why did every principal speak in the same stilted, formal way? Ari wondered. "What *did* happen?"

"The children were lined up waiting to go back inside from recess," Mrs. Flaherty explained. "Mrs. Dyer didn't see anything out of the ordinary until Megan suddenly turned and swung at Jacob and hit his ear." Jacob, of course, had started blubbering almost immediately. At least, that was Ari's interpretation. Jacob was the sort who blubbered.

"What did he have to say?" she asked with assumed calmness.

"He claims he didn't do anything."

"Claims?"

"No one saw him."

Which meant that Mrs. Flaherty likely had the same doubts she did, Ari thought. "Then he said something. Mrs. Flaherty, you know as well as I do that Jacob's been a troublemaker since kindergarten."

"Apparently not in this case."

"Oh, come on! He's always done things when no one's looking and gotten away with them. Once he grabbed Megan's snack when he'd finished his, and when she tried to get it back, the teacher thought she was taking his."

"Well—"

"And another time he threw spitballs at Shannon Souza, but no one saw that, either."

"Mrs. Evans, in both cases the teacher disciplined him."

"As well as Megan and Shannon."

"Well—"

"He must have started it somehow."

Mrs. Flaherty folded her hands on her desk and gazed at Ari. "Mrs. Evans, I know no parent likes to think their child can act out like this."

"Megan doesn't."

"This isn't the first time Megan's misbehaved."

That rocked Ari. "What?"

"Megan didn't tell you?"

"No," Ari said, stunned, but understanding Megan's reasons, too. When Ari was young she'd never told her mother when she'd gotten into trouble at school. Eileen had always found out, of course, which had made the resultant discipline that much worse. For the first time, Ari sympathized with her mother. "What has she done?"

"Talking in class, several times. Not doing her work when she was supposed to. Bothering the other children when they were working. At first she got warnings, but Mrs. Dyer had to put her name on the board. You know that she puts a child's name on the board with checkmarks for each breach of discipline, and when there are three checks, the child has detention."

"But Megan never has."

"No, having her name on the board seemed to settle her down," Mrs. Flaherty agreed. "But she did get sent to me yesterday."

"What? Why?"

"For talking back to Mrs. Dyer."

"Megan?" Ari's voice rose in disbelief.

"Mrs. Evans, we were all as surprised as you are. Megan's always been a well-behaved little girl. This pattern is troubling." Mrs. Flaherty's gaze was almost pitying. "Of course, she's been under a lot of stress lately."

"Yes. The divorce upset her."

"I meant, what happened in your shop."

That rocked her again. In her concern for Megan, she'd forgotten the events of the past days. "I've tried to keep that from her."

"Children know these things. Even if you haven't shown that you're upset, she senses it."

Something occurred to Ari. "Has there been a lot of talk about it in school?"

"Among the teachers, of course."

"I meant among the kids. Children know these things," Ari mimicked, which earned her a frown.

"Be that as it may." Mrs. Flaherty tapped together some papers that were on her desk, while Ari marveled again that someone actually spoke in such a way. "We do have a problem."

Ari nodded. "What do you suggest I do?"

"I'm sending her home for the day. Of course, this is not a reward for her."

Ari wanted to roll her eyes. "Megan likes school."

Mrs. Flaherty nodded. "I'm going to make an appointment for Megan with the school counselor."

"What will she do?" Ari asked, surprised by the fierce surge of protectiveness she felt.

"She'll talk to Megan. The best way to deal with children of this age is to have them draw pictures to express their feelings." Mrs. Flaherty rose. "We'll find out whatever's wrong."

Ari stood up, too, wanting nothing more than to leave this office and get to Megan. Her feelings were so mixed and muddled that she couldn't figure them out. "Thank you," she said, and went out.

In the outer office, Megan sat forward on a chair, with Jacob across from her. He was blubbering again, this time to his mother, who shot Ari a venomous look. All Ari's attention, though, was on Megan, who was stiff, her eyes on the floor. *Poor kid*, she thought. Why hadn't she realized that Megan was so affected by what had happened?

Someone had brought her things to the office. Ari helped her get into her jacket and picked up her backpack. "Lots of homework tonight?" she asked as they walked out.

Megan nodded, her gaze still down. Acting by instinct, Ari dropped the backpack and went down on one knee, doing what she wished she'd done when she'd first saw Megan, before going into Mrs. Flaherty's office. She pulled her close. "Oh, honey," she said as Megan started crying, and rocked her back and forth, murmuring soothing nonsense.

After a while Megan calmed down, and Ari rose to her feet, reaching for the backpack. "Come on, kiddo," she said, holding out her hand. "Let's go get some ice cream."

✄

The phone was ringing as Ari and Megan walked into the house sometime later. "Oh, heck," Ari said, lunging at it before whoever it was could hang up. Megan, head down, walked past her and put her backpack onto the counter, and it was only then that it occurred to Ari that she could have let the answering machine pick up. Too late now. She'd get rid of whoever it was, and then go take care of her daughter.

"Ari?" Diane's voice came over the receiver.

Ari straightened. Diane's voice sounded strained. "Di, what is it?"

"That detective of yours."

"He's not my detective," Ari protested.

"Huh."

"He's not."

"You had lunch with him the other day."

"Yes, but he only wanted to ask me some questions."

"At the bandstand?" Diane said skeptically. "I know he's cuter than Ted—"

"Oh, for heaven's sake, Di!"

"Well, he is."

"All right, yes, he is, but he's still just a cop and I'm still just a suspect."

"Even after what Ronnie Dean said?"

"There's still this small amount of time when I could have done it, and you know I could conceivably have reason to."

"Yeah, right. You're working together, aren't you?"

"What makes you say that?"

"I know you, Ari."

"Damn," Ari said after a minute.

"Strong language for you."

"No one's supposed to know. He could get in trouble."

"So could you," Diane pointed out.

"You're my friend."

"Yeah," Diane said, with more skepticism than Ari had ever heard from her. "Anything I tell you will go back to him."

"No, it won't."

"No?"

"Viking honor," Ari said.

Diane laughed. "God, I haven't heard that since high school!"

"Did I ever go back on my word?" Ari demanded. "Did you?"

"No," Diane said finally.

"What did he want Saturday? You never did tell me."

"No, my lawyer doesn't want me to talk. But, Ari, I can't keep things from you."

"What happened, Di?

"He thinks it's me, Ari. Your detective, not the lawyer. Even though I told him I would never use my yarn that way. Hell, I sat there and spun so he'd see what it was like. I told him all about how I process yarn and how I go to wool shows to buy rovings and fleeces and to see what everyone else is doing. I told him I wanted to make a go of it. And what did he do?"

"What?" Ari asked, though she knew the question was rhetorical.

"Nothing. Just nodded, the way he does. He doesn't talk much, does he?" she said bitterly.

Ari let out her breath. "Not when he doesn't want to tell you something, no."

"So he thinks I did it." There was silence for a moment. "Or Joe."

Ari took a deep breath. "He wouldn't. You wouldn't."

"Yeah. He didn't come out and say it, but, come on, Ari. I'm not dumb. If it's not me, it has to be Joe."

"But why would he? And how could he have done it? He was at home, wasn't he?"

"Of course he was," Diane said quickly.

This time Ari was quiet. She knew her friend. Diane was keeping something from her. "What happened, Di?"

"Edith offered to buy the farm."

"She didn't!"

"Oh, she did, and for a decent price, too. Not what it's worth, but still. She wanted to add it to the Robeson property and develop it. I'll tell you, Ari. If the police hear about that, we'll be in trouble for sure."

"Why? It takes away your motive."

"Yeah? It means she was threatening us both ways,

with that development of hers, and then wanting to take our land. I hope no one knew about that."

"They won't hear it from me," Ari said absently, her head still whirling.

"No?"

"For God's sake, Diane! I already told you I won't say anything."

"I know," Diane said, her voice small. "I'm sorry,"

"I'd hope so," Ari said, still ruffled. "You refused, of course."

"We didn't have the chance."

"Di. You didn't agree? Did you?"

"No," she said, though there was a note in her voice Ari couldn't interpret. "But a farm's hard work, and you know small dairy farms are having a rough time. That's one reason I took up spinning."

"You were tired of spending money for yarn and decided to make your own. Di, did you consider it?"

"Are you kidding? You know I love this place. It's Joe who wanted to."

"You're kidding!"

"Nope."

"But why? The farm's been in his family for years."

"He hates it, Ari," she said softly. "He always has."

"I had no idea."

"No one does. He wanted to be a lawyer."

"Joe?" Ari said incredulously.

"Yes, but he had no choice. His parents always assumed he'd take the farm over, even though his sister really wanted it."

"Do his parents know?"

"That he doesn't want to work here? No."

"No, I mean about Edith's offer."

"Are you kidding? That would've had them back from Florida in an instant."

"Yes, I suppose." Diane's in-laws, though retired, still kept close tabs on what was going on on their property. "That's all you'd need, your mother-in-law here."

Diane snorted, but when she spoke her voice was serious. "It's a problem, Ari."

"Well, you can't sell the land now," she said prosaically. "Not with Edith dead . . ." Her voice trailed off.

"Yeah," Diane said in response to Ari's unvoiced thought. "It gives me a motive, doesn't it?"

"Di, no one will believe you had anything to do with Edith's death."

"You sure about that? I'm not."

"Do you have an alibi?"

"Yeah. Pat Sylvia saw me."

Ari shifted uneasily in her chair. There was that something in her voice again. "What is it, Di?"

Diane paused. "The day Edith was killed . . ."

"Yes?"

"Joe went out."

"When?"

"Around five."

"Di—"

"I know. It looks bad."

"But why?"

"Oh, Ari." She sounded miserable. "We had such a

fight, about selling the land. And you know how Joe is when he gets mad. He got in his truck and just took off. I don't know where he went."

"Diane, he didn't kill Edith."

"I know."

"He didn't. How could he have gotten into my shop? And besides, he didn't have as much reason as you . . ."

"As much reason as I have," Diane finished for her. "The police don't know that, though. Oh, Ari, what will I do if the police find out?"

"I don't know," Ari said, a leaden feeling in the pit of her stomach. By rights of their agreement, she should tell Josh about this. By rights of friendship, though, she owed it to Diane not to, and friendship won. "I won't say a word."

"Oh, Ari, you won't?"

"Did you really think I would?"

"I don't know."

"Di—"

"I'm sorry! But I'm so scared."

"I know," Ari said, still a little nettled by Diane's assumption, still torn about her decision not to tell Josh. "But everything is going to be fine."

"I hope so." Diane paused. "Thanks for listening to me."

"What are friends for?"

"Yeah. I know. Oh, shit."

"What?"

"The police are here again."

"They are?" Ari asked, alert.

"Yes, your friend and some others. Shit."

Right, Ari thought. "Maybe it's nothing."

"Ha. Bye," Diane said, and hung up.

Ari closed her eyes and replaced the receiver in the cradle very, very carefully. Police at the Camacho farm meant only one thing. Diane was in big trouble.

Josh stood beside his car, search warrant in hand, and surveyed the farm again. Under the best of circumstances a search could be difficult, but on this farm, with all its outbuildings, the prospect was daunting, even with other officers to help him search. Josh thought he knew where he'd find the key piece of evidence, though. That pile of scrap wood in the shed had been bothering him since he'd seen it.

The sheep weren't in evidence this afternoon, which was a relief. Diane met him at the side door, her face set and stony. It was true she had an alibi, but something was wrong here. Somehow Edith Perry's death was connected to this farm. "Mrs. Camacho," he said formally.

"Detective." Her voice was frosty, and as formal as his. "Is there something I can do for you?"

"Yes." He set his foot on the bottom stair leading to the porch, feeling at a distinct disadvantage. "I want to search your house."

"Absolutely not," she snapped back.

Well, it had been worth a try, though he'd known from her face that she wasn't going to cooperate. "It will be to your advantage, if you have nothing to hide—"

"Oh, can it. I don't know what you're expecting to find, but you're not looking anywhere without a search warrant."

He gazed at her for a moment, and then reached into his inner pocket to produce the warrant. "I have one here."

"Let me see it." She held out her hand for the document and then studied it. "Damn it. House, barn, shed—I don't know what gives you the right."

He gazed at her steadily. "My job does."

"Ha." She looked up. "Are you going to search now?"

"Yes. The other officers and I."

She looked past him toward the other policemen, her lips set in a tight line. "Then I'd better call our lawyer," she said, and stalked back into the house.

Sometime later, Josh, hands on hips, stood outside near one of the barns, frustrated. While they had taken away several brown paper evidence bags containing pieces of wood of various shapes and sizes, along with several battered baseball bats and canes, the search had basically turned up nothing. There was just too much stuff. A lot of things accumulated in old houses, Diane said with a trace of malice. Thus the rooms in the attic were filled, the shed was packed almost to capacity, and the barns held old machinery and odds and ends. Diligent though the searchers were, there were so many places to hide things that their task seemed impossible, especially since that stack of wood in the shed hadn't yielded anything remotely useful. There was a slight possibility that they would find something. There was, however, a much stronger one that they wouldn't. It had been a week since Edith's death. That left ample time either to destroy evidence, or to hide it so well it might never be found.

Beside Josh stood Joe Camacho, who was obviously aggrieved. He was a short, stocky man, with a square face and dark curling hair; he wore green work pants and a sweatshirt proclaiming in faded letters that he was a Freeport Townie. He seemed an odd match for Diane, who was tall and slim and even in jeans had a kind of elegance, but the two of them presented a united front to the policemen who had invaded their home.

The Camachos' lawyer was not happy about the search. Nor did he look happy now as he talked with Diane, Josh noted as he watched from across the farmyard. She had, as she'd said to Josh, incriminated herself. She'd also made a valid point. What had passed between her and Edith was no secret.

"What are you looking for, anyway?" Joe asked abruptly, his hands shoved into his pants pockets.

"You know I can't tell you that," Josh said.

Joe snorted. "Don't know what you think you're gonna find."

"You never know."

"All this because of that damned yarn."

Josh looked at him. He had the feeling Joe wasn't referring just to the murder weapon. "Your wife works hard at it," he commented.

"Too damned hard. I wish she'd get over it."

"What do you mean?"

"This hobby of hers. Takes her away too much from the dairy."

"She's making money."

"Yeah, for what that's worth." He glared at Josh. "You get your kicks out of sticking your nose into people's lives, Detective?"

"It's my job."

"Yeah."

Josh didn't take offense at the skepticism in the other man's voice. He'd heard worse. "Diane told me how much work it is."

"Yeah, Diane's a worker. I'll say that for her. Look, don't get me wrong." He turned. "I'm damned proud of Diane and what she's done."

"But you don't like it."

"Hate it." He thrust his hands deeper into his pockets. "I hate sheep and I hate yarn. The farm should come first."

Josh cast him a swift glance. It was the first time he'd heard anyone express that particular sentiment. From this man, it might be significant.

From the barn, there came a sudden shout. "Detective!"

"Excuse me." Josh strode toward the shadowy coolness of the barn, and snapped on rubber gloves. "What is it?"

"This." One of the searchers turned toward him. "We found it in that pile of scrap over there."

Josh glanced over at the small pile of lumber, some

obviously used, some new, and then carefully took what looked like a wooden stick. It was only a few inches long, smooth on one side and beveled on one long edge; rough and untreated on the other. The smooth side had been painted white, and had chipped. It looked like a window stop, and like the sticks used to make the garrote that had killed Edith.

Stepping outside, Josh looked at the house. No, those didn't look like replacement windows, he thought. In fact, he'd bet they were the originals, with sash weights and pulleys intact. This piece of wood might have come from one of those windows. He could readily find that out.

The jagged edge at one end of the stick, however, was what held his attention. If this was what he thought it was, it was strong evidence against the Camachos, evidence he'd paradoxically hoped not to find. He couldn't be certain, but it looked to him that at least one piece of the garrote had been broken off this particular stick.

CHAPTER 9

It was late afternoon. The day had dragged, with no news about what was happening at the Camacho farm, and Ari was glad to see it come to an end. She was about to close up when the bells over the shop's door jangled. "Ari?"

"In here, Diane," Ari called from the office, straightening abruptly. There was a note in Diane's voice she hadn't heard since Diane's mother had died several years ago. "What happened?"

Diane stood in the doorway to the office, her face pale and her jaw set. "You didn't hear?"

"About the police? No, not since I talked to you. Let's go into the back room. I'll put some water on for tea."

"I'd rather have a beer," Diane muttered.

Ari turned in surprise from running water into a kettle. There was a time when Diane had been a heavy drinker. She had, in fact, dropped out of college because of it. At some point, though, she'd caught hold of herself, and to Ari's knowledge she rarely touched a drop. "What happened?" she asked again.

Diane dropped into a chair at the dinette table. "He asked a lot of questions."

"About what?"

Diane fidgeted, and then slumped. "He had a search warrant."

"Oh, no." Ari sank down at her desk, her fingers clutching the edge. "What was he looking for?"

"I don't know. Joe saw something, though."

"What?"

"The damndest thing, Ari. Joe said they took an old piece of wood from a window."

"Like what?"

"A window stop. You know, the piece on the side where the sash weight is."

"Oh, my God." Into Ari's mind flashed the image that had haunted her for days, of the yarn tangled about Edith's throat and the two sticks twisted in that yarn. Discarded wood from a window. Of course.

"What?" Diane demanded. "You know something, don't you?"

"I can't tell you."

Diane's eyes narrowed. "The wood means something, doesn't it? What?"

Ari spread her hands helplessly. "Di, I'd tell you if I could, but I've been told not to."

"By the police?"

"Yes."

"Damn it, Ari!" Diane jumped to her feet. "I'm your best friend."

"I know, but I still can't tell you."

Diane stalked to the door and then pivoted. "I'm going to be arrested, you know. Or Joe is."

"But you have alibis."

"I'm Joe's alibi. You know that. They'll find a way to break them somehow. You watch." She took a step toward Ari. "Why won't you help me?"

"Di, please." Ari braced her hands on the table. "I can't. I wish I could, but I can't."

"Yeah." Diane's lips set in a firm line. "Fine," she said, and strode out of the room. A moment later Ari heard the shop door slam shut, the bells ringing discordantly.

Behind Ari, the kettle whistled. Distracted, she turned to stare at it, and then let out a breath. Two minutes ago, she'd been making tea for Diane. How short a time for so deep a rift to develop between them. They'd argued in the past, but never like this. Never over something so serious. Their long friendship had probably just ended.

But what could she have done? She plopped down at the table again, resting her chin in her hands. She really had been warned by the police not to say a word about the garrote. A window fitting. No wonder the two pieces of wood looked familiar. Just last year the Camachos had replaced the sash weights and ropes in their windows. Probably they had done the same with the surrounding wood. If so, someone had found it handy.

"Trouble?" Laura asked from the doorway.

Ari looked up. She should have expected Laura to come in at some point. After all, she'd hardly missed a day since the murder. *How much of the conversation had she overheard,* Ari wondered. She had to have seen the garrote, but she'd yet to say a word about it. "The police searched Diane's farm."

Laura walked a little farther into the room. "Did they find anything?"

"I don't know."

Laura gave her a look, and then smiled. "Perhaps Detective Pierce can tell us."

Ari grimaced. This part of the case had gone beyond her, which meant she had to find out more about what was going on. Little by little, all the important parts of her life were being threatened: her freedom, her livelihood, and now her most enduring friendship. Diane couldn't have killed anyone. "I suppose I should call him."

"No need, dear," Laura said cheerfully. "He'll be here in a few minutes."

"What? How do you know that?"

"Oh, he said he might come by."

Ari looked at her suspiciously. "Aunt Laura, did you ask him to?"

"Why, yes, dear."

"Good God!" Ari stared at her. "Why did you do that?"

"I thought you'd like to be brought up to date."

"Are you matchmaking?"

"Would I do that?"

"Yes."

"He is a fine-looking young man," she said thoughtfully. "And you do like him."

Ari put her face in her hands. Would this day never end? "Only as a friend."

"Friend, my foot. I don't think he looks at you that way."

"No," Ari agreed. "To him I'm a nuisance." And he was going to arrest her best friend.

"Oh, hardly that, dear."

"Aunt Laura—"

"It's time you woke up and faced facts," Laura interrupted her, in the brisk voice she used so rarely that it always drew instant attention. "You're an attractive woman, but you're not getting any younger. If you want to get married again, you need to start working on it."

"I don't want to get married again, Laura. You of all people should understand that."

Laura dismissed her very brief, and very much in the past, marriage with a wave of her hand. "Oh, that. I was young."

"Twenty-four, weren't you?"

"Yes, but he was a jerk, dear."

Ari rolled her eyes. Privately, she agreed that her uncle Mike wasn't exactly personable or intelligent. Laura, on the other hand, was both gregarious and devious. "Laura, what's on your mind?" she demanded.

"I just want to see you happy, dear," Laura said, giving Ari her most innocent look.

"Bullsh—baloney." Ari's eyes narrowed. "You want me to try to find out what's happening in the investigation."

"Of course I do. Don't you want to know?"

Of course she did, especially after Diane's visit. Thank God her aunt didn't know of her agreement with Josh, or she'd want in. Ari already had enough of Laura's well-meaning meddling in her life. "Were there a lot of people at the funeral?"

"Yes, more than I expected." Laura hung her coat on the metal rack. "Herb put on a luncheon at the Century House afterward. You were missed, dear," she added.

Ari doubted that. She did suspect, however, that she'd been a topic of conversation. "I'm sure I was," she said dryly.

"It was actually sadder than I thought it would be."

"Well, it's about time people take Edith's death seriously. I know she wasn't well liked, but still."

"Yes," Laura agreed. "Everyone's been concentrating on what's been happening since."

"As well as the sensationalism of it. I hope that will die down soon."

Laura went into the front room. "I'm tired of working on this sweater," she said. "I was thinking about making another scarf to put on display. Something cheery for winter, but simple. What do you think about the garnet eyelash yarn?"

Stripe it with pink and white and it will be perfect, Ari thought involuntarily. "Why don't you make a red beret to go with the purple scarf first? You can knit in spangles to make it fancy. Your friends in the Red Hat group will love it."

"That's an idea. Red mohair?"

"Yes. I put some aside this morning," Ari said. "You'll have to thread the spangles on the yarn first."

Laura made a face. "I hate doing that. I think I'll start from the top of the beret and work down. If I put the spangles only on the bottom, I won't have to use too many."

"However you want to do it. You'll be the one wearing it."

"Yes, I will, won't I? Now, where are those size-seven circular needles?"

"Here," Ari said, taking them from a lower shelf on the sales counter. She kept needles aside for the use of her staff, so that they didn't have to open packages that were meant for sale. "And some double-pointed ones, too."

"And the mohair?"

"Why don't you bring it home?" Ari suggested. "It's nearly time to close up."

Laura looked up. "With Detective Pierce coming?"

"He'll be too busy, after being out at Diane's."

"Maybe not, dear. Here he is."

Ari cursed silently as the door opened. She wasn't sure how much she could take. It had already been a difficult, emotional day, considering her two conversations with Diane. "You look tired," she said, surprising herself.

Josh nodded. "I am."

"Did you find anything?"

He looked from her to Laura. "You know I can't say."

"Ah. Then you did," Laura said.

Ari studied him. There was more than tiredness in his eyes, but she didn't know what it was. "I think you should go home and get some rest."

He shook his head. "I still have work to do."

Ari walked him to the door. "I imagine we'll be hearing the results, anyway."

"Probably. Listen, Ari. Lock up tight."

She frowned. "Why?"

Again he shrugged. "Just a feeling. Don't take risks."

"I won't," she said, perplexed, and watched as he crossed the street to his car.

"And you say you're not involved with him, dear," Laura said behind her.

"I'm not."

"Then what was that about?"

Ari shrugged. Like Josh, that was something she couldn't answer.

She didn't see Josh again until the next day. She was studying the packing list for a new shipment of yarn when she heard the door open. "Oh!" She whipped off the half glasses she hated to admit she needed for reading. "Josh."

"Hi." He ambled into the room, looking better than he had the day before, though just as serious. The familiar blue cooler swung from his left hand. He glanced at Laura, relaxed in the rocking chair Ari kept for her customers' comfort, her needles flying. "How do you do that?"

Laura held up the red hat, which was far enough along and had enough stitches that she was now using the circular needles, and beamed at him. "Easy. Look." She waited until he was bending over her. "Right-hand needle through the stitch on the left-hand needle, but behind it. Loop the yarn over the right needle, pull the needle back from the yarn, and pull the stitch off the left needle. Simple knitting stitch, Detective."

"I see."

"Knit and purl. All knitting comes from those two stitches."

"I thought you used straight needles."

"Oh, no, not always. I'm knitting in the round so the hat will have no seams."

"Oh." He pulled at his ear.

"Doesn't your mother knit, Detective?"

"My mother's an accountant," he said, as if that explained everything.

"Ah." Laura nodded. "Left-brained."

"I suppose." He turned to Ari. "Ready?"

"For what?" she asked.

"Lunch." He held up the cooler.

Somehow she kept from glaring at her aunt, who, she was certain, was behind Josh's visit. She doubted Laura's help would be needed much longer. "Lunch? Are you kidding?"

"No."

She stared at him consideringly. Something else was going on besides Laura's attempt at matchmaking. "All right. Where?"

"I thought the bandstand again."

"Okay," she said after a moment, and walked out of the shop with him.

"You know," she said, after they'd walked for a few minutes in silence along Union Street toward the water, "Laura's starting to figure out what we're doing."

He didn't answer right away. "I guess it was too much to hope that she wouldn't."

"She's not the only one. Diane thinks you're telling me things, too."

He gave her a sharp look. "You didn't tell her anything, did you?"

This time, Ari hesitated. "No, but it was hard. I think I've lost her friendship."

"I'm sorry. I didn't mean for that to happen."

She nodded. "I know. Everyone else thinks we're dating."

"We expected that."

"Yes, it's probably because of these romantic lunches by the water."

"Romantic." He smiled briefly. "Not quite."

"No," she agreed, though she didn't know why that made her feel just a little bit down.

"We both know why we're in this," he went on. "It bothers me more that people have guessed about that."

"I'm not going to be in it much longer, though, am I?"

"Don't know."

"Well, I don't know what more I'll be hearing, or what I can ask about. Diane has an alibi."

"Yes."

Ari looked down at her feet, shuffling through the first of autumn's fallen leaves. Soon the maples along Freeport's streets would be ablaze with color. "You don't sound so sure."

"Ari, it's getting to the point when I can't tell you much more."

"You know you can trust me," she said as they reached the bandstand.

"I do," he agreed. "But it's what you just said. People are starting to figure out what you're doing. I don't want someone getting the wrong idea."

She looked at him sharply. "You don't think Diane did it."

"Don't know."

"Do you really think someone will come after me?"

"I don't know. We still don't know why your shop was chosen. A body in a yarn shop." He snorted. "Sounds like a bad mystery novel."

"You and Laura. She said the same thing." She huffed out her breath. "Why isn't anyone taking Edith's death seriously?"

"Believe me, I'm taking it extremely seriously," he said, voice tight.

"As a case," she persisted, as they neared the bandstand. "No one seems to care about her."

"Well, she wasn't too well liked, was she?"

Ari sat down on the top step of the bandstand, her arms around her knees, and stared at him. "Are you that used to death?"

Josh was opening the cooler and taking out sandwiches. "No."

"You can't let yourself care, can you?"

He shrugged yet again. "A cop sees everything, especially in a big city. Too many drive-by shootings, with innocent victims getting hit. Too many homeless people freezing to death. Too many husbands beating up their wives." He took a deep breath. "Freeport's different."

"Is that why you came here?"

"Partly," he said, without elaborating.

"We have our share of problems, you know."

"Yeah. Nothing in comparison, though."

"Doesn't a body in a yarn shop qualify?"

"No, that's unique. You don't come across something like that too often."

"No." Like him, she stared out at the water, and then sighed. Last week's events had affected her mood. "What did you bring today?" she asked, forcing herself into brightness.

The sandwiches turned out to be smoked turkey with cranberry chutney on whole-grain bread, with the inevitable Cape Cod potato chips and Diet Coke. The day was overcast and uncomfortably humid, and the breeze off the water was a welcome relief. "I hate this out-of-season heat."

"Isn't anyone buying yarn?"

"Besides that." For a few minutes, they ate together in a silence that was once again companionable, each gazing out at the harbor. No fishing boats were out there today. "Diane told me what you found."

He paused in the act of taking a bite of his sandwich. "Did she?"

"Yes. You're not going to tell me, are you?"

"No."

After all she'd helped him with, that struck her as wrong. "That's not fair."

"Don't act like a kid, Ari. You know I can't always talk about things."

"You found a piece of wood," she said flatly. "A broken window stop."

"Yup," he said after a moment.

"Does it match up with the ones the yarn was tied around?"

"Don't know yet. It's at the state police lab."

"But does it look like it?"

Once again, he didn't answer right away. "Yes."

"Oh, damn." Ari put her face in her hands for a moment, and then looked up. "Isn't that kind of stupid, keeping something that could link her to the murder where anyone could find it?"

"Not just anywhere. We had to search a shed, and a barn," he said glumly.

"Oh, really?" Ari asked with a certain malicious relish. She was well acquainted with the Camachos' shed. "Joe's father used to be a dealer at a flea market. Diane used to complain because he usually came home with more than he'd sold. She took me through there once." She grinned. "There's a lot of baby furniture and old flying saucer sleds."

"And old auto parts. Greasy auto parts," he added.

"Use it up, wear it out, make it do, or do without," she said lightly, quoting the old New England axiom for saving money. "It makes sense on a farm with old equipment."

He gave her a sour look. "We actually found the window stop in the barn," he said, bringing the conversation back to business. "Not buried too deep, either." He looked at her. "Do you happen to know if they've done any work on their windows lately?"

Ari hesitated. For once, she didn't want to share any information with him. "Why?"

"I think you know why. You said Diane told you about it."

Ari took a deep breath. If she answered him, she'd be getting Diane into deeper trouble. Why had she ever gotten herself into this? "They replaced the sash weights and ropes last fall."

"Ah. I see."

"Wouldn't it be stupid of them to use the scrap?"

"Criminals do stupid things."

"They're not criminals!" Ari flared.

He looked at her. "What do you mean, 'they'?"

"I don't know. I guess I mean Joe, too. Oh, Lord." A thought struck her, and she straightened, cheerful again. This might redeem what she'd just said. "Diane doesn't have a motive."

"Sure, she has."

"Nope. Not from what she told me."

"What is it?"

"Did you know that Eric Hall inherited the Drift Road land?"

"Yeah, we did know that."

He hadn't told her, she noted. "He's not going to develop it."

Josh went still, and then continued chewing. "Now that's interesting. Where'd you hear that?"

Ari recounted the conversation she'd had with Eric. "So you see," she said when she'd finished, "Diane doesn't have a motive." Not counting the fact that Edith had wanted to buy the Camacho farm, she added silently.

"Why didn't you tell me this last week?"

"Things got in the way," she said a little guiltily. Megan's problems had pushed other things from her mind.

"Hall didn't control the land when Edith was killed."

"Still," she argued, "he was here. He had a motive."

"He couldn't get into your shop."

Ari fell silent. "Damn it," she said. "This stinks."

"You shouldn't have gotten involved," he said, almost gently.

"Josh, she has an alibi," she said earnestly. "And she wouldn't have abused her yarn like that."

"Joe might have."

"I don't believe it. Yes, I know he hates her spinning, but he loves her." Her sandwich forgotten, she dropped her head in her hands. "How can I get her out of this?"

"I'm not sure you can."

"This stinks," she repeated.

"Yeah." He balled up the waxed paper he'd used for wrapping the sandwiches and stuffed it into the cooler. "It usually does."

"How do you stand it?"

"Someone's got to do the job."

"I know."

Josh closed the cooler and stood up. "I've got to be getting back."

"So do I." Ari dusted off the back of her olive linen pants and looked up at Josh as they started back toward the center of town. "Will you let me know what you find out?"

"You'll be hearing about it," he said obliquely.

Which meant she wouldn't know anything before everyone else did, not until Diane was arrested. *Huh.* Not if she could help it.

They parted cordially enough at the door of the yarn shop, and she went inside, thoughtful. Diane was in deep trouble. The hell of it was, Ari thought, she didn't know how she could help.

The piece of the window stop that had been sent to the state police crime lab was indeed a match for the two pieces used in Edith's murder. Josh contemplated the report, which detailed that fact at length. The paint didn't match the windows at the Camacho house, though; it had lead in it, while the paint chip Josh had taken from the house was latex. There were, however, fingerprints on the board, though there

hadn't been on the other two pieces. Josh wasn't surprised. Even the most intelligent criminals sometimes
overlooked the simple precaution of wiping weapons
clean.

Ari had said something that bothered him,
though. It *had* been stupid of either Camacho to
keep that board in the barn, unless their intention
had been to hide it in plain sight. Whatever else
Edith's murder had been, it was not a stupid one.
Someone had put some planning into it and chosen
a place and a weapon that would implicate several
people. Someone had come prepared to make a
weapon. That she—or he—had done so while Edith
was there showed a cool kind of nerve. So did the
fact that he—or she—had probably wiped the narrow boards clean while they were still attached to a
body. He didn't know if either Diane or Joe could
have done it, but finding the broken board in the
barn was strong evidence, apparent proof that that
part of the weapon had been made there. It showed
nerve, too, but a different kind. A kind of nose-
thumbing, a belief that the police almost certainly
wouldn't find it. It *was* stupid, and neither one
struck him as being stupid.

Josh pulled at his earlobe. He was tired. The
clamor to arrest Diane was as strong as it once had
been against Ari. There were differences, though.
The evidence was stronger, and so was the motive.
The only problem was that both Joe and Diane had
alibis. Unless he broke those somehow, there'd be no
arrest. In the meantime, the trail Edith's killer had

left was growing colder. The only thing he could do was to keep on digging.

Glancing out the window, he grimaced. The weather had turned, and the gray drizzle matched his mood. Shrugging into a windbreaker, he went out and drove to Marty's to get something to eat at his desk. For once he decided to forsake his more adventurous tastes for a favorite from his younger days, pastrami drenched in messy Russian dressing on rye bread. Comfort food, his mother would call it, reminding him of his old eating habits. That and potato chips.

"Hey, Joe," a hearty voice boomed near his ear. Startled, Josh turned to see an older man, burly with a thick shock of white hair. He was dressed in the baggy green work pants and sweatshirt that were the apparent uniform of the working man in this area. "Where you been hiding?"

"Nowhere," the other man mumbled, and Josh took a second look. Joe Camacho. Their eyes met for a moment. Joe's were hostile. Josh nodded and turned away to face the deli case, his every sense on alert.

"Stopped by to see you the other day," the big man went on.

"Yeah? I gotta go, Manny. Got work to do."

"Yeah. Say, where were you the other morning?" Manny's voice moderated a little as the two men walked away. Josh left the counter to wander down an aisle, as if in search of something.

"What morning?"

"One day last week. I was on my way down to the fish market. Early, Joe, so where were you?" Manny dug Joe in the ribs with his elbow as he marched toward the door. "Don't have anything on the side, do you?" he said, his voice moderating to what he probably thought was a whisper.

"Hell, no. Diane would kill me." Joe stood impatiently at the cash register, jingling change in his pocket. To Josh's practiced eyes, he looked nervous.

"Just giving you a hard time. Can't see you going out with someone early on a Tuesday morning."

Tuesday? Josh's head whipped around. Joe was gone, trailed out the door by Manny, whose voice was now only a rumble. *Hell,* he thought, considering the implications of what he had just heard.

"Excuse me," a woman's voice said behind him, and he became aware that he was staring fixedly at women's sanitary products. He gave the woman, who was looking at him with raised eyebrows, a weak smile and turned away. Hell, it was too good to be true. It was too coincidental to be real. If Manny whatever-his-name-was was right, Joe had been away from the Camacho farm early last Tuesday morning.

He was still standing there, stunned, when he heard his name. Turning, he went back to the deli counter to get his sandwich. *Tuesday,* he thought again. The day Edith Perry had been murdered.

CHAPTER 10

"I don't want to get Joe into trouble," Manny Rego protested when Josh had him come into the police station for a talk the following day.

"Mmm-hmm." Josh leaned back in his chair. "You said you went by the Camacho farm," he prompted.

"Yeah, I went by there last Tuesday. Or was it Wednesday? Nah, Tuesday. See, I remember, 'cause that was the day I had to refuse some lobsters from one of my suppliers. Too quiet, you see. If they ain't movin', they're close to dead, and I can't sell dead lobsters. Anyways, I was going to the fish market—"

"Which one?" Josh asked.

"Mine. Says 'Macklin' on the outside, but that was the old owners. Thought I'd keep the name, seeing as everyone knew it. Anyways, it was early, like usual. I got a lot to do, what with the cleaning and the setup, and I got to get to the fish houses first."

"You drove by the Camachos'?"

"Yeah, like usual, and then I thought I should talk to Joe."

"About what?"

"What? Oh, nothin' important. Joe was talkin' about having a clambake. Kinda late for that, what with leaves fallin' and all, but he usually puts one on for his workers. See, you can't tell the weather this time of year," he said, leaning forward. "Your basic clambake, you have on the beach or at a pit. You get some stones nice and hot, put seaweed on top of 'em, and then clams, and then more seaweed—"

"Yes, I know," Josh said, because he had a feeling Manny could go on for hours discussing the intricacies of a clambake. "What did he have to say?"

"Nothin'. He wasn't there. I was thinkin', he could have a clam-boil instead."

"So that was it?"

"Yeah, that's all. Besides, Diane makes a hell of a cup of coffee."

Josh nodded. "What time was this?"

"Eh? Early, like I said. Five o'clock, maybe? Naw." He shook his head. "A little earlier, 'cause I got to the market at five, like I always do."

"You didn't see Camacho's truck?"

"Nope. 'Course, he coulda been up and about at work someplace else, but I never known him to do that so early. During calving season, yeah, but that's different."

So it was. Most farm animals had their young in the spring, not at the end of September. Again Josh waited as Manny delivered a few more rambling monologues, without telling him any more of substance. Finally he sent the man home. Where, he wondered, had Joe been at that time of the morning? He suspected he knew the answer. Christ, Joe Camacho. How would Ari react to that?

Frowning, wondering why the answer to that question mattered, at last he got up from the desk. It was time to tell the chief, and eventually the D.A., about this.

Josh pulled into the Camachos' driveway that afternoon after his talk with Rego, a police cruiser behind him. Both the chief and the D.A. agreed that there was enough evidence to bring Joe in. He had motive and the means to kill Edith, even if it didn't seem, to Josh, the kind of murder Joe would commit. Apart from that, though, that block of time when he'd been missing had to be explained.

Joe's truck was in the garage; Diane's Jeep was in the driveway. That both simplified and complicated matters. Diane was already hostile toward him, and together the two of them could stonewall. On the other hand, the question stood stark and clear: Where had Joe been that morning?

"Where did you go the morning Edith Perry was killed?" he asked Joe a few moments later. This time, instead of Diane's workroom, they were in the formal parlor, as if the Camachos had already guessed the gravity of the situation. He was sitting in an old wing chair that needed major repairs to its springs, while

Diane and Joe faced him from the humpbacked sofa, faces stony, united in their closeness. Outside in the hall were the two patrolmen Josh had brought along, as backup if Joe put up a fight.

"He was here," Diane put in swiftly. "I told you that. So did Pat Sylvia."

"That was around six, though." Josh kept his gaze on Joe. "What about earlier?"

"Yeah, I was out and about," Joe said, not looking at Diane.

"Anywhere in particular?"

"Down to the beach. I like to see the sunrise."

That took Josh aback for a moment. "Do you do that often?" he asked, skeptical of the answer. Not only did Joe not strike him as a poetic type, but the sun rose much later now than five A.M.

"Once in a while."

"Joe's been working hard lately," Diane put in.

Josh glanced quickly at her. "On what?"

"Just stuff," Joe said vaguely. "There's always a lot to do on a farm."

If that were so, it didn't make sense that he'd left it early that morning. "Where else did you go?"

Joe stared back at him, solid, stolid. "Nowhere special. I just drove."

"Did anyone see you?"

"You know the answer to that."

Josh paused. "I take it that's a no?"

"Yeah. No one saw me, far as I know."

"So you can't account for your time?"

Joe's eyes, hostile and yet resigned, met Josh's. "No."

"You were at the yarn shop."

"No."

"No!" Diane protested.

"You had a key," Josh went inexorably on.

"No, it never left my key ring!" Diane said.

"You had motive. And you had the weapon."

That made Joe and Diane look at each other in confusion. "What weapon?" Joe asked.

"The yarn came from the shop, not here," Diane put in.

Josh shook his head. Though the town would have to turn the results of its investigation over to Joe's defense, Josh had no intention of telling him about the window stop yet. "You had the weapon," he repeated, "and you can't account for your time."

Joe slumped. "I didn't do it."

Josh looked at him as he rose, to signal to the patrolmen in the hallway. "I have to ask you to come with me," he said, and reached into his inner pocket for the arrest warrant. "Joseph Camacho, you're under arrest for the murder of Edith Perry."

✄

"Did you hear?" Ruth Taylor said, flinging open the door of Ariadne's Web a short time later.

Ari, kneeling on the floor where she was straightening some yarn in a bin, looked up. "No, what?"

"They arrested Joe Camacho."

"What!" Ari shot up so fast that she lost her balance and hit her elbow against the counter. "Ouch. No! When?"

"A couple of hours ago. Now, who would have thought that?"

Ari busied herself with picking up the yarn that had tumbled to the floor when she jumped up. *Not Joe*, she thought, and at the same time thanked God that it wasn't Diane. "He couldn't have done it," she said.

"They must think so." Ruth, her eyes avid, leaned her elbows on the sales counter, where Ari had taken refuge. "I wonder why."

"I don't know."

"You know more about this investigation than anyone else. After all," Ruth said coyly, "you and that Detective Pierce seem to spend a lot of time together."

"Mmm," Ari said, ignoring Ruth's implication that there was something between her and Josh, bothered more by the hint that she was in the know about the police's thinking. She hadn't forgotten Josh's warning about possibly being in danger, should the wrong person find out what she was doing.

"Mike Thomas saw Joe going into the station with that detective," Ruth went on, "and then Carol Ferreira told me. Her niece is a secretary for the police, you know."

Of course. News like this would spread fast in Freeport. Troubled, Ari listened with only half her attention to Ruth chattering on, inserting a noise of feigned interest only occasionally. By the time Ruth left, she had a headache. By the time the door opened in midafternoon and Josh strolled in, Ari's temper was at the boiling point.

"I see you've heard," he said mildly, apparently in answer to the look she threw him, and leaned his elbows on the counter.

Ari nodded curtly and pretended to be interested in a yarn catalog. After a moment, though, she looked up. "You might have warned me."

Josh stole a quick look around the shop. For once it was empty of customers. The only other person there was Summer, who was in back checking a new shipment of supplies against a packing list. "We can't talk here."

"No," Ari agreed, and though she was still annoyed, some of her ire faded. There was something about his eyes. "Summer, can you come out front? I need to go into the back room for a while."

Summer came out, her eyes speculative and interested. "Okay, but if anyone wants to see you—"

"I think you can handle things," Ari said, and shut the door behind her and Josh. "Want something to drink?"

"A Coke would be good." He took the can she handed him from her small refrigerator, then watched as she filled the kettle for tea. "It's been a day."

"I'll just bet." She slanted him a look as she sat at the table, more relieved than she wanted to admit. Her shop was safe. It was a disloyal thought to have when her best friend was in such trouble. There was no denying, though, that she'd been more nervous than she'd realized. "I really didn't think it would be Joe. I thought Diane was the one who was in for it."

He shook his head. "No, her alibi held up. We can't place her here."

"But you can place Joe? Here, of all places?" Her voice rose as her anger returned. "With his own wife's yarn?"

"People do irrational things." He gazed toward the door leading into the shop. "God knows that. Stupid things. But ..."

She leaned forward. "You have your doubts."

Josh crossed his arms on his chest. "He looks good for it. He had access to a key, motive, and opportunity. And means," he added.

"The window stops you found?"

"They match."

"And?"

"You haven't heard? He can't account for his time."

"Oh," she said, and rose to pour hot water into a mug. "What about Eric?" she asked, as she had once before.

"Edith's son?" Josh frowned.

"You know that he could have done it. Oh, Lord, listen to me." She briefly closed her eyes. "I'm blaming one friend to free another." She sat down. "I didn't bargain for this."

"Welcome to police work."

"I suppose. But what about Eric? He was in town that night, I told you that. And you know he had a motive. I don't care that he claims he didn't know he was inheriting. Where's the proof of it?" She dunked her tea bag in the cup, and then rose to throw it away. "Does he have an alibi?"

"None that we can find. He says he was out running that morning, but no one saw him."

"Well, then?"

"He did tell me something interesting when I questioned him."

"What?"

"His mother wanted to buy the Camacho farm."

"Oh, Lord."

"You knew that, didn't you?" he said accusingly.

Ari let out her breath. "Yes."

"And didn't tell me?" He sat back, steely-eyed, suddenly very much a policeman. "I could consider that obstruction of justice."

"I'm not on the case officially. You said so yourself."

"You're the one who wanted to investigate."

"I know." She looked down at her mug. "But doesn't that lessen Joe's motive?"

He shrugged. "Do you really think they wanted to lose their farm?"

"Mmm." Partnership or no, she wasn't going to tell him what Diane had confided to her concerning Joe's attitude about the farm.

"It's better for them now. When I questioned him, Eric said he's not going to develop the land."

"I know, but how could Joe and Diane have known about that? No one knew Eric was going to inherit it."

He studied her. "Are you holding out on me?"

"No."

"You wanted to be in on this investigation, Ari. You know what that means."

"Yes." She sighed. "Except I still can't believe it of Joe."

"I told you, he looks good for it."

Something about his tone made her look sharply at him. "You don't believe it, do you?"

He didn't pretend to misunderstand. "The evidence is strong."

"Evidence can be planted."

"C'mon, Ari." He gestured impatiently. "Do you know how often that really happens? God knows I've seen a lot, but nothing like this."

"Didn't you ever investigate this kind of killing in Boston?" she asked, momentarily diverted.

"Once or twice." He shifted restlessly in his chair. "Nothing like what you're suggesting. Most criminals aren't very smart. Usually there's something they ignore, or they think we won't find out about it."

"Like the window stop?"

"Yeah."

"It could have been left there on purpose. Were there prints on it?" she asked suddenly.

"Yes, but they're smudged."

"But wouldn't you expect Joe's to be on it, since it came from his house? Did it come from his house? Did you take paint samples?"

"Yes, but that's a no-go. When the Camachos redid their windows, they repainted, too."

"So there's no proof the board's actually theirs."

"Chances are—"

"You're talking about a cold-blooded killing. Joe's not like that."

"He's smart enough."

"But not cool-headed enough. Especially when . . ."

"When what?" he said sharply.

"Nothing."

He regarded her in silence. "They had a fight that morning, didn't they."

"I don't know."

"They did." He nodded. "One of the workers said they were barely talking to each other."

Ari sagged in her chair. Oh, poor Joe. And poor Diane. Yet she might be able to help. "Say they did." She set down her cup. "I know Joe. If they fought, he just slammed into his truck and drove off. I've seen him do it," she said, before Josh could speak. "Wouldn't he have had to go to the barn for the window stop?"

"He could have had it in the truck."

"So when would he have made the arrangements to meet with Edith? I haven't heard that anyone saw them together."

"We're checking his cell phone records. Diane's, too."

"You won't find anything," she said confidently. "And you still have to explain why here, and why with Diane's yarn."

"She told me herself that he doesn't like her having sheep."

"Oh, get real! Do you see that as a reason?"

"People do stupid—"

"Things. I know. This isn't stupid. It's hostile. Joe's not like that."

He regarded her for a moment. "The problem is," he said finally, "that we don't always know what people are really like."

"I still don't see it. I know Joe doesn't like the sheep, but he wouldn't do that. He's just not that malicious." It was her turn to study him. "You don't think he did it."

Once again he took time answering. "Let's just say I have my doubts."

"I knew it!" she crowed. "I knew you didn't buy that load of malarkey."

"Malarkey?" he said, smiling for the first time.

"Malarkey," she answered firmly. "That's all it is."

Josh looked thoughtfully at his soda can. "The evidence is strong, though. It'll be hard to beat."

"Unless we keep looking for the real killer."

He looked up at that. "The case is closed."

"Does that mean you're off it?"

"Except for a few loose ends, yeah. It's the D.A.'s now, not ours, and he thinks we have enough to go to trial."

"Not as far as I'm concerned."

He gave her a long look. "I hope you're not planning anything."

"Maybe you can't do any more looking, but I can."

To her surprise, he didn't burst into protest. "Supposing you're right."

"I am."

"If you are, do you realize what you'll be up against? Someone who's already killed." He held up a hand to forestall her protest. "Now, wait, hear me out."

"I'll be careful."

"It may not be enough." He sat back, arms crossed on his chest again. "You've already been a target."

"I have? When?"

"As you said, why your shop?"

"Don't you see, that's why I have to do it?" she burst out. "Whoever killed Edith went after me, too. How can I let someone try to ruin my life?"

"He—or she—might well try again."

Ari set her chin stubbornly, a look her mother would have recognized. "He—or she," she said, deliberately mimicking him, "thinks the murder's been solved. Case closed, as you said."

Josh rubbed at the back of his head. "I can't help you, you know."

"I know." Ari nodded. It was what she'd expected, and yet her spirits sank. If she went on with the investigation, as she'd just insisted she must, she'd be alone, without any backing. It was a frightening thought.

"Not officially, anyway."

That made her look up. "What do you mean?"

"You promise to be careful?"

"Of course I do. I'm not stupid."

"And let me know whatever you find out?"

She sucked in her breath. "You'll help?"

"Yeah, but quietly. If I get found out there'll be trouble."

Again she nodded. She couldn't guess what the consequences to him would be. "I know."

"For you, too, you know."

"Oh?" she said in surprise. "Why?"

"Obstructing justice, for one thing."

"For Pete's sake."

"I'm not kidding."

"I don't care. I have to do this."

"Why?"

"For Diane, and myself, too." And because of curiosity, and a sense of things not finished. "My livelihood's been threatened."

"All the more reason for you to stay out of it, Ari."

"I'll be careful. Are you really with me on this?"

"Only if you don't hold anything back from me again."

Ari looked down into her cup. "I promise," she said finally, reluctantly.

"Good. Now, let's think of how we're going to do this. . . ."

The phone rang while Ari was adding up a customer's purchases. "Ariadne's Web," she said, wedging the receiver between her ear and her shoulder.

"Ari? It's Susan. Did they really arrest Joe Camacho?"

Ari gave the customer her change, along with a distracted smile. "Yes, it's true."

"Of all people! It just shows you that you never really know someone."

"He's innocent."

"There must be some reason for them to arrest him. I'm so relieved."

"Relieved?" Ari asked, startled, and mouthed a

"thank you" to the customer as she handed her her bag.

"Aren't you? My Kait's not in danger anymore."

"She never was, Susan."

"Wasn't she? You were."

"I was not," Ari protested, in spite of what she really believed.

"Of course you were. Now that's all behind you. You don't have to worry about the shop anymore."

Ari frowned slightly. So Susan had reached the same conclusion that others had, that for some reason Ari had been a target. "It's a hard thing, though."

"Oh, I would imagine. You would think, though, that since Diane's your friend and—"

"Susan, I'm sorry," Ari interrupted her. "We're pretty busy here and I can't really talk."

"I'm sorry," Susan said. "I'm just stunned."

"I know. Susan, I have to go—"

"There's something else," Susan said quickly. "Kaitlyn wanted me to call, too."

"Oh?" Ari shrugged and grimaced at a customer who was holding up a skein of yarn, to indicate an apology for not being able to help.

"Yes. She's finished the website. I think you'll be pleased with it, Ari."

At the moment, the website held little interest for her. "I'm sure I will. Tell her to call me about it."

"Oh, wait, I have another call," Susan said.

Ari sighed as the phone went temporarily dead. She hated call waiting. "I'm sorry," she said to the customer. "I'll be right with you—yes?"

"That was Kait," Susan said. "She heard the news, too."

Ari let out another sigh. "Susan, I really have to go—"

"I won't keep you. Just one more thing. Kait wants to come in some night to install the website, but I—"

"Susan!" Ari said, more forcefully. "I have to hang up."

There was a brief silence. "I see," Susan said, sounding offended, and abruptly hung up.

Ari stared at the receiver for a moment before putting it down. "I am so sorry," she said, coming out from behind the counter to go to the customer. "Can I help you?"

"Susan Silveira?" the customer said shrewdly.

"Yes."

"She thinks the sun rises and sets on that girl."

"I know. Now, what can I do for you?" she asked, and listened as the customer explained her dilemma about which yarn to pick for a project. Her project seemed supremely unimportant at the moment. So did the damned website. Joe had been arrested for murder. That was what she'd have to do something about.

CHAPTER 11

Joe Camacho was arraigned on Tuesday in New Bedford Superior Court. As the arresting officer, Josh was present. So was Ari, sitting stony-faced on one of the benches, and so, of course, were the media. When the short hearing was over, Joe was bundled back into the sheriff's van and returned to the Bristol County House of Correction. There he would remain until his trial, since bail was automatically denied in cases of first-degree murder.

Parking was always hard to find on the narrow and busy streets near the old courthouse. As a result, Ari had had to park several blocks away. After dodging several persistent reporters, she finally made her way down William Street. She had just unlocked her car door when she heard her name called. Steeling herself for more curiosity and questions, she turned, and blinked in surprise. Herb Perry, Edith's widower, was hurrying down the hill toward her.

"Mr. Perry!" she said in surprise. She'd spoken to him only once since Edith's death, to give her condolences. She certainly hadn't expected to talk to him today. *But why not?* she asked herself. Before Joe's arrest, Herb had been considered a suspect. In her mind he still was.

"Ariadne." Herb wasn't much to look at. He was about the same height as Edith had been, and as thin and compact. They had looked alike, more like brother and sister than husband and wife. His white hair was thinning on top, and his features, which probably hadn't been extraordinary to begin with, had coarsened with age. Yet his eyes were bright and alert. Warning bells went off within Ari.

"I'm sorry about everything," she blurted. "Really sorry. It was a terrible way for you to lose your wife."

"It was." Hands in his pockets, he looked away. "Christ, I'd've never picked Joe as a killer. Hell of a nice guy, is Joe."

"Yes." Ari fiddled with her keys. Being with Herb under the circumstances made her uneasy. "Is there something you want to talk to me about?"

"Yeah, but not here. Suppose I come by your shop?"

"Good heavens!" She stared at him. "Do you know what people will make of that? Everyone will be coming in to find out what we're talking about."

He shook his head. "It's nothing much. Can't do it till tomorrow, though. Got Eric coming by tonight. What d'you think?"

Ari thought quickly. She could ask her mother to

stay with Megan for a little while, pleading the amount of work that had piled up this past week. She wasn't sure that her mother would be fooled, but she would probably agree.

"All right," she said finally. "Tomorrow I'll stay at the shop for a little while after I close up." At six P.M. it wouldn't yet be completely dark. She would also keep the shade on the door up and the lights on, and stay where people outside could see her. She hadn't forgotten that this man might have killed his wife, though with someone in custody she didn't think Herb would be a threat to her.

"Okay. Has to be after six, though."

"Fine, that will be after I close. You know where it is? Dumb question. Of course you do."

"Yeah. I worked there once, you know."

"Worked where?"

"In your building, when it was a hardware store."

About to unlock her car, Ari jerked her head up in surprise. Oh, no. It couldn't be true. It was too coincidental to be real. If she came across this in a novel, she'd throw the book against the wall.

"Well." *What did she say to that?* she wondered. "That was a long time ago." And the locks had been changed, so she had no reason to worry.

"Yeah. Oh, Christ." He was glancing up the street at some people hurrying toward them. "Reporters. I gotta get out of here."

Ari was surprised that the press hadn't followed Herb there in the first place. "Me, too." She wrenched her car door open and all but fell inside. In her rearview mirror she could see Herb, sprinting with surprising speed for someone his age, toward a huge boat of a Cadillac parked across the street. The reporters were in hot pursuit. She breathed in a sigh of relief when she saw him get safely inside before they could reach him.

The encounter made Ari's stomach queasy with nerves and doubts. As she waited glumly at the approach to the New Bedford–Fairhaven Bridge, though, she started to settle down. Since the bridge was closed to cars to let a fishing boat head out to sea, she had plenty of time to think. She even felt some anticipation. She wasn't taking her friend's arrest meekly. She was going to do something about it. Being alone with a possible murderer might not exactly be wise, but she didn't really think anything would happen. She'd be very, very careful. Her only real worry was what he wanted to talk to her about.

A little while later, Ari stepped into her shop. The bells over the door chimed, rang, and then suddenly clanged as they fell down with a *whoosh* and landed with a discordant thud on her shoulder. "Yikes!" she exclaimed, jumping to the side and staring up at the doorjamb where the bells had hung. "How the heck did that happen?"

"Are you all right?" Laura demanded, hurrying toward her from behind the sales counter.

"I think so." Her hand to her shoulder, Ari continued to stare at the doorjamb. "I'll have one heck of a bruise, though."

"Maybe you should have it checked, dear."

"No, I'm okay. More surprised than anything."

"Then come have a cup of tea." Laura bustled into the office. "Was it ghastly this morning?"

Ari grimaced. "It wasn't fun. I'd better check to see what happened here, before a customer comes in and gets hurt."

"I think the damage has already been done."

"Regardless." Ari climbed onto a small stepladder and frowned at the screw holes she'd drilled for the bells. "Hmm. Both look a little rough," she said after a moment. "I don't think I could screw it back on where it was."

"But how could they have just pulled out?"

"I don't know. You know what this looks like?"

"What?"

"I think the top screw came loose, probably from the door opening, and then put too much strain on the other one. That's why they came out. Ouch." She rubbed her shoulder again as she climbed down. "I'll have to drill new holes and put them up again."

"Maybe Ted can do it. After all, you're hurt, dear."

"Huh. I know more about using power tools than he does. Anyway, I'd rather wait until we're closed, so no customers are coming in." She turned and walked into the shop, wincing as she shrugged off the Scandinavian cardigan her grandmother had made her long ago. "Has anything interesting happened today?"

"Not particularly. There were a few people in, but most of them didn't buy anything."

Ari nodded. "I thought things would slack off, now

that everyone thinks the murderer's been caught. I do imagine that once people get back from the arraignment they'll be coming in."

"Why don't you go home, Ari? You should put ice on that shoulder."

Ari stood in the doorway to her office, considering the idea. She rarely took time away from the shop, and she was suddenly tired of being there. The last week had been difficult, and her shoulder did hurt. "Yes, I think I will."

"The best thing you can do, dear. Can you drive?"

"I'll manage." Ari looked up at where the bells had once hung, and sighed. She'd rehang them tomorrow. It promised to be an interesting day.

Kaitlyn walked in late the next afternoon. "Hey," she said, stopping at the door and looking up. "What happened to the bells?"

"They just fell off," Ari said from behind the sales counter.

"By themselves? Weird."

"They landed on Ari," Laura said, looking up from the rocking chair, where she was now working on the garnet fake fur scarf. "On her shoulder."

Kaitlyn looked at Ari. "Are you all right?"

"Yes, just a little sore."

Laura shot her a look. "Too sore to put them up again."

"I'll do it for you," Kaitlyn offered.

"Thanks, but I didn't bring the drill. One more day won't matter. You look happy today."

"I got an 'A,' Ari!"

"On one of your designs? That's wonderful."

"Yes. I asked if I could submit something for extra credit, and he really liked it."

"Terrific. Is it one I've seen?"

"No, but I'll bring it in." Kaitlyn followed Ari into the office and sat down at the desk. Her eyes fixed on the computer screen.

"Do you mind if I watch?" Laura had come into the office, too, and was peering at the screen as Kaitlyn brought up the web page.

"Well, okay," Kaitlyn said shortly, after a moment.

Ari heard Laura huff in surprise, or offense, behind her. But then, she and Kaitlyn never had liked each other much. "Of course," Ari said. "You'll be using it, too. Show us, Kaitlyn."

"Okay." Once again Kaitlyn led Ari through the website, from the opening page to the last ordering screen. When she was done, she sat back and looked at Ari questioningly. "What do you think?"

Ari blinked. She had been concentrating on her shoulder rather than on the computer. "I think it looks fine."

If Kaitlyn was offended at this less than enthusiastic response, she didn't show it. "Should I put it up on the net, then?"

Oh, why not? "Yes."

Kaitlyn's face brightened. "Good! It'll take a few

minutes. I have to transfer the files from here to the web host." She worked in silence for a while, hitting various keys. "There," she said finally, sounding satisfied and triumphant. "Done."

Ari leaned forward. "Really? Just like that?"

"Yeah. Let's change seats, and you can call it up. Type in the address—there, look at that!"

"My goodness," Ari murmured, sitting back as the logo Kaitlyn had designed for her appeared on the screen. "It works."

"Of course it does. Oh, look at that." Kaitlyn was grinning. "Finally, one of my designs is successful."

Ari shot her a surprised glance. "Of course it is."

"It looks good," Laura said from behind them.

Ari hoped that only she heard the grudging note in Laura's voice. "This is so strange."

"What?" Kaitlyn asked.

"To think that anyone in the world could see this."

"I keep telling you, Ari, that you should go online more," Laura said.

"It wastes too much time."

"You'll have no choice now, once you start getting orders," Kaitlyn said, and turned as someone called to them from the shop. "Mom? What are you doing here?"

"I came to see how the website is doing," Susan said. "What a nice job you did, Kait."

"Yes, didn't she?" Ari said, as surprised to see her as Kaitlyn was. Susan was not a knitter.

Kaitlyn fidgeted a bit. "I thought you were showing a house this afternoon."

"Oh, I am, but I wanted to see this first," Susan said. "I'm so proud of you."

"Mom," Kaitlyn protested.

"She did very well," Laura said calmly, and then turned as she heard a voice in the shop. "We're in here, Barb."

"What are you doing?" Barbara Watson, one of Ari's regular customers and Laura's crony, looked into the office. "What happened to the bells?"

"They fell." Ari was beginning to feel claustrophobic, with everyone clustered around her. "We're looking at my web page."

"Really? Let me see." Barbara peered over her reading glasses. "It's about time you entered this millennium, Ari."

"Exactly what I've been telling her," Laura said.

"Are you going to have any patterns available?"

"Of course I am. That's the whole point."

"I didn't mean that. I meant, sample patterns."

Ari stared at her. "Give them away, you mean? The whole point of this is to make money."

"A lot of people have put free patterns online," Barbara said.

"Really? Why would they do that?"

"Sometimes it's the only way for people to publish their ideas," Kaitlyn said quietly.

Ari turned to her. "Have you done that?"

"What, and lose my copyright? If I tried to publish in print later, I wouldn't be able to because of that." She paused. "When I was first learning how to make web pages, I did put a design on my own site, though, a simple one. A scarf in garter stitch."

"Well, anyone can make one of those, so that's okay."

"It was for beginners," Kaitlyn said defensively.

"And it was nice," Susan said firmly. "Of course, though, she's right. Why give something away for free?"

Barbara was leaning over Ari's shoulder. "Ari, haven't you ever looked at anything to do with knitting online?"

"No. I told you, I think the Internet is a waste of time." She sat back. "Once I start looking at things, I tend to keep going, and I have too much else to do. I have this shop." She waved her hand toward the selling area. "Running your own business is twenty-four/seven. So is being a mother. I have to find some time to work on new designs. And somewhere in there I have to get housework done."

"Have Ted pay for a cleaning lady for you. He has enough money," Laura said dryly.

"I'd have to clean the house first."

The women around her broke into sympathetic laughter. "Too true," Barbara said. "I rush around like crazy picking up clutter each week before mine comes. She even told me once that I'm dirty."

"What? And you kept her on?"

"Good cleaning people are hard to find. Seriously, though, it's not a bad idea, Ariadne. I can ask my cleaning lady if she has an opening, or if she knows someone else."

"Maybe." Ari was frowning at the screen. "People

really put their patterns online without expecting payment?"

"I hate to say it, but I've gotten some good ones that way."

"Hmm. Maybe that's an idea. What do you think?" she turned to ask Kaitlyn.

"Why?" Kaitlyn said.

"As samples. You know I do that every now and then in here. It gets people to see what I do, and I usually get customers from them."

Kaitlyn was frowning. "Well, if you want to."

"I'll think about it. I think I'll check out some other sites here tonight," she added.

"Where are Ted and Megan going tonight?" Laura asked. Since Edith's murder, Ted had called every night before closing, and last night Ari had mentioned that she would be staying late at the shop tonight, without saying why. To her pleased surprise, Ted had offered to take Megan out for supper.

"Megan wants to go to Chuck E. Cheese." Ari's smile was wicked, as she thought of Ted in his designer suit at the popular and noisy children's paradise.

The women around her laughed again. "Still, I'll stay, too, shall I, dear?" Laura said, when they were quiet again.

"Oh, no, don't be silly," Ari said, alarmed. She didn't want anyone here to witness her meeting with Herb. "Aren't you going out to dinner tonight?"

"I'll cancel."

Ari turned to look at her, though her shoulder cramped. "You'd actually cancel a date?"

"A date?" Barbara looked at Laura with interest. "Who is it, and why haven't we heard about it?"

Laura's face was red. "It's nothing much."

"My mother fixed her up with the new science teacher from the high school," Ari said, her smile diabolical again. It served Laura right, for all the times she'd interfered. "This is, what, the second date?"

"Second! And you never told me, Laura," Barbara said.

"It doesn't matter," Laura protested. "Ari has a beau, too, now."

"That cop?"

"Maybe we'll double with Laura," Ari said lightly, knowing no one would take her seriously. "If he has time."

"With Joe arrested, he should," Susan said.

"Maybe," Ari said, and listened with only half her attention as the conversation shifted to the events of the past days. At last, though, the women left. Laura stepped back from the computer.

"That was rotten of you, Ari," she said.

"Serves you right." Ari stretched and put her hand to her shoulder again. "Ouch."

"I do think you should rest your shoulder, dear."

"For goodness sake, it's not broken, only bruised." She pushed back her chair, grimacing again. "Maybe I will go home for a while now. Megan will be home from school soon. I'd like to spend some time with her before she goes out. Can you hold down the fort?"

"Of course I can, dear."

Laura's bright tone instantly made Ari suspicious. "Laura, what are you planning?"

"Why, nothing, dear."

Ari raised her eyebrows skeptically. She didn't quite trust Laura where the shop was concerned. "Don't you dare rearrange anything while I'm gone."

"Oh, I wouldn't dream of it, dear."

"I can stay," Kaitlyn volunteered. "I don't have much homework tonight."

Ari quickly calculated the damage to her payroll if Kait did stay. "Thanks, Kait, but I don't think you have to. It's been quiet today."

"Yes, I'll be fine," Laura put in.

Ari cast Laura another suspicious look as she took her pocketbook from a desk drawer. "I hope so."

"Don't worry so much."

From the door Ari looked back at Laura, who was already gazing about the shop, and sighed. "Okay. I'll be back later," she said, and went out.

✂

Ari walked back into the shop just before closing. Laura, counting the money in the cash drawer, looked up. "I didn't think you'd be back."

"I told you I would be." She looked around. "All right. What did you do in here?"

"Nothing," Laura said innocently. "I just moved a few samples around."

"And some yarn, I see," Ari said.

"Well, dear, I do think that Chanel jacket wasn't displayed quite right. That's lovely chenille you used, and the fake fur collar is wonderful."

Laura is a force unto herself, Ari thought as she walked into her office. "I had a reason—oh, never mind."

"Did Megan get off all right?"

"Yes." Ari gave Laura an unholy grin as she came back out onto the sales floor. "You should have seen Ted's face when he found out where they're going."

"Serves him right."

"No, not really. He's good with Megan."

"Yes, now, but when you were married he didn't pay much attention to her."

"He didn't pay much attention to me, especially during tax season."

"I think, dear, that you should start seeing that policeman."

"No!" Ari said in mock surprise. "I didn't know that."

"Yes, dear. He's a nice man."

"He is," Ari agreed. "He's also wrong about Joe."

"Don't hold that against him, dear. He was only doing his job."

"True." She looked over Laura's shoulder. "How did we do today?"

"Pretty well. A lot of people came in to talk about Joe. I looked at knitting sites," she added.

"Knitting sites? Oh, on the web."

"Yes, between customers. Actually, do you know the first thing I did?" Laura grinned. "I searched for myself."

"What do you mean?"

"I looked up my name."

"Did you find anything?" Ari asked, intrigued.

"Mostly genealogical information about different Sheehans, or various Lauras."

"I never thought of doing that," Ari said. "Maybe I will tonight."

"You're still going to stay?"

"Yes."

"Kaitlyn volunteered to come back in, if you need help."

"I told her not to. I can manage."

"I think she has some designs she'd like you to look at."

Ari's heart sank. She had no heart for telling Kaitlyn that yet another of her designs didn't work, although maybe that had changed. The girl did have talent. "I'd rather she waited until her shift on Saturday."

"She sounded disappointed. To tell you the truth, I felt sorry for her." Laura went into the office and came out, throwing a heavy cardigan around her shoulders. "Her life's not easy."

"I know. She needs the money."

"So do you, dear."

"Of course I do, but Kait's different. Leaving RISD hurt her."

"If you ask me, I think she was a little spoiled before. Maybe it's hard for her with her father losing his job, but Susan has to be making a good amount in real estate, with prices the way they are." She rooted through her pocketbook. "Now where are those keys—there they are." She paused by the door. "Are you sure you don't want me to stay?"

"And miss your hot date? Don't be silly." Ari reached for the sign on the door and flipped it to CLOSED. "Good night, and have fun."

"Yes, dear." In spite of her earlier concern, Laura had brightened up. "I'll see you in the morning."

"Yes," Ari said, and after closing the door, turned the lock. Laura's obvious anticipation sent a pang of jealousy through her. Certainly it was time for Laura to have some happiness, she thought. She herself wouldn't be meeting a man tonight, though. Only Herb.

Sighing, she walked in to her office and logged on to the Internet. She should have checked out her competition long before this. After all, she'd gone to regular yarn shops before opening her own, hadn't she? It made sense to do the same online. Though Kaitlyn had already done so when she was designing the site, to get an idea of how others had put theirs together, the final responsibility was Ari's. It really was high time she entered the twenty-first century.

Her fingers were poised to type her name into a search engine when Barbara Watson's words floated back to her. Free knitting patterns. Now who would put those on the web? Intrigued, Ari searched first for Kaitlyn's own site. It was professionally done, and the directions for the scarf, featured in a colorful picture, were clear and concise. Kait did have a future, Ari thought again, if only she'd stop trying so hard.

Typing some more, she sat back, waiting for results. "Free knitting patterns," she read aloud, scanning one group of type. It had a web address highlighted at the bottom. Below, there was another grouping and then yet another. She glanced up to see the number of results for her search, and blinked. It numbered in the thousands. "That many?" she muttered, and clicked on the address for the first site.

A web page came up on her screen. On it was the owner's name, and the proclamation that all the patterns she provided were free to anyone. Ari clicked on the link for Aran sweaters. The site was nicely designed, she thought, with a background of pastel-colored stockinette stitch, and ornate lettering. Surely the designs wouldn't be as amateurish as Kaitlyn had implied.

They weren't. The photographs showed various models wearing beautifully made sweaters, with links to the instructions for each one. The illustrations themselves, though, were of varying quality, some in color and some in black and white, some fairly large and some small. There was something about them, especially the one on the lower right. . . .

"Heavens!" Ari stared at the screen. She knew that sweater. It was the fisherman sweater she'd made when she was a teenager. When she clicked on the picture the directions came up, densely printed and still familiar to her after all these years. That project was the hardest she'd done at that time, and she was still proud of it. It also had come from a booklet published by a yarn company, not the person who claimed it now.

Disturbed, she went back to the main screen and clicked on other links. Norwegian sweaters were displayed, again with obviously posed photographs and again with directions in tiny print. The same held true for children's and babies' items, for men's sweaters, for afghans. Some of the sites were for businesses that sold patterns, like hers. Others gave credit to the original publishers. A lot of them offered original designs, free of charge. Too many, though, had been pirated.

Ari was more than disturbed now. She was angry and appalled, as she leaned back in her chair. Kaitlyn had mentioned designers losing their copyrights if they published online, but this was far worse. This was direct infringement, direct theft. She wondered if the publishers knew. She wondered if her own designs had been stolen.

Again she bent over the keyboard, tapping furiously. There were fewer results on her search for her own name. The site for the shop wasn't listed yet, but Kaitlyn had told her to expect that. What results she had were chiefly genealogical, and there were far more than she'd expected. Evans might be a common name, but Ariadne certainly wasn't.

Modify the search. Beside her name she typed the word "knitting." This time there were far fewer results. The companies that had published her patterns had them listed, giving her the credit. The clothing company that occasionally turned out high-end knitted goods from her work promoted her on their site. There was even a reprint of the article *Vogue Knitting* had done on her a few years back, with a link to a pattern. The rest of the results were again mostly genealogical.

Finally she pushed back from her desk. The Internet was all very well, but she had just spent a lot of time at the computer that she could profitably have spent doing paperwork. Besides, Herb would be coming soon. She checked her watch and made a little noise of surprise. It was well after six. Where could he be?

Just then, she heard a soft swishing sound from the sales floor. Ari turned her head sharply. "Hello?" she called. "Herb?"

Absolute silence. Still, she wasn't alone in the shop. She could sense it, though she heard no more sound. A chill shuddered up her spine, and instinct made her fumble for a weapon, any weapon. Absurdly, what her fingers latched onto was a ruler. *What damage can I do with that?* asked a cool, rational voice in her mind, but she clutched the ruler tightly anyway. Hardly breathing, she slowly got up, wincing when her chair squeaked as she moved.

At that moment, the lights went out in the shop.

That same primal instinct for defense had her diving for the light in her office. With it backlighting her, she would be an easy target. The computer screen glowed eerily, and in the shop the shadows left by the setting sun obscured everything. Had someone moved over there behind a display counter? The shadow was caused by the lights of a passing car shining through the store window.

Time seemed to pass in a slow, excruciating eter

nity. Frightened of leaving her office, frightened of staying and being trapped, she was reaching for the phone to call the police before she realized she couldn't call out. Her computer was still connected to the Internet.

A board creaked on the sales floor, and suddenly Ari had had enough. She wasn't going to cower here, no matter what might happen. And she wasn't without defenses. She'd played soccer and football when she was younger, and she still knew how to tackle an opponent. She hoped her kicks were still as powerful as they had been when she'd sent soccer balls flying.

She quickly barreled out of the office, head down, ready to butt whoever was after her in the stomach. "Shit!" someone said in a muffled voice, suddenly standing. Ari was finally facing her attacker. *Medium height,* she thought, still cool, still rational. Medium build, too. The hair was covered and the face was obscured. And the figure was holding some kind of stick high in the air.

It was a long stick, with a long reach. Ari charged, hoping she'd pass her assailant before he could swing the stick at her. A long stick, thin, with a crook at the end. She'd have to give details to the police. She'd have to—

And then the stick slashed down.

CHAPTER 12

Ari dreamed of Aran sweaters. Knit three, purl two, work a cable. The directions so befuddled her that she had to keep rereading them, with the frantic conviction that she'd never get it right. She dreamed of Scandinavian sweaters, their distinctive eight-pointed star design worked in bright green. She dreamed of a dress made of crocheted granny squares in neon shades: bilious yellow and irradiated pink and poisonous green. It had a high turtleneck collar of a firebright orange. *Wait a minute.* Granny squares were used in afghans, not in dresses. The thought was so absurd that she pulled free of the dream.

Only gradually did she become aware of other things. A beeping sound, bright and continuous. Footsteps. And a soft swishing sound, just like . . .

She came fully awake at that, frightened, though she didn't know why. What she did know, though, was that she was in a hospital. She closed her eyes, still seeing in her mind the images of bland beige walls, striped curtains next to her bed, and monitors that beeped and flashed. Definitely a hospital, but why?

There was a sudden growing pressure on her arm. She opened her eyes to see that it came from a blood pressure cuff inflating. "Oh," she said.

The nurse who stood by a machine, watching the numbers on display, glanced at her. "Good," she said. "We thought you were waking up."

"Why?"

"Because of your vital signs."

"Oh," Ari said again. Now that she was awake, she was aware of pain in her head, throbbing and persistent. "Am I in the hospital?"

"Saint Luke's," a voice said nearby.

Ari turned her head to see Josh lounging against the windowsill. At the foot of the bed, Ted glared at her. His hands were balled into fists, and his head was thrust forward belligerently. "Jeez, Ari, what've you gotten yourself into now?"

Ari closed her eyes against the pain in her head. The last thing she needed to deal with just now was Ted's anger. "Why am I here?"

"You don't remember?" Josh said.

"No."

"You were attacked in your shop. What were you doing there that late?"

"Megan," Ari said, suddenly remembering. "Where is she? Is she all right?"

"About time you asked. With your mother."

Thank God. She winced as she looked toward Josh,

backlit by the bright sun streaming in through the window. "Is it morning?"

"Early afternoon," Josh said.

"Afternoon! Oh, she must be so scared."

"Call her," Ted said, his tone more normal. *Why, he is concerned*, she thought with surprise. "Here's the phone."

"In a minute." Some of the pain had left. "Do you know who did it?" she asked.

Josh straightened. "No. I was hoping you could tell me. When Herb——"

"What is that noise?" she asked sharply, hearing that soft swishing again.

"What noise?"

"That whispery sound."

Josh looked toward the nurse, who, in the act of rolling out the machine used for taking vital signs, had paused at the bottom of the bed to note something on a chart. "Push that again," he said. The nurse, frowning quizzically, moved it a foot or so farther. "That noise?"

"Yes." It reminded her of something, just tantalizingly out of reach. Something familiar, but unknown. "I can't remember."

"That's okay." His voice was soothing. "That happens after a head injury. It'll come back to you."

"Yeah." Ted finally straightened. "I want to catch the bas——"

"It's all right, Ted." She smiled at him, finally seeing his concern. Ted's strongest emotions sometimes were covered by anger.

"Yeah, but you gave us a scare last night."

"Last night," she said, concentrating. "Yes. It had to be. The bells fell off the day before. I couldn't put them back up because my shoulder hurt."

"Then he came in the front door?" Josh asked, alert now.

"Yes," she said in surprise. "That sound. That's what it was."

"What, the front door?"

"Yes. I didn't even realize I'd heard it."

"We found the back door open, though."

"The back door?" She frowned, and winced. "Ouch. Does that mean he got out that way?"

"Or she."

"Or she." After all, they'd been referring to the murderer as a female all along. And surely this attack was tied to the murder. "It was after hours," she said. "Herb Perry wanted to talk to me about something."

"We know," Josh said. "He found you, or so he says. Could he have a key?"

She frowned. "I don't think so. He worked in my building once, when it was a hardware store, but I had the locks changed." She looked up at him. "Did he do it?"

"Herb Perry?" Ted said skeptically. "I can't see it."

Neither could she. "What did Herb have to say?"

"He called it in. He said that someone was standing over you, holding a stick high." He paused. "If Herb's telling the truth."

The stick. There was something about that. . . . "Long," she said. "Round and thin. It had—Josh, it had a crook on the end."

He bent forward abruptly. "Are you sure?"

"Like a cane. I think. Oh, I don't know." She moved her head fretfully. "I just don't."

He blew out his breath in frustration. "How thick?"

"I don't know. It was shadowy, hard to tell. I'm sorry."

Josh leaned back against the wall, his eyes opaque. "Hmm."

"What?"

"Nothing."

"Meeting him without telling anyone was damned stupid, Ari," Ted put in.

"I know," she said meekly. "It's connected to the murder, isn't it?"

"Maybe. Who knew you were going to be there?"

Again Ari concentrated. "Herb, of course," she said finally. "Laura. Kaitlyn was there, and her mother. She put my web page up finally." She frowned. "No one else—oh. Barbara Watson. A couple of other customers at closing. Laura might remember who they were. But, Josh." She looked at him. "I had the lights on. Anyone could've guessed I was there."

"That narrows it down," he said dryly. "Who's Barbara Watson?"

"One of Laura's friends. But she couldn't have done it. She's close to six feet, and thin."

"You saw who did it?" Ted said sharply.

"Good heavens. Yes, I did," she said in surprise. "I concentrated on her—him?—so I could tell you. Medium height. No. Just a little above. Tallish for a woman, not so tall for a man. Medium build, ditto. Not—you know something?" She stared at him. "Not really feminine-looking. Not the right shape. Or maybe the clothes were baggy. I don't know."

"It's okay," Josh said. "That helps."

"I wish I remembered more, but the lights were out."

"Yeah, I know." He looked away. "Herb Perry isn't tall, or heavy."

"But the way she moved—"

"She?"

"Maybe he," she admitted. "Kind of fast and easy. Herb's not young."

"But he walks a lot. Did you know that?"

"Yes, now that I think of it. Damn." She put her fingers to her head as the pain flared again. Someone moved closer to her. *Josh*, she thought, and opened her eyes to see Ted bending over her.

"You're damned lucky," he said. "If you'd been hit any harder you wouldn't be here."

Ari closed her eyes again. She had no doubt that whoever was after her had meant to kill. But why? With Joe in jail, the killer had to be feeling pretty safe. What possible threat could Ari be to her?

"Can you think of anything else?" Josh asked.

"I told you everything I remember," she said, hearing petulance in her voice. "I'm tired."

"I'll stop bugging you, then." Josh stopped at the door. "Don't worry. I've got things under control."

"Look," Ted said, belligerent again. "I want Ari protected."

"I'll have someone on her tonight."

"Tonight?" Ari said. "Why?"

"You have to stay another night," Ted explained, and turned back to Josh. "What about afterward? If anything happens to her, I'll slap a lawsuit on you so fast—"

"Ted," Ari said, before he could go on. "Please."

Ted glanced at her and subsided. "Sorry, Ari." He took her hand. "But, hell, you gave me a scare."

"I'm sorry. Ted, what about Megan?"

"I'll bring her by later."

"I'll see you later, Ari," Josh called from the door.

Ari raised her hand to him, both sorry and relieved to see him go. "Poor kid. I can't imagine what she's thinking. She's already had a hard time." She looked up at him. "Did she tell you what's been bothering her?"

"No, but maybe she will tonight."

"Tonight?"

"I'm going to stay with her."

"Oh, good. She needs you, Ted."

"Yeah. When you're better, Ari, could we talk about me visiting her more?"

"Maybe. Not now, though."

"Yeah." He hesitated. "You look tired."

"I am. I think I'm going to sleep."

"Okay. I'll stay a while."

"Thank you," she said, too tired to voice her surprise. Instead she snuggled down as best she could in the unyielding hospital bed. She was aware of Ted standing beside her bed, and yet he wasn't the one in her thoughts. It was Josh. If anyone could find out what had happened to her, he would.

"That guy has the hots for you," Ted said, startling her just as she was beginning to drift off.

"What?" She stared at him groggily.

"That cop. He's got the hots for you."

If her head hadn't ached so much, Ari probably would have laughed. "He's investigating what happened to me."

"You ask me, he's investigating *you*."

This time she did laugh. "Ted."

"I'm serious, Ari."

"I know." She closed her eyes. "You're wrong. Anyway, why does it matter to you? We're divorced."

"Yeah."

The flat tone in his voice made her look at him again. "Ted, I can't exactly argue with you now."

"No," he said after a moment. "Sorry. But you and I've got to talk one of these days."

"Okay," she said, and closed her eyes again. Josh would take care of things, she thought. She could count on it.

✂

The next day Ari was a little shaky on her feet but otherwise all right. Back in her shop she felt safe, not only because of the throngs of customers who were drawn by this latest sensation, but because of the police car that cruised by at irregular intervals. She had no doubt that she owed that to Josh. Anyone intending her harm wouldn't be able to predict the cruiser's movements. Laura also seemed to be there all the time, just now muttering darkly about getting a gun. "You can't do that," Ari said in a harsh whisper. Across from her a customer seemed to be studying a fine-spun skein of Heilo yarn from Norway, but Ari had no doubt she was listening to every word.

"You need protection, dear," Laura said tranquilly.

"Having you here all the time is protection enough. Not to mention that you bring me back and forth from home. That's when I make a good target."

"Exactly. If I get a gun, no one will bother us."

"Laura, you don't know how to shoot."

"I'll learn."

Lord help her. "Really, I don't think whoever attacked me will do it again."

"Why not?"

"For one thing, I'm alert now. Plus, the police are watching me, not only here but at home."

"Have Josh Pierce stay over," Laura suggested.

"Laura!" Ari protested, and the customer glanced over, eyes avid.

"He'll keep you safe."

"Good God." Ari shook her head. A ghost of a headache whispered along her scalp. She'd have them from time to time, she'd been warned, sometimes with migraine force. This one, thank God, hadn't yet developed into anything. "Has the world gone nuts?"

"Yes," Laura said quite seriously. "Certainly it has, when someone as decent as you is hurt."

"And someone like Joe is arrested."

Laura regarded her, head tilted to the side. "I wonder how Diane is doing. Why don't you go see her?"

"She'd probably run me off the farm. I think she blames me for what happened to Joe."

"Now, that's just silly. How could you be to blame?"

Ari shrugged. "It's all tied up with me."

"I think she knows better. Has she called you since you were in the hospital?"

"No." And that hurt. She and Diane had been friends nearly all their lives. Before this, Diane would have been as fiercely protective as Laura. Now her allegiance had changed. Oh, Ari expected her loyalties to be with Joe, but the total lack of contact with her hurt. Not being able to talk to her best friend about everything that had happened hurt. There was a giant void in her life.

"Call her, dear," Laura urged her. "It'll make you feel better."

Ari doubted it, but she smiled and touched Laura's hand. The customer had come to the counter, bearing enough skeins of yarn to make a traditional Norwegian sweater. It was a big sale, making Ari smile. To her relief, the topic of what had happened to her, and its consequences, died for the moment.

She wasn't as nonchalant as she tried to appear, though. She was uneasily aware that there was someone out there who meant her harm. That person could get to her at any time, in spite of the police. If enough time passed with no sign of trouble, they probably wouldn't guard her anymore. She knew that their resources must be needed elsewhere, but their absence would leave her alone and vulnerable. That fueled her determination to find the real killer. There was now no doubt in her mind that Edith's death held a threat against her.

The phone rang. "Ariadne's Web," she said absently, and her eyes grew wide as she heard the voice on the other end. "Just a minute," she cut in. "I'm going to put you on hold." Ari pressed the hold button and put down the receiver. "Laura, I'm going to take this in my office."

Laura shot her a look. "Is everything all right?"

"Yes, yes." The headache threatened again as she went into her office, but again she ignored it. This was too important a call. "You're the last person I expected to hear from," she said into the phone.

"I heard you were back at work," Herb Perry said.

"Yes."

"I didn't hit you, Ariadne."

Ari still wondered about that. "Then who did?"

"There was someone standing over you when I came in. You shouldn't leave your door unlocked," he said reproachfully.

"I didn't."

"Anything can happen nowadays, even in Freeport. I used to tell Edith that." He broke off, and then continued in a constricted voice. "She wasn't as careful as she could've been. Used to think no one would ever bother her." He laughed, a mirthless sound. "Thought no one would ever dare."

So why had she been killed, and why, Ari wondered yet again, in her shop? Someone reckless, she thought, someone used to taking risks. The problem was, she didn't know anyone like that. At least, she didn't think she did. But then, people she thought she knew were turning into strangers. Herb had always seemed genial to her before, but what was he really like? "Do you still have a key to my building?" she asked abruptly.

"Look, how could I if you changed the locks? I hope you're going to do that again, young lady."

Ari smiled faintly at the fatherly tone in his voice. "Yes, the locksmith was here yesterday. But, do you?"

"No. Yeah, I worked in the hardware store, and yeah, I cut keys, but only duplicates. Who's your locksmith?"

"Keysmith."

"Jack Morgan's business. Yeah, he and I go way back. Maybe he gave me a key," he said sarcastically. "Maybe I used Edith's."

Ari went still. "What did you say?"

"Hey, didn't you know? Edith had a key."

CHAPTER 13

Ari gasped. "Edith had a key?"

"Yeah. Thought you knew."

"No," she said, stunned. "How did she get it?"

"Because she was looking to buy the building."

That plan, which had caused Ari such concern, didn't seem important now. "My God, Herb, she let herself and her killer into the shop."

"You think?"

"Yes. I've been wondering how they got in. Have you told Josh Pierce?"

"That detective? Nah. Why should I?"

"Because someone got into my shop and killed your wife!"

"Not with her keys."

"How do you know? It's the most likely answer." But why here?

"Come to think of it, how'd someone get in the other night?"

"No one knows." She put her fingers to her forehead. The headache was settling in, in earnest. She'd have to get home soon to rest, or she'd be in rough shape.

"You sure you locked your door?"

"Yes." But had she, Ari wondered? She couldn't remember. An action like that was automatic, easy to forget.

"Hell, Ari, someone got in the other night. I thought you were dead at first."

"You saw the person, didn't you?"

"Yeah, but not very well. He was holding up a stick of some kind—"

"You saw it?"

"Sure. I saved your life, you know."

So she'd been told, though she wondered about that. "What did sh—he look like? And the stick?"

"Baseball bat, I think."

"Baseball? But—" she began, and stopped herself.

"Yeah. What else? Anyway, I couldn't see much of him. Why weren't your lights on?" he said accusingly.

"They were, and I *did* lock the door. This wasn't my fault." At least, not in the way he thought. "What did the person look like?"

"Short. Thin. Definitely a man."

"How could you tell?"

"The way he moved. Fast, no fussing, not like a woman."

Ari gritted her teeth. "Couldn't it have been an athletic woman?"

"With that build? Nah. Nothing up front, if you know what I mean."

Again Ari bit back a retort. She'd had no idea that Herb could be so offensive. Unless he was deliberately misdirecting her. "What did you want to see me about?"

"Oh, yeah. I'm still gonna buy the building, Ari."

Oh, Lord, just what she needed. It seemed her business was threatened after all. "Oh."

"Yeah. I gotta negotiate with Bill Harper again," he said bitterly. "He put it back on the market. He's got that Silveira gal as an agent, and she's a shark."

"I thought Susan was *your* agent," Ari said in surprise.

"Nah. She was Edith's at one time, but not mine. Anyways, I don't think I'll have to raise your rent, unless I have to pay too much."

That was a relief, though the prospect of its happening in the future was a concern. On the other hand, Bill Harper, the current owner, could also raise the rent anytime. "When will the sale go through?"

"Not for a while. I've gotta reach an agreement with Bill, and then wait for the closing."

She had a reprieve, then. "You'll let me know?"

"Yeah. Damn shame this had to happen to you," he went on. "Edith liked your patterns."

"She never bought any of them, as far as I know."

"Yeah? Maybe she borrowed them."

That sounded more like it. "Maybe."

"Anyways, I'm sorry about what happened to you. You're a good gal, Ariadne."

Ari rolled her eyes at Laura, who had just come into the office. "Yes, well. Thank you, Herb. I appreciate that. You do know how sorry I am, too?"

"Yeah, well." He fell briefly silent. "Look, I've taken up too much of your time. See you around, maybe?"

A chill shivered down her spine. "Maybe," she said, and hung up. "Ugh."

"Herb Perry?" Laura asked, eyebrows raised.

"Yes." Ari looked up. "I didn't know he was such a jerk."

"Well, dear, I always did think he and Edith deserved each other."

That startled a laugh out of her. "Maybe they did. Oh, Laura." She leaned back. "Do you ever get the feeling you just don't know people?"

"All the time. Look at Ted."

Ari laughed again, the last of the unease left by Herb's phone call fading. "Yes, once upon a time you thought he was something special."

"Even I can be wrong," Laura said, not a bit abashed. "Now, I didn't come in out of nosiness, though I'll admit I wanted to know who called. Detective Pierce is here."

"Josh? Good. I was just about to call him."

"Why?" Laura asked curiously.

"I'll tell you later. Is he out there?"

"Along with five customers."

Ari blew out her breath. At most times she'd welcome so many customers, but now it just meant there were that many people who might overhear. "All right." She followed Laura out of the office, checking a smile when she saw Josh frowning at a sweater splashed with random designs of bright colors, making a stained-glass effect. "Detective."

Hands in pockets, he turned. "Interesting," he said, indicating the sweater with his chin.

"Isn't it? Summer designed it."

"You've got two good employees working for you."

"Yes, they're both talented. Summer's a little older and a little steadier, though. She's working her way through UMass Dartmouth. But come into the back room." She lowered her voice. "I've got something to tell you."

Six pairs of eyes followed their progress across the shop. "Is there any special reason you're here?" she asked as they came into the back room.

Josh sat at the battered table and nodded when Ari held up a can of Coke from the small refrigerator. "Just came by to see how you are. Busy, I see."

"Oh, I've caused another sensation. It'll die down." She winced. "Bad choice of words."

"Yeah." He leaned forward. "Is everything okay?"

"Yes. Oh, but I have something to tell you. Herb Perry just called."

His attention sharpened. "What did he want?"

"Josh, he told me Edith had a key."

"What? To the shop?"

"Yes, because she was going to buy the building."

He frowned. "That doesn't seem right."

"No, it doesn't, does it? I'll have to ask my landlord about that."

"We didn't look at her keys."

"Remember, I gave you my original key, so you can just compare it to what Edith had."

"Fine." He sounded grim. "This changes things."

"I think so, too. All the keys I had floating around—that doesn't matter now, does it?"

"Don't know that yet, but it's something to look into."

"It rattled me," she said frankly, popping some aspirin in her mouth and washing them down with Diet Coke. "Good heavens, I've been through all this because of Edith!" Her brow wrinkled. "Could Herb have done it?"

"Killed Edith? We looked into it."

"And arrested Joe instead."

"He seemed the most likely."

"But Herb had access to a key." She leaned forward. "He had a motive, since he inherits her property. Except for the Robeson farm, of course. He had opportunity, and maybe the means. And you know he could have attacked me."

"I know." He looked troubled. "We ruled him out because we had no reason to think he had access to a key. Now, I don't know."

"He seems just as strong a suspect to me as Joe."

"Except why here, Ari? Answer me that."

"Maybe to look the building over before they bought it. I wouldn't have put that past Edith. Eric could have gotten the key, too!"

"That's reaching. How would he know his mother had it?"

"Ask him. You might be surprised."

"Maybe." He sounded skeptical. "But Herb, now . . ."

"Is it enough to reopen the investigation?"

"Maybe. I don't know. The D.A. seems pretty certain Joe's our man."

"But would he stick to that if we told him about this new evidence?"

"We?"

"All right, you. Would he?"

He paused. "Maybe. I think he might have doubts, since you were attacked."

She leaned forward again. "Josh, do you think Herb has a copy of the new key to the shop?"

"I'll check with your landlord, but I doubt it, after what happened."

"Then who attacked me? Herb *says* he found me, but . . ."

"I know. He could have been your attacker. We searched his house for the weapon you described—"

"When was this?" she asked in surprise.

"You were still in the hospital. We didn't have to get a search warrant, he just let us in."

"And?"

"Nothing."

"He said it looked like a baseball bat."

"I don't think so, not after what you said. And . . ."

"What?" she said, when he didn't go on.

"Look, don't tell anyone this."

"What?"

"Edith was hit with something similar."

"What!" she exclaimed. "Do you mean the murderer—"

"Keep it down." He glanced toward the door leading into the shop, though no one could have heard them, and then back to her, looking harassed. "We've got to keep this quiet."

"I know, but . . ." She frowned. "Edith would have noticed if Herb had brought something like that with him."

"We didn't find anything that resembled a cane or a bat. Are you sure that's what it was? Remember, it was dark, and you suffered a trauma. You might not remember correctly."

"It was a cane." She frowned. "Or something like it."

"Somehow I can't picture one of Freeport's senior citizens going after you."

The thought was so ludicrous that she smiled. "Like Ruth Taylor? She used a cane once when she hurt her knee," she said, and paused, startled.

"What?"

"Josh, she might have had a motive."

"What?" he asked, looking skeptical.

"Her grandson. Do you know how proud she is of her grandchildren?"

He grimaced. "The first time I met her, she showed me pictures. So?"

"Her grandchildren are always over at her house. I heard Edith complain about it more than once."

"Why?"

"Because they play baseball and street hockey. It's a dead-end street and it's safe. . . ."

"What?" he prompted, when she didn't go on.

"I don't know," she said, frustrated. "Something was trying to get through then, a memory or something."

nting to do something like that. "I don't know who can trust anymore."

"Look, don't worry. You've got protection."

"For now."

"For as long as I can manage it."

She smiled. "Thank you."

"But I can't come by anymore."

"Why not?"

"I'm not supposed to be telling you any of this."

"I have the right to know what I'm facing. Anyway, Joe's in the clear. That's one thing."

"Diane isn't."

"She wouldn't do it! We've been friends for too long."

"You never know. Anyway, the official theory is that it was an ordinary break-in."

"You know it wasn't." It was better than the theory that Diane had attacked her, though. No matter how matters were between them, she knew Diane wouldn't hurt her. "Darn it. What are we supposed to do?"

"*You're* not supposed to do anything."

"You're here talking to me, with the door closed, so you can't really believe that."

"Nevertheless, you can't go snooping after this."

"But if I find something out—"

"You're not going to keep at it, are you, after what's ppened?" he demanded.

"Of course I am. Someone attacked me, and we h know it wasn't random."

"Damn it, Ari, you can't."

"Don't force it. It will come."

"I hope so. Anyway, I don't think Ruth's gra
dren really bother anyone very much, but ther
been some problems."

"Broken windows?"

"One or two."

"Edith was her neighbor," he said thoughtfully.

"Yes. I think she called the police once or twice."

"I don't know, Ari. It doesn't seem like a strong enough motive."

"Well, no," Ari admitted. "Ruth has a temper, though."

"This was a cold-blooded crime, Ari. There was too much planning involved. Besides, she's old."

"She goes to the YMCA every day to swim."

"That's right. She told me that." He sat back. "I've never seen a town where all the senior citizens are in such good shape. Now that our list of suspects has grown, you have to be more careful."

"I don't understand it, Josh. With someone in ja
shouldn't the murderer think she's safe?"

"She thinks you know something, Ari," he said
garding her gravely.

"But I don't!"

"I'm not the one you have to convince."

"Then you think she might try again? Or
added hastily. Herb might be a suspect in th
but somehow she still thought of the murc
woman.

"It's possible."

Ari shuddered. It was hard to imagi

"I have to. It's my life now, Josh. I have to do something."

"This isn't a high-school prank."

"I know that," she said impatiently. "I'll be careful."

"It might not be enough. Damn." He frowned at her. "You're asking for trouble."

"What can I do, Josh? If I sit back, she'll come after me again. You know that, and you know the patrols won't be coming by forever. If I don't help find my attacker now, I'll be even more vulnerable when you and the police move on to different cases."

"Yeah." He gazed thoughtfully at her. "But maybe there's something we could do to keep you safe."

"What?"

"We could start dating."

CHAPTER 14

Ari burst out laughing. "I don't think I've ever had such a gracious invitation before."

"You know what I mean," Josh said. "It wouldn't be real."

For some reason that nettled her. "I didn't think you cared."

"Sure I do."

"Not that way," she said, and remembered uneasily what Ted had said about Josh in the hospital.

"I'm not talking about *that way*." He leaned back. "I'm talking about getting together once in a while. Dinner, a movie, like that."

"Not late," she said swiftly, a little annoyed and a little pleased. He was kind of cute. "Not with Megan."

"Couldn't she stay with your mother?"

This sounded like a lot more than just discussing the facts of a case, she thought. "She's clingy right now. Having me in the hospital scared her."

"Okay, I can see that. Well, I can't keep you from asking questions. But when do you expect to tell me anything you find out?"

"By phone," she said reluctantly.

"With people in the department listening in? No. Besides, you worry me."

"It worries me. But I'm not going to do something stupid. I'm not a heroine in a gothic novel who goes outside investigating strange noises in only her nightgown."

"No?" he said, and there was a strange spark in his eyes. Humor, Ari thought, and something else.

"No. I'm not that stupid."

He grinned at her. "Good. The thing is, though, people talk to you. Even if you didn't ask questions, you'd hear things."

"I might not if they think I'm passing them along."

"So let's go to dinner and a movie."

Ari looked at him suspiciously, but he seemed sincere. If he had an ulterior motive, there was no sign of it. "Are you really serious about this?"

"Yup."

"You know what people will think."

"They'll think what we want them to. If the murderer thinks we're seeing each other, maybe she'll relax."

"And your chief, too."

His face reddened a bit. "Yeah, that, too. God knows I'd be busted down to checking parking meters if he finds out I've involved you."

Ari stifled a smile at the image of Josh as a meter maid. "You didn't involve me. I involved myself."

"Doesn't matter. It works out the same."

"I suppose." She pursed her lips. "So if we're not really dating, what will we be?"

"Friends," he said promptly. "C'mon, Ari. You know what people have thought of us from the beginning. Laura's even tried to matchmake."

"I didn't think you knew about that," she said, surprised and mortified.

"She's pretty obvious."

"True." Ari looked away. She was tempted. Hadn't she wondered what it would be like to date again? "I don't know."

"Yeah, you do." He grinned at her. "You ever have any fun, Ari?"

"Of course I do."

"Like in high school?"

That silenced her. It seemed like so long ago since she'd been free to be herself. True, she had a business to run now, and a child to raise. And yet . . . She smiled, slowly. "Okay, then," she said, suddenly recklessly decisive. "Let's do it."

The shop was quieter when Ari walked out of her office. Josh had left a few minutes earlier. Now Ariadne braced herself for Laura's questions about Josh's visit. To her surprise, though, Laura simply came over from where she was straightening out some of the bins of yarn, then smiled.

"No one's here?" Ari asked.

"Not just now," she said, and went on with what she was doing.

Ari busied herself at the sales counter, checking the register and a few messages from customers. At last, Laura came over and joined her. "Well?" she said, expectantly.

"Well, what?"

"What did Detective Pierce want?"

Ari sighed. "What took you so long?"

"Why, what do you mean?"

"To ask me about him."

"I thought I'd be discreet, dear."

"Huh."

Laura's eyes were very wide. "I know you don't want me poking into your business."

"That's never stopped you before."

"It's only because I care."

Ari looked at Laura's expectant face, and gave in. "He asked me to go out tomorrow night," she said, knowing that that would get on the grapevine soon enough.

Laura plunked down on the rocking chair. "Well! I never thought he'd do it."

"Not because you didn't try."

"Well, yes, dear, I do think he's a nice man."

"He is." She hesitated. "As long as he was involved in investigating Edith's death, though, he couldn't very well ask me out." It was only a little fib, she told herself.

"I never thought of that. So where are you going?"

"Dinner and a movie."

Laura made a face. "How boring. Are you at least going to Providence?"

"No, to the Lucky Dragon and the Oxford."

"But they show second-run movies."

"No, this weekend it's a foreign film we both want to see. Don't look like that, Laura. He's on call tomorrow night, so he can't go out of town."

"I suppose it's better than nothing."

"Sorry to disappoint you." Ari rose. "Since it's so quiet, I think I'll go to the market. Do you mind?"

"Why, no, of course not."

"You can call me if it gets busy," Ari said. She distrusted the gleam that had come into Laura's eyes.

Laura glanced speculatively at the bins of yarn. "I don't imagine we'll have a rush of people."

"Probably not." And if not, Laura was likely to go around the shop rearranging things. Ordinarily that would drive Ari wild, but today she didn't really mind. Laura had done a great deal for her in these past weeks.

"Thank you, dear. Now, get out and enjoy the day."

Enjoy the day. Right, Ari thought a little later, as she went into Shaw's market. It was as busy as she'd expected, since the store started its weekly sales on Fridays. Grabbing a cart, she headed for the far corner of the store. The store was so large, and laid out so oddly, that she preferred to start at the back. Milk, she thought, reaching for a bottle. Kids' yogurt for Megan.

Peanut butter and bread, of course. Then back she went, picking up what she needed, absently navigating the half aisles and full-length ones and the odd angles that made the store like a maze. It would be good to have this task out of the way.

At last she reached the produce section at the front of the store. Apples, potatoes, broccoli, and onions. Salad makings, too. She was examining a head of lettuce when a voice spoke next to her. "Why, Ariadne Jorgensen."

Ari turned to see a tall, spare lady with graying hair. "Mrs. Mailloux!" she exclaimed, genuinely glad to see her former history teacher. Sarah Mailloux was one of the few teachers graced by the pranks she and Diane had played in high school, such as toilet paper strewn from her bushes and car. She'd retired to Williamsburg, Virginia, a few years ago, having fallen in love with the town when she'd read a series of historical novels based there. "I heard you were here on vacation."

"Yes, I've been here nearly a month."

"My mother's been wondering why she hasn't heard from you."

"Oh, I've been so busy with my grandkids." She gestured toward three children, two boys, one girl. One of the boys sat in the miniature car attached to the front of her cart, but the other boy, who was about Megan's age, was inspecting every peach, and the girl was tossing an apple into the air and catching it. "No, Mia, don't do that," Sarah called, though the little girl ignored her completely. "I can't control them," Sarah confided as she turned back to Ari. "I hate to say it, but they're spoiled."

"By you, or Leslie?"

"Oh, my daughter, of course." Sarah's smile was rueful. "Not Mémère. I'm afraid I can't talk long."

"I understand. Megan gets impatient if I start talking to people, too," Ari said. "But I'll bet you're enjoying every minute."

"Oh, yes. We've gone all over the place, and I've had a marvelous time catching up with friends. I've even managed to get some golf in."

Another golf nut, Ari thought. Josh was right. Freeport did have more than its share of active, fit senior citizens. "Is Mr. Mailloux here, too?"

"No, he's back in Williamsburg, doing some work on the house. He'll be up next week." She sighed. "The time has flown."

"Yes, it has."

Sarah's gaze sharpened. "But I haven't told you how distressed I was to hear about Edith Perry."

Ari sighed. "Yes, I can't believe she was murdered. How horrible."

"And to think I saw her just a few days before." Sarah moved her cart to make way for another shopper. "And now you've been attacked. Are you feeling all right?"

"Yes, just an occasional headache. I was lucky."

Sarah shook her head. "Sometimes I think the world's going to hell in a handbasket. To think of Joe Camacho, of all people, in jail."

"He didn't do it," Ari said swiftly.

"No, I don't think he did. Peter!" she called sharply to her grandson. "Don't you dare eat those grapes."

The boy made a face. "Aw, but Mémère—"

"Not until we pay for them." This time Sarah sighed. "I'd better get the little monsters home before they tear up the place."

"Yes, I have to go, too." Ari turned her cart to walk beside Sarah. "But come into the shop next week. I've got some new patterns and yarn I think you'd like."

"Yes, I'll do that. That's a lovely sweater, by the way. Did you design it?"

"In a way. It's based on a traditional Icelandic design." The sweater was predominantly teal, with rose and pink in a zigzag design at yoke and waist, knitted in heavy Lopi yarn.

"I like it. Edith did, too, now that I think of it."

Ari frowned. "Edith? But this is the first time I've worn it."

"Is it? Maybe it was something similar, then. She did say it was your design."

Ari frowned. "When was that?"

"When I saw her, just before she died."

"But she never bought my patterns," Ari said.

"This time she did."

"What did it look like?" It was possible Edith had seen the sweater when she had it on display and had adapted it herself. She had been an expert knitter, after all.

"It was just a plain piece of paper, with the directions and a nice color picture."

Ari stared at her. None of the pictures on her patterns were printed in color. It cost too much. "Are you sure?"

"Why, yes. I remember exactly because she was excited about it. As excited as she ever got," Sarah amended. "You see, she said that she could finally afford to buy one of your designs." Sarah eyed her curiously. "I never thought your prices were high, but you know how Edith was. Have you marked them down?"

"No. How could she have—"

"Oh, no," Sarah said at the same time, turning sharply around at the sound of long, rolling thunder. Apples were everywhere on the floor, some still rolling, to come to rest beneath counters and near people's feet. In the midst of the disaster stood Mia, looking both frightened and guilty. "Mia! What did you do?"

"I only wanted an apple, Mémère," Mia said.

"Oh, what am I going to do about this—where is Kyle?"

"He's there. Uh-oh, Mémère. He's been bad."

"What? Oh, no," she said, starting toward Kyle, who held a half-eaten peach in his hand. "I'm sorry, Ari, but I have to go."

"Yes," Ari said, stifling both a smile and gratitude that it wasn't Megan who'd caused the problem. "Will you come to the shop so we can talk more?"

"Yes, of course," Sarah said distractedly. "Tuesday?"

"Yes, fine," Ari said, and turned toward the checkout counters, feeling blindsided. The mystery surrounding Edith, and herself as well, had just gotten deeper. How in the world, Ari wondered, had Edith gotten a pattern that hadn't been on display before her death?

Ted was waiting for her when Ari came home. "Where have you been?" he barked as soon as she walked in the door.

"Where do you think?" Ari held up a bag as she pushed by him. "Shopping. What are you doing here on a Friday?"

"I'd like to have Megan tonight."

"Tonight!" Ari stared at him as she dropped her bags on the kitchen table. "That's not part of the agreement."

"Yeah, well, we've worked around it before."

Ari frowned as she began unloading the grocery bags. "You could have called."

"I did. I called the shop, and Laura told me you were gone. Your cell phone's not on, and you weren't here. So I thought I'd just come."

"Ted, I've really had enough of this."

"Of what?"

She gestured toward him. "You, being here all the time, when you never were before. It's driving me nuts."

"It's only because I care."

"If you cared this much before, we'd still be married!" she shouted.

"Hey." Ted held out his hands, palms out. His eyes were surprised, as they always were on the rare occasions when she lost her temper. Even she admitted that her anger could be an awesome thing. "You don't have to yell. I was worried."

"You badger me." She pointed an accusing finger at him, nearly connecting with his chest. "You accuse me and you yell, Ted, not me, and you make me feel in the wrong. Do you think I brought any of what happened on myself? Do you? Do you think I want it? Jeez, Ted." She turned her back to him, gripping the edge of the counter. "You've got no right to tell me what to do anymore."

"We've got Megan to think about, Ari."

Ari stood still, her head turned a little to the side. He was right. As Megan's parents, they shared a bond that would never be broken. "I'm tired of it, Ted," she said, quieter now, but no less passionate. "I've got enough problems without you acting this way."

"I'm sorry," he said after a moment. "But this whole thing's gotten to me."

"It's gotten to me, too."

"I know." He leaned back against the wall, his attitude at odds with his stylish Italian tailored suit and expensive leather shoes. "We have to think of what it's doing to Megan, too."

"I know," Ari said, after taking a deep breath.

"She said anything to you?"

"No."

"Okay, let me ask that a different way. Have you spent enough time with her for her to tell you anything?"

"Have you?" she shot back.

"It's why I'm here early. I heard she got in trouble in school for fighting."

"Who told you that—oh, Mom, I bet."

"Yeah."

It figured. For some reason, her mother had always liked Ted. "I wish she hadn't."

"Hey, someone had to."

"I was going to," she said defensively.

"Yeah," he said after a moment. "I guess you would." For all their problems, each agreed that the other tried to be a good parent. "Got any idea what it was about?"

Ari spread her hands helplessly. "I don't know. The boy she fought with has always been fresh, but . . ."

"Megan isn't."

"I know."

"I think you're too wrapped up in what's going on."

"Yes, of course I am. Someone attacked me, Ted." She paused. "But I don't ignore Megan."

"Okay, but how do you think she feels about everything? Especially since you're dating that cop."

"How'd you find out about that—oh. Mom," she said again. "We're just going out to dinner."

"Yeah? I'm telling you, Ari, he's got the hots for you."

Ridiculous. "Ted, sometimes I wonder that you keep any clients, the way you talk."

"I can talk sophisticated with the best of 'em, babe." Unexpectedly, he grinned at her, and for a moment Ari remembered what had drawn her to him in the first place: his self-deprecating sense of humor and honest outspokenness. Unfortunately, that latter trait was hard to live with. "Ted, what are we fighting for? We both care about Megan."

"Are you dating that cop?"

She hesitated. "You've dated other women."

"Yeah, but—"

"So why is this different?"

"Because Megan doesn't see it when I date."

The unfairness of that enraged Ari again. "That's not fair, Ted! Yes, I'm going out with Josh. Why shouldn't I?"

"Megan needs stability now, not a new man in her life."

"Ted, are you jealous?" Ari asked curiously.

"Nah. We're divorced."

"I meant about Megan."

He was quiet a minute. "Yeah, maybe."

"You don't need to be. She knows who her father is. She loves you, Ted."

Ted shrugged. He never had been good at expressing emotions. "Yeah, well I love her, too." He looked away. "So where's he taking you?"

"The Lucky Dragon for supper, and then a movie at the Oxford."

"Are you kidding me?"

"No."

"He splashes money around, doesn't he? Chow mein sandwiches and a second-run movie."

"A foreign one this week."

He snorted. "It's still a cheap date."

"Ted, I am not a cheap date!"

He looked surprised again. "Didn't say you were, Ari. But, jeez, he could treat you better."

"We're not serious."

"No?" His look was skeptical. "I saw the way he looked at you in the hospital. He's interested, all right."

"You're wrong, Ted.

"If you believe that, I'll sell you the Fairhaven Bridge."

That made her laugh. "No, thanks."

"Nah," he said, grinning. "Bad deal. But look, Ari. Go slow here, will you?"

"Why?"

"Because he's a cop, and you were a suspect. What's his real reason for this?"

That cut too close to home for comfort. "Just for fun. Don't you think I'm allowed that? Especially after everything."

"Yeah. Of course you are. I just want you to be careful."

"I will," she said, surprised and touched. "Nothing's going to happen to me, Ted."

"Hope not. Ari, I really want—"

"Here we are," Eileen Jorgensen called cheerfully from the hallway, cutting Ted off in the middle of what Ari was certain was going to be another attempt at reconciliation. Megan trailed behind her, her face sullen. "All ready to go."

Ari glared at Ted. "You were confident, weren't you?"

"Hey, she wants to go," he insisted.

She smiled down at Megan, hoping she hadn't heard the angry exchange between her parents. "Hi, sweetie. This is going to be fun, isn't it?"

"Yeah." Megan looked down at the floor.

"You've got Kitty with you?" Ari asked, though the white, round-faced stuffed animal was tucked under Megan's arm. Clutched in her other hand was a clear vinyl tote bag, filled with vials of lip gloss, dolls, and various stickers.

"Uh-huh."

"And all your makeup, I see."

"Uh-huh."

There was something else in the bag, something familiar. "Megan, is that a knitting knobby?"

"Yup." Megan pulled out a long, narrow spool with four prongs on the end. Colorful yarn was wrapped around the prongs, and from the hollow center of the spool a long knitted cord dangled. "Nana bought it for me."

"That was nice of her," Ari said, after giving her mother a surprised look. She knew better than to remark that she herself had learned how to knit using a knobby.

"Uh-huh. Mom, do I have to go?"

Surprised, Ari dropped to her knee. "Megan, what is it?"

"Hey. Don't you want to spend some time with me?" Ted protested at the same time.

"You don't want to go, Megan?" Ari asked.

"C'mon, Ari, don't make a big deal of this."

"Ted," Ari said sharply, turning to him. "Just wait. Honey, can you tell me why?"

For answer, Megan shrugged. "I just don't want to."

Ari frowned. "Did something happen in school today?"

"I don't remember."

Which meant that Megan didn't want to tell her, Ari thought. "Honey, you'll have a good time with your father. You know that."

"Waterfire's this weekend," Ted put in. "You like that, don't you? You like the bonfires and the music. Hey, tell you what. Let's go on one of the gondolas on the river."

"Mom." Megan's eyes were pleading. "Please."

"Megan—"

"Please, please, please? I don't want to go."

"Megan, I want to spend time with you, too," Ted said.

"Daddy's right," Ari said reluctantly, though if it were left to her, she'd keep Megan home. "You know I have to work tomorrow, and I'm going out tomorrow night. So what'll you do? Stay in and watch TV all day?"

"I never see you, Mommy."

"C'mon, kid." Ted had picked up Megan's backpack. "Let's get a move on."

Megan looked up at Ari. "Mom?"

"Daddy's right, honey," Ari said, making a painful decision, and then rising. She couldn't face those big sad eyes anymore. "You have to go. You'll have fun."

"Mommy." Megan flung her arms so hard around Ari's waist that she nearly toppled over. "Mommy."

Ari knelt again, returning the hug. "Honey, everything's okay."

"Will you be here when I get back?" Megan whispered.

Oh, poor kid. "Of course I will. Where else would I be?"

"I don't know."

"Right here, sweetie. Tell you what. Let's go to McDonald's."

Megan's face brightened. "Now?"

"Now?" Ted said at the same time. "I thought we had an agreement."

"Not right yet." She grinned at Megan, who already looked more cheerful, and got up. "Come on." She held her hand out to her daughter, who slid her own into it, somewhat to Ari's surprise. Megan, newly independent, didn't like to hold her mother's hand anymore. "Maybe you'll get a good toy there."

"Yeah. They have princess things now, Mom. Krissie came in with a crown yesterday."

"Really? Maybe you'll get one. We'll be quick," she added to Ted, whose face was dark.

"Don't take long."

Ari simply smiled at him and went out, Megan clinging to her hand. That was one problem averted, if only for the moment. Something was bothering Megan, and of all Ari's troubles, this was the most serious. The yarn shop, her estrangement from Diane, even Edith's murder, paled by comparison. Maybe it was time to put all this investigating nonsense into second place in her life, where it belonged. Let Josh do his job. There were some things that were more important.

CHAPTER 15

Ari went into the shop earlier than usual the next day and tried to busy herself with paying bills, though she wasn't able to concentrate. Yesterday's problems had kept her awake the night before and left her feeling uneasy about Megan, even though Megan had called from Ted's last night, sounding more cheerful. There was nothing she could do about that, Ari thought now, though in hindsight she wished she'd let Megan stay home. Sometimes she despaired of ever getting the mommy thing right.

A knock on the door broke Ari out of her reverie, and she looked up to see Kaitlyn. "What are you doing here so early?" she asked as she opened the door.

"I figured you might need some help, with everything going on," Kaitlyn said as she came in.

"I can't pay you for extra time."

"I know, but I had nothing else to do." Kaitlyn looked a little lost. "It's no fun being at home."

Ari cast her a sympathetic look, but decided not to say anything about it. "Do you have a game after this?" she asked, looking at Kaitlyn's outfit. She was dressed in a short plaid pleated skirt, worn with knee socks and heavy shoes, much like soccer spikes. Kaitlyn might not like going to UMass Dartmouth, but she'd taken advantage of the sports program there. In summer it was softball; in winter, basketball. This season's game was field hockey.

"Yeah, but I'm not playing. I don't feel up to it."

Ari peered at her. Kaitlyn did look a little pale. "Are you feeling all right?"

"Yeah, just a little tired. Do you mind that I came dressed like this?"

"No, not at all."

"I figured I wouldn't have time to change."

"It's actually a nice style," Ari said. "All you need to add to make it preppy is an oxford shirt and a cable sweater. Or a sweater vest."

"Yeah." Kaitlyn perked up. "Hey, maybe I'll design one. Retro's always in. Only in some fun fur or funky color."

"That's a thought," Ari said neutrally, though she hoped that Kaitlyn would keep her design conservative this time. "If you don't, do you mind if I do?"

"We-ell—"

"Never mind." Ari spoke quickly. She hated the thought of someone stealing her own ideas. "That was wrong of me."

"Yeah. It was. I mean, Ari, how would you feel if someone wanted something you made for nothing?"

"As a matter of fact, I've given designs away. Oh, that reminds me. Edith didn't buy any patterns here recently, did she?"

"No," Kaitlyn said, sounding surprised. "You know that."

Ari nodded. Last night she'd called both Laura and Summer, and they'd said the same thing. "You didn't by chance show her anything I was working on?"

"Why would I do a thing like that?"

"Okay. I have to ask. According to Sarah Mailloux, Edith made a sweater from one of my patterns."

"Who?"

"She used to teach history at the high school."

"Oh, yeah, I remember. She retired before I had her." Kaitlyn made a face. "I was glad. I heard she was an old witch."

"No, she wasn't. She was hard, but fair."

"So they all say."

Ari stared at her. "Kaitlyn, why are you so prickly this morning?"

Kaitlyn stared down at the sales counter. "I had a fight with my dad."

"Oh. I'm sorry. I was just wondering."

"Yeah." There was silence for a moment. "How did Mrs. Mailloux know they were your patterns?"

"I assume Edith told her. She was admiring the sweater I had on yesterday—"

"Which one?"

"The teal Icelandic. Anyway, she said that Edith had a pattern for it."

"It doesn't mean it was yours. Anyone can make Icelandics in bright colors, rather than neutrals."

"True, but she said—"

"The thing is, I can't see Mrs. Perry paying anything for patterns," Kaitlyn went on. She was leaning on the counter as she talked, and her face had cleared. "You know, I think she was downloading free patterns from the Internet."

"What makes you say that?"

"I saw her once in the library with some." Kaitlyn looked down. "We argued about it."

"Why?" Ari asked, surprised.

"You know how I feel about that. Anyway, it wasn't much of an argument. My mom came along and that ended that."

"Why didn't you say anything about it before?"

"Think about it. Would you want to admit arguing with someone a few days before she was killed?"

"No, I suppose not."

"But you know, Ari, it really frosts me."

"What?"

"The idea of Mrs. Perry getting free patterns."

Ari frowned as remembrance flooded back. "Do you know, I was looking at some patterns on the Internet the other night?"

"When?"

"Just before I was hit."

"Really? But that couldn't have had anything to do with it, could it?"

"I don't see how."

"Ari, did you search for your own designs the other night?"

"Online, you mean? Yes, but all I kept finding was the *Vogue Knitting* pattern, ad nauseam. Oh, and genealogical stuff."

"Oh. Well, maybe you're okay."

Ari peered at her again. "Kait, are you sure you feel all right?"

"Yes. But, you know, it's not fair," she said, with more spirit. "I mean, suppose someday someone wants to have one of my patterns for nothing? We work at those things, Ari. Why should we give them away?"

"We shouldn't, of course. The problem is that a lot of people who knit make little variations on patterns, so they think that's all we do. They don't realize how much work we put in." She smiled again. "Like your candy-striped hat."

"I still think that could work," Kaitlyn said stubbornly. "Maybe as a Christmas novelty."

Ari bit back a smile. Someone might like it, though. Everyone's taste was different. "Maybe."

"Hello," a voice called from the door.

"Laura," Ari said in surprise, turning. "What are you doing here? I didn't expect to see you today."

"I need a new project." Laura gazed aimlessly around at the yarn bins.

"Do you mean you didn't find anything yesterday?" Ari's tone was sardonic.

"No, dear. Do you have anything for me to do?"

"Not at the moment. Why don't you look at the patterns on the rack and choose something from there?"

"Maybe I will. By the by, how is your head today?"

Ari reached up to touch her scalp. "It's still sore, but I'll survive."

"I hope it won't keep you from your date tonight."

"Date?" Kaitlyn's face brightened. "Ari, you're dating someone?"

Ari closed the cash drawer. "Josh Pierce," she said, managing to appear calm. The truth was that she was feeling nervous about seeing Josh, though it wasn't really a date. Of course not.

"Oh, cool. He's cute for an old guy."

"Old!"

"Old for me, anyway. He's got to be in his thirties."

"You're making me feel ancient," Ari complained, reminded again of just how young Kaitlyn was. "I'm almost thirty."

"Oh. I didn't mean—"

"Forget it. Anyway, it doesn't mean anything. We're really just friends."

Kaitlyn gave her a sidelong glance. "Yeah, right."

"Yeah, right," Ari shot back, feeling unsettled. It *was* possible that her arrangement with Josh would develop into something more personal. Just now she had nothing to discuss with him about the murder, or her attacker. Unless something else happened, she never would. Not that she wanted anything to happen, she thought hastily. But if something didn't break soon on this mystery, she'd go nuts.

Ari closed early on Saturdays, when most people were busy with other things. All told, it had been a mixed week, she thought as she counted her receipts, starting off with people coming in for gossip and then buying; and then, except for yesterday, continuing with weather that was too nice for people to want to buy yarn. In other ways it was mixed, too, at home and at the shop, with Josh. She was getting increasingly nervous about their date tonight. She'd be glad when it was over.

She was glum as she pulled the store door firmly shut behind her and headed for home. The shop wouldn't be open again until Tuesday, and the intervening two days yawned before her with nothing to do and no one to see. Megan was with Ted, her mother was doing chores, and Laura had decided to make the rounds of the discount stores: Building 19, Ocean State Job Lot, and Family Dollar. Worst of all, though, she no longer had a best friend she could turn to. Chances were that the friendship between her and Diane, though old and precious, was over. Even if she and Diane did mend things in some way, it would never be the same.

Ari stopped in front of her house, reluctant to go in. Without Megan, the house would be unbearably empty. Ari was well aware that she hadn't paid Megan the attention she needed since finding Edith's body. Last night's trip to McDonald's had helped, but Ari had never believed in quality time versus quantity time. They needed to be together more. Something was wrong with Megan, she thought, and wondered if she'd ever find out what.

And what was she going to do about Ted? He was driving her crazy, with his calls and his jealousy. He hadn't seemed quite so interested in her when they were married, which was a major reason for their divorce. On the other hand, she thought, smiling to herself, if he'd been so attentive, so meddlesome, she would soon have been climbing the walls. It was a good thing Ted hadn't been killed instead of Edith, or Ari would probably be in jail now.

That thought brought Herb Perry to her mind again. She knew it was an axiom that most murders were committed by one's nearest and dearest. Add in a financial motive, and Herb looked suspicious indeed. So did Eric, though no one could prove that he'd still been in Freeport when his mother was killed. Neither of them had an alibi, and Herb could have attacked her. He could easily have finished her off, she thought, shuddering. Unless he had been interrupted. Unless he wasn't guilty. Though he was thin enough, and fit enough, somehow he didn't fit her memory of her attacker. Probably he really had caught the attacker in the act, though his description of her didn't match.

Her? Yet again, Ari frowned at the implication of that word. At first she'd thought there'd been nothing overtly feminine about her attacker, and neither had Herb. Yet somehow she was certain her attacker had been female, as she'd long suspected the murderer was. The description would certainly fit any number of knitters Ari knew. Someone Edith knew, too. She had to have trusted whoever had lured her into the shop in the early morning, or someone she had no reason to fear. That sounded like either Herb, or an as-yet-unknown female. The problem with any suspect was how she'd gotten the yarn to make the garrote, assuming she'd brought the weapon with her.

A motorcycle rode by, the roar of its engine startling her. She'd been standing before her house for a while, she realized. Ronnie Dean must be going nuts wondering what she was doing, she thought, and smiled. Still, the thought of going inside was unappealing, and not just because the weather was nice. She had nothing to do, no one to see. She didn't even have anything she wanted to eat. She could make a salad, but she didn't want to. She wanted something solid, comforting. A meatball sub, she thought suddenly, something she loved but rarely allowed herself to have. She'd treat herself to one, and maybe some Lindt truffles, if Marty's had any. After this week, she deserved it.

Marty's was doing a brisk business. Ari had to park in the back, and then pass a number of people sitting at the picnic tables overlooking the inlet. Light sparkled like refracted diamonds on the bay, and the maple trees were more colorful than they had been just a few days earlier. Her spirits lifted a little. Maybe she'd stop at the library to see if they had any new mysteries in, and maybe she'd find something to do outside, too. The garden, which wouldn't last much longer, needed some attention. The physical work would be a good antidote to all the stress of the week.

At the deli counter inside the store, she ordered her sandwich and a Diet Coke, having decided that she'd eat outside, too. While she was waiting she might as well get her candy, she thought, and headed away from the counter. She turned into an aisle and came face to face with Diane.

Neither said anything for a long minute. There was too much to say; there was not enough. Diane broke the silence first. "Hi."

"Hi," Ari answered, almost shyly.

"How've you been?"

"Busy. You?" Ari said, and then wanted to kick herself. She had a fair idea of what Diane's life was like at the moment.

"Yes. Going to Dartmouth a lot."

Ari briefly closed her eyes. Of course Diane would go to visit Joe at the Bristol County House of Corrections, where he was awaiting further legal action. "I'm sorry. I wasn't thinking."

"Yeah, well, it's okay."

Ari nodded. "My sub should be ready—"

"I'm waiting for a salad," Diane said at the same time, and gave Ari the first hint of a smile. "I didn't feel like cooking."

"Neither did I. I'm going to eat outside. Want to join me?" she said impulsively.

Diane looked around the store. "No."

"Oh." Ari's spirits deflated. Diane probably didn't want to have a thing to do with her.

"Not here," Diane went on. "There are too many people."

"Do you want to come back to my house?"

Diane shook her head. "I have to get back. Would you want to . . ."

"Yes," Ari said, spirits rising again. Maybe things weren't as bad as they'd seemed a little while ago.

"Ari, sub's ready," Marty, at work behind the deli counter, called. "Yours, too, Diane."

"I'll follow you out," Ari said as they moved to the counter.

"Good. See you there."

The maples on Acushnet Road were almost as pretty as the ones in town, Ari thought. She reflected irrelevantly on their choice of cars. Diane drove a shiny black Jeep, while she drove a boxy Subaru station wagon, a real mama car, even though she really would rather have something sporty. A Mercedes roadster, maybe. But she didn't want to be a minivan or an SUV mother; at the least she'd save on gas.

The sheep were cropping the grass in front of Diane's house when Ari pulled into the driveway. Once she had gotten caught in the middle of the flock when they were heading to the barn for their evening meal. Diane, laughing, had rescued her from what Ari later called "attack sheep." The memory made her smile.

Diane slammed the door to the Jeep, her face serious. Ari's stomach, and her hopes, plummeted. Though they'd been cordial enough at Marty's, things might go much differently now that they were alone.

A lot hinged on the next few minutes. In spite of all they'd been through in the past, their friendship could be over.

Diane stared at her for a moment, and then lunged, enfolding Ari in a fierce hug. "Ari." Her voice was choked. "I wanted to see you, but I just didn't know if I should."

"Me, too." Ari's hug was just as tight. "I thought you were mad at me."

"Pissed off," Diane said, and pulled back, glaring at her. "Damn, Ari, I'm still mad."

"I couldn't warn you," Ari protested. "I wanted to, but I couldn't."

"Yeah." Diane stared at her for a moment and then turned away. "Come on in."

Ari followed her into the kitchen, her nervousness returning. Their friendship had been tested before, but never like this. "Di, I'm sorry."

"Yeah, I know." Diane filled a teakettle. "Tea or soda?"

"Thanks, I've got a drink." The silence was awkward, broken only by the sounds of paper bags crinkling as each took out her lunch. "How is the spinning?"

Diane shrugged as she put plates on the table. "It's been hard to get to, with everything going on. I need to, though. If Joe's convicted, I don't know what'll happen to the farm."

"Can you run it yourself?"

She shrugged again. When the kettle began to whistle, she poured water into a flowery bone china cup and put it down beside her salad. "Probably, but the problem is that we've got a mortgage from when we built the new barn." She looked down at her cup as she dunked her tea bag up and down. "How's your business?"

"Booming." Ari rested her cheeks on her hands. "Di, you wouldn't believe the people coming in. Everyone wants to know everything. Thank God they usually buy something, even the expensive stuff."

"Edith wouldn't have."

"Di, that's awful," Ari said, but she grinned. There was a subtle shift in the atmosphere.

"But true. Gossip's free, yarn isn't." Diane set down her fork and reached out to cover Ari's hand. "I'm glad you're here."

"Me, too. I didn't know if you'd want to see me."

"Oh, yeah, but after last time . . ."

"I know." Ari looked down at their hands. "I heard the police searched here, again."

"Yeah." Diane pulled back, her face drawn, and made a production out of tossing her salad. "At least this time we know why."

"What?"

"A cane, or something like that, our lawyer said."

"They can't think you attacked me!"

Diane straightened. "Was that what was used on you?"

"I think so." She frowned. "I'm not really sure."

"Well, of course they found one. Joe's uncle used one when he got sick."

"Aluminum?"

"No, wood."

"Good."

"Why?"

"They'd be looking for something with my blood on it, or maybe hair. They'd show up on wood."

"Huh. All anyone would have to do with something like that is throw it in the woods. Who'd keep it around?" Her face lengthened. "Not like that piece of window stop."

"No. And see, Diane?" Ari leaned forward. "That's how I know you couldn't be guilty. You're not that stupid."

"Tell that to the police."

"I know." Ari took a bite of the meatball sub, wiped tomato sauce off her face, and frowned. "You know, Diane," she said when she could, "whatever hit me—I'm not sure it was a cane, but I think I've seen something like it before."

"Where?"

"I don't know. I keep trying to remember, but I can't." She took a sip of soda. "I thought it could be Herb, but my landlord didn't give him a new key to the building."

"How do you know that? Oh." Diane set her cup down. "Your friend."

"Well, yes." Ari looked down. "He talks to me a little."

Diane leaned forward. "He does?"

"Yes. Di, don't tell anyone. Don't tell your lawyer. Don't even tell Joe."

"Why not?"

"Josh could get in trouble."

"Oh. Josh, is it?"

"Yes, Josh. The case is supposed to be closed. If anyone finds out he's still working on it—"

"Is he?"

"Sort of. If anyone finds out, he'll be yanked off it so fast your head'll spin."

Diane leaned forward. "Do you mean he's doing it on his own?"

"Yes."

"Wow! Why?"

"He's not satisfied."

"Ari! Do you mean he thinks Joe's innocent?"

"He's leaving things open. But you can't tell anyone, Di."

Diane's grin was broader. "Do you think I'll be able to hide it?"

Ari almost groaned. Sometimes Diane was transparent in her emotions. "You can't tell anyone. Viking honor?"

"Viking honor," Diane said, and held up a finger to either side of her head, in imitation of a Viking helmet. "It's such good news."

"Josh is the only one who has doubts. Well, no, the D.A. does, too, after my attack, but the investigation   is officially closed. If you say anything, Joe won't have a prayer."

That brought Diane back to earth. "Oh. That's true, isn't it?" She leaned forward, arms crossed on the table, eyes intent. "But Ari, what is he going to do?"

"We don't really know."

" 'We'?" Diane leaned forward. "Ari, are you seeing him?"

"Well, sort of."

"What does that mean?"

"Well, we are going out tonight."

"Are you kidding?"

"It's no big deal. There aren't many available men around here," she said defiantly.

"Too young, too old, or too married."

"Di . . ."

"So you're not really sleeping with the enemy?"

"He's not the enemy!" Ari exclaimed, and then reddened. "No, of course not. We're not. Really."

"Yeah, right," Diane said, smirking. "So if you're not dating, what are you really doing?"

Ari took a deep breath. "I guess I'm still investigating. But, Di, don't tell anyone that, either."

"Ari." Diane stared at her. "After getting attacked?"

"I don't know why that happened," Ari said swiftly. "It might not even be connected."

"Yeah, right," Diane said again.

"Okay. It has to be, especially with the same weapon. Oops. You didn't hear that from me."

"You mean, that was a cane, too?"

"Herb thinks it was a baseball bat."

"Herb." Diane snorted. "He keeps his brains in his—"

"Diane."

She grinned. "Back pocket. What?" she said innocently.

"Nothing," Ari said, but she gave Diane a look.

"Could Herb have done it?"

"I don't know. He hasn't been ruled out yet."

"It would be nice."

"If it were him? Yes. Convenient. But why'd Edith get killed in my shop? That's what I keep coming back to."

"There has to be a reason."

"I don't know what. Oh."

"What?"

"Guess who I saw yesterday," Ari said.

"Who?"

"Mrs. Mailloux."

"Oh, yeah. I saw her the other day, too."

"Where?"

"At Marty's. Where else?"

"Shaw's, in my case. Diane, she told me something."

"What?"

"She said Edith had one of my patterns."

"She actually bought one from you?"

"No, of course not. And the picture was in color, and I hadn't put it out yet. It's a new design."

Diane stared at her. "Then how . . ."

"I don't know, but someone's stealing my patterns. And I wonder if whoever it is killed Edith."

CHAPTER 16

"What?" Diane exclaimed. "Who?"

"I have no idea," Ari said.

"Yes, you do. Someone you trust. Who has access to your patterns?"

"Well, that's the problem. It could be anyone. Kaitlyn and I racked our brains this afternoon and couldn't come up with anyone."

"Hmm." Diane looked thoughtful. "You have them on your computer first, right?"

"Yes, so?"

"Maybe someone hacked into your computer."

"What? What are you talking about?"

"Oh, come on, even you have to have heard of hackers. Someone could have gotten into your computer online and stolen the designs."

"That's ridiculous. Who'd do such a thing?"

"Anyone with computer knowledge."

"Do you know how?" Ari demanded.

"Well, no. It's a little too advanced for me. But maybe someone does."

"No," Ari said firmly. "That's going a little too far. There has to be a simpler answer."

"Okay. Someone at the printer's?"

"No. No. Ridiculous. My patterns don't make much money. Who'd risk his job for that?"

"Maybe it's not for the money."

"What do you mean?"

"We've thought from the beginning that someone has a grudge against you. That's why Edith was killed in your shop."

"Do you think Edith would have been murdered anyway?"

"It's a possibility." Diane pursed her lips. "I think someone had reason to want her dead. Getting at you was probably just a side benefit."

"Some benefit."

"Yeah. Ari, where else do you keep your patterns, besides your computer? In your office?"

"Yes. In a file."

"And the pictures to go with them?"

"In another file. Why?"

"Someone could have stolen them from your office."

"I can't believe that," Ari protested.

"Who could get into there?"

"No one."

"No? Not Kaitlyn? What about Summer, or even Laura?"

"They all have alibis for Edith's death. So much for that theory," Ari said, and fell silent.

"What is it?"

"Di, I think there are times when anyone could have gotten in. If there's only one of us working, and we have to go into the back room for a customer, no one's covering the sales desk."

"Who have you done that for?"

"I don't know. Anyone. Everyone. Well, not everyone, but a lot of people. People who special-order yarns, or want something I haven't put out yet, or even . . ." She grinned. "Once in a while I've run to the bathroom when there's a customer in."

"Someone you trust, obviously."

"Yes, but I couldn't give you names."

"Maybe you should start thinking."

"It seems so absurd. I mean, isn't it a little far to go to get a free pattern?"

"It's not that, and you know it."

"I know." Someone had a grudge against her, she thought, and shuddered. "I wonder if anyone else knows about Edith having my pattern."

"I can ask around."

"Thanks, Di. If you happen to see Mrs. Mailloux, would you ask her about it? She was supposed to call me last night, but she didn't." She grimaced. "Those grandchildren of hers are holy terrors."

"Sure, I'll ask her, and anyone else I see."

"Be careful," Ari said, alarmed. "You don't want to tip her off."

"Her?"

"The killer."

"Get real. Do you really think someone will come after me because of stolen patterns?"

"I don't know. I don't know what set her off." She slid off the stool. "I have to get back. I've got things to do before I go out."

Diane walked her to the door. "Is Megan with Ted?"

"Yes."

"Why did you ever hook up with him?"

"He was wearing a designer sweater."

Diane laughed. "Only you, Ari."

"In homespun yarn," Ari added.

"Well, that still wouldn't have done anything for me. Maybe you'll have better luck with the cop."

"Don't be silly."

"He's better-looking than Ted."

"Oh, honestly." Ari got into her car. "It's not like that."

Diane stepped back from the car, grinning knowingly. "Yeah, right."

"Yes, right," Ari retorted, and started her car. Diane was so wrong, she thought as she turned around and started down the drive. She and Josh were friends, and sometimes co-conspirators. That was all.

The Lucky Dragon wasn't quite as pedestrian as Ted had implied. While its menu did include chow mein sandwiches and such ordinary fare as chop suey and egg foo yong, it was better known for its more gourmet items and its quality. Among other things, it boasted the only Mongolian grill in the area. After some deliberation, Ari and Josh decided on crispy lemon chicken and tea for her; beef with asparagus and Tsingtao beer for him. It wasn't a date, Ari told herself, but it was unexpectedly fun to be out with a man again, with no hidden agenda. At least, not the usual one.

"I saw Diane today," she said, reaching for a fried noodle and dipping it into sweet sauce.

"Oh?" Josh's look was guarded. "What'd she have to say?"

"Lots of things. We've been friends for too long to let a little thing like murder separate us."

He grinned at that, an honest-to-goodness grin. She felt absurdly pleased at that reaction. "Or vandalism and destruction of school property."

"Mmm-hmm." She sat back as their waitress placed cups of hot-and-sour soup before them. The mention of school reminded her of Sarah Mailloux, who hadn't been far from her thoughts since yesterday. Ari wondered why she hadn't called. "Anything new?"

"Nope. Uh-oh."

"What?"

"Don't turn around, but it's Gerry Macklin and his wife. I said, don't turn around."

Ari turned back from smiling at Macklin, who was a town selectman. "There. Now we're an item."

"Yeah. So much for being subtle."

"I didn't think we were supposed to be subtle. Isn't the idea to throw everyone off the scent?"

"Yes, but . . ."

She glanced quickly up at him as she spooned up some soup. Not for the first time, she wondered what this evening was about. Was it about Edith's murder, or was it indeed a date? "So there's nothing new at all?"

"No." His face was grave. "It's not looking good for Camacho, though."

"Does the chief know you're still investigating?" Ari asked.

"No, but he knows I'm not satisfied with the case against Camacho." He leaned forward. Anyone watching would think it was for romantic reasons, Ari thought. "Have you ever thought that maybe he is guilty?"

"No. Not for a minute."

"The evidence is strong."

"So who hit me? Your case has holes."

"Most cases have holes. That doesn't mean we've arrested the wrong person."

"You don't believe that."

"Unless something new comes up, I may have to."

Ari sat back, fuming, as the waitress set down their entrees. "Are you saying that Diane attacked me?" she asked when they were alone again.

"You said your attacker was a woman."

"Not Diane."

"How do you know?"

"Because she wouldn't. It certainly wasn't Joe."

"True." He was quiet for a moment. "The chief asked if I had anything new today."

"Oh." Ari passed the rice to Josh as she pondered the implications of that. "Do you?"

"No."

Josh's expression spoke more of discouragement than conviction. Maybe going in another direction would help.

"Edith Perry was getting my patterns from somewhere."

Josh speared some asparagus. "So?"

"Not from me."

"So she borrowed them from someone."

"Josh, she had the pattern for a sweater I wore yesterday for the first time, and not the way I had it printed."

That made him look up. "What are you saying?"

"I think someone's stealing my designs."

He frowned. "How different was it?"

"The picture with it was in color. My patterns are in black and white. Besides, I didn't put it out until after Edith died."

"Who told you this?"

"Sarah Mailloux. She used to be my history teacher, and she knew Edith."

"Far as I can tell, everyone in this town knew Edith."

"Well, yes, that's true. But, Josh, someone stole that pattern."

He sat back. "Any idea who?"

"No. Diane and I went over and over it this afternoon, and we couldn't think of anyone."

"Someone who works for you, maybe?"

"Yes," she said reluctantly. "Or one of my customers." Quickly she outlined all that she and Diane had discussed. "Josh, I'd hate to think it of someone I know. I mean, I've had people shoplift before. One of my grandmother's friends took a pattern once. That hurt."

"Someone you know likely killed Edith," he pointed out. "Ari, I'm sorry, but having your patterns ripped off doesn't seem that important when someone's been murdered."

"All right, so it's not. But that's my livelihood, Josh. Someone's stealing my work. Don't you think it could be connected?"

"Maybe." He picked up his fork, and then set it down again. "Ari, have you thought that it could have been Edith herself?"

"What? How? She never came into the shop."

"She had a key," he pointed out.

She thought that over. "No," she said finally. "Edith was a lot of things, but I can't see her as a thief. Yes, I know that taking things off the Internet is technically stealing, but it probably doesn't feel that way to most people."

"Okay. You never know what's going to be important in a case, though. This is a loose thread, and it does concern her, but I doubt she was killed for it."

Ari pushed aside the paper-thin slice of lemon that adorned a piece of chicken. It seemed important to her, no matter what Josh thought. But then, she was closely involved with this. "The only one who'd have a motive for that would be me, or who-ever's selling them, to keep from being found out."

"It's pretty thin. I've known people to kill for less, but I can't see it. Wonder who did sell it, though."

"Yes, and how? If someone's peddling my designs around here I'd've found out before this."

Josh ate a moment in silence. "Maybe whoever's doing it isn't from around here."

"What do you mean?"

"Mail order. I don't know how Edith found out about it, but—"

"The Internet," Ari said suddenly, sitting up straighter. "That has to be it."

He frowned again. "Why?"

"I'm not the only one with a website." She leaned forward. "Josh, there are whole sites of pirated de-signs. That's what I was looking at just before I got hit. I remembered that yesterday."

"Who could have known you'd be doing that?" he said, alert.

"I told you, I don't know. Strange." She pursed her lips. "It's awfully coincidental, isn't it?"

"Did you find your designs?"

"No. I found some odd genealogical things, but not my patterns."

"Maybe we should—damn. That's my pager. Do you mind?" he asked as he reached for his cell phone.

"No, of course not," Ari said, sighing at the inter-ruption. In spite of their conversation, she'd been en-joying herself. This was what it must be like to be married to a cop, she thought, and brought herself up short. *Not hardly.*

Josh folded up his cell phone with a snap and gestured to the waitress. "I've got to go."

"What is it?"

Josh had turned to the waitress. "The bill, please, and we'd like our food wrapped." When she left he said, "I probably shouldn't tell you, but there's been a knifing in a bar."

"Was anyone killed?" Ari asked, hand to her throat.

"Not yet. Some drunks in a fight, probably. I'll drive you home."

"Thank you," she said, and let him escort her out, annoyed and disappointed. So much for her evening out, she thought glumly.

Sunday was gray and misty. Ari had treated herself to a special breakfast of fresh malassadas, a Portuguese version of fried dough, and hazelnut-flavored coffee, and had read both the New Bedford *Standard-Times* and the Boston *Globe* from front to back. The bar fight that had taken Josh away last night had proven to be not much of anything, according to the local paper; one man was in the hospital with minor knife wounds, and the other was in jail. Both awaited charges for their little escapade. From Josh himself she heard not a word. When they had decided that they weren't really dating, he'd apparently meant it.

Laura, on the other hand, had called as soon as Ari came in the night before. She'd heard about the stabbing on her police scanner, and guessed correctly about the abrupt end to Ari's evening. Ari quickly changed the subject, bringing up instead the intriguing possibility that someone was stealing her patterns. She wasn't really surprised when she found out that Laura already knew. Sarah Mailloux had told Ruth Taylor, among others, and so the word had spread. Sarah apparently knew nothing beyond what she'd told Ari, which meant that she had no new clues as to where Edith had gotten the pattern. She and Laura speculated on the problem for a few minutes, without reaching any conclusion.

Now Ari faced a house ringing with silence, without Megan's busy presence. Ted wouldn't be bringing her home until five, which meant that the day stretched out before her, empty and lonely. She might as well work on that new idea she'd had, Ari thought, bringing her dishes to the kitchen and rinsing them in the sink. It would at least pass the time.

She was just bringing up her design software at her computer when her doorbell rang. Startled, she went to the door, gazing out the side windows first, and then resting her head on the jamb with her eyes closed. Josh. Of course. Just when she looked her best, she thought sardonically, still in her robe and slippers, though it was early afternoon.

Josh looked surprised when she opened the door. "Am I interrupting something?"

"No." She stepped aside so he could come in. "I tend to be lazy on Sundays. If you want to wait in the living room, I'll go get changed. There's coffee in the kitchen," she called over her shoulder as she dashed for the stairs.

"Thanks," he called after her.

A few minutes later she was back, wearing jeans and a loose brown pullover knitted in reverse stockinette stitch. She'd pinned her hair up in back with a clip, and wore only soft moccasins with no socks on her feet. She definitely looked less than her best, especially compared to last evening, when she'd taken pains with her hair and makeup. "Sorry to keep you waiting," she said a little breathlessly. "I didn't expect anyone."

"Sorry." He was standing, looking awkward. "Maybe I should have called first."

She waved him over to a brown corduroy recliner, and settled onto the sofa that was upholstered in a sturdy plaid, nudging back some of Megan's toys as she did so. For all her design expertise, Ari hadn't done much to fix her house up. This room was childproofed because Megan had to play somewhere besides her room, but the parlor was as boring as it had been when she and Ted first moved in. It held the same beige-painted walls, the same wide walnut coffee table, the same Indian print rug. "No, it's okay. So last night wasn't much of anything?"

"What? I thought—oh, the stabbing, you mean?"

"Yes." *Had he thought she meant their brief evening together?* she wondered, and hoped her cheeks weren't red.

"No, just two drunk idiots. Look, I'm sorry about last night."

It felt unexpectedly cozy sitting with him, with the rain now coming down in earnest outside. "It's okay. I understand."

"I'll make it up to you," he promised.

"Okay," Ari said, uncomfortably aware of something hanging in the air between them, and wondering just why he was here. "Have you found out anything new?"

"About Edith? Not since last night."

"Oh."

"But I got to thinking." He leaned toward her. "About your patterns."

"Laura called last night. She's been asking her friends about them, but no one's seen them."

"Then where did Edith get the one she had?"

"If she did," Ari said doubtfully. "Mrs. Mailloux could be wrong."

"Could be." He nodded. "I think we should find out."

"How?"

"You mentioned the Internet last night. Where's your computer?"

"In the kitchen."

He walked into the kitchen, and she followed. "Why don't you log on?"

"Okay," she said doubtfully, sat in the chair he held out for her, and clicked on the icon for her online service. "I know this was my idea, but it seems strange."

"What does?"

"The idea of someone stealing my designs. It's not

as if I'm a big-name designer. I could have been, but I'm not."

"Seems to me you could still be," he said as he drew a chair over.

"Maybe. Darn it." She pounded her fist on the edge of the computer table. "Ow. It makes me so mad. Stealing what I've worked on—when is it going to end?"

"What?"

"Everyone's life has been turned upside down. When is it going to end?"

"I'd like to know that myself."

"Maybe Laura's right," she said. "Maybe I am the target."

"Maybe." He leaned forward again as the computer linked up with the Internet. Ari was deeply aware of his nearness. Once again, Ted's words about Josh and his interest in her returned, making her feel just the slightest bit uncomfortable with him.

"What should I look for?" she asked, edging away a little.

"Try searching for your name."

"I told you. I already have," she said, but obediently she entered her name into the search engine. The results were exactly as she'd predicted: genealogical, along with several references to her pattern in *Vogue Knitting*. She scrolled through several screens, but nothing new came up. At last, Josh had to admit defeat. "Now what?" she asked.

"Try a pattern. What was the one Edith Perry had?"

"*The New Icelandic.*" She typed it in. "Not very

original, I know, but it fit. Yikes." She stared at the thousands of results the search produced. "We'll never get through all those."

Josh leaned over her shoulder, closer than she'd expected. She glanced up at him. *Hmmmm . . .* "Try another one," he said.

"Okay. *Country Sheep.* Yikes," she said again. "Maybe if I add my own name—there. Still too many, but . . ."

" 'Sheep breeding,' " Josh muttered as he read the screen. " 'Black Sheep.' Good name for a rock group. 'Big Sky Country'?"

"Montana."

"I know that."

"I think they had range wars there, sheep farmers against cattle ranchers. I'm not sure. Oh, look, there's that darn *Vogue* article again." She clicked on the link, and this time the sweater she'd designed for the magazine was displayed. Ari smiled at the picture of her first major success. It was a deceptively simple cable sweater, but she had made so many variations in the cables that it almost looked like a fisherman sweater. Since she'd made it with white cotton yarn, though, and included cables in the neck ribbing, it retained its classic appearance. "I always liked that one," she went on as she scrolled down the page. "It's nice-looking, but easy."

"If you say so. What's that link at the bottom?"

" 'More patterns like this,' " she read. "Probably goes back to the *Vogue* patterns."

"Give it a try."

"Okay," she said, and clicked on the link. A moment

later another picture came up. The background was of multiple pastel-colored balls of yarn, while to the side was a border made up of similar, but brighter, yarn. There was no name given for the designer of the site. There were, however, small pictures of sweaters, bright and colorful, muted and classic. "Good God!"

"What?"

"Those are my designs."

Josh leaned still closer, making her pull away a little. "Are you sure?"

"Yes." She pointed to one photograph, then another, and yet another. "All of them. Look." They watched as a picture of the oatmeal-colored sweater with autumn-colored leaves splashed across it, which Ari wore in the picture on her website, appeared. " 'Autumn Leaves,' " she read. "That's not my name for it."

"What is?"

" 'October.' Josh?" She looked up at him. "Someone *is* stealing my patterns."

Josh at last sat down, after pulling his chair closer to hers. "More than that. Whoever did it hacked into the *Vogue Knitting* site."

"Is that what happened?"

"Yes. It's illegal," he said grimly.

"So is theft."

"Yes." He frowned. "Someone who knows how to use a computer did this. Who do you know who could?"

"Aren't hackers usually teenage boys?"

"Ari, would a boy be interested in sweater patterns?"

"You never know."

"Can you think of anyone?"

"I don't know. I hate the idea that someone I know could do this to me." She frowned. "Kaitlyn, I guess. She designed the page for the shop. Summer, too. She had to learn web page design for school."

"Maybe they have boyfriends who can hack into a machine."

"I just can't see it." She frowned again. "Laura," she said reluctantly.

"Laura?"

"Yes. Diane, too."

"I wonder if Herb Perry knows how."

She stared at him. "He could. The senior center has classes on Internet use all the time."

"Well, that narrows it down," he said dryly.

"Why would anybody do this?"

"Money."

Kaitlyn, she thought again. Summer. They were both students with considerable computer experience, and they both could use the money. So, she admitted reluctantly, could Diane. She dismissed Laura out of hand. Her aunt wouldn't do this to her. "She's not charging too much for the patterns. Why do we always say 'she'?" she added.

"Because it's probably a female. Let's try buying one."

"Whoever it was will know it's me."

"We'll get some information, though," he said. "One order for 'Autumn Leaves.' Name, address—I'll make up a credit card number—hey. Look at that."

"What?"

"An address to send a check to."

She leaned forward again. "A post office box in Boston?"

"Probably the main branch. A good anonymous place."

"Couldn't you stake it out? The police, I mean."

"I don't know." He sat back. "This is mail fraud."

"Mail fraud!" She stared at him. "That means the feds, doesn't it?"

He grinned at her suddenly. "Ari, you read too many mysteries."

"Why?"

"Stakeouts, feds—you talk like a cop."

"But it does involve the feds, doesn't it? I mean, the post office is federal."

"Postal inspectors handle that." He stared at the screen. "Damn it."

"What?"

"Internet crime goes across state lines. Do you have any idea what it's like when the Fibbies—"

"The what?"

"FBI. Do you know what it's like when they get involved?"

"They take over?"

"Bingo."

"But they won't care about a local murder, will they?"

"Maybe. I don't know. If it's connected with this, it could be considered a federal crime. The lawyers will fight over that."

"If we find out who did it."

"We will. Print out the page, will you? Damn," he said again, as his pager went off. "Excuse me a minute." He took out his cell phone and moved away.

"Of course," she said, sitting back and immediately regretting the loss of the closeness that had grown between them in the last few minutes. *Oh, grow up, Ari!*

Josh came back as she was pulling the last of the pages from the printer. "I have to go."

"I figured." She looked up. "Another knifing?"

He frowned. "No. No one really knows what."

Ari rose quickly. "Something bad?"

"Don't know. I'll call you," he said, grabbed the printout, and just like that was out the door.

Ari stared after him, and then turned to shut down the computer. She didn't like the look on his face. Something was up, something serious. Something that affected her? The thought made her shudder. *I've got a bad feeling about this.*

The phone rang a few minutes later. "Are you all right?" the voice on the other end demanded without first greeting her.

"Of course I am. Why wouldn't I be?"

"Oh, thank God. I had my police scanner on. There's been a mugging."

"A mugging! In broad daylight?" Ari's hand flew to her throat. "Who?"

"I don't know. But you're okay?"

"Yes. Oh, Laura, I'm sorry. You thought it was me?"

"I've been calling you for the last ten minutes and your line was busy."

"Well, that should have told you something."

"You could have been calling for help."

"Well, I wasn't. I was online."

"Online? You?"

"Yes. Josh and I—"

Laura's voice changed. "Interesting."

"It wasn't like that." Ari sat down on her couch and propped her feet on the coffee table. "Wait till you hear what we just found out," she said, and told her what she and Josh had discovered.

"So that's it," Laura said when she was done.

"Yes."

"Hmm. I think we should order some."

"Whoever it is will recognize our names," Ari said, as she had to Josh.

"I wasn't thinking of us. I know. Cousin Liz, in Sandwich."

"Would she do it?"

"She's a good sport. She reads mysteries, too, dear."

Ari nearly groaned. Josh was right. All of them read too much. "Okay, then. Should I call her?"

"No, I'll do it. It's been a long time since we talked. What is the web address?"

"I'll get it—"

"Wait. There's my other line. Do you mind?"

"No, of course not," Ari said, and waited, listening to the electric hum of the empty wire. After a few minutes, though, she hung up. Usually Laura returned right away, having told the second caller that she'd call back, but not this time. Something was up.

A few minutes later the phone rang again. "Ari." This time Laura's voice sounded strained. "Did you hear?"

"No, what?"

"I thought someone might have called you."

"No. Why? What is it?"

"That was Ruth Taylor who called."

"Oh? About last night?"

"Ari, get your mind off romance," Laura said impatiently. "This is serious."

Romance? Hardly, Ari thought. "What is it?"

"She said someone was killed."

Ari sat up straight. "Who?" she demanded.

"Are you sitting down?"

"Yes, yes. Who is it?"

"Well, dear." Laura took an audible breath. "It was Sarah Mailloux."

CHAPTER 17

"No!" Ari exclaimed. "Laura, you don't think—?"

"What?" Laura said.

"Oh, this is awful. It's my fault."

"How can it be?"

"What she told me about the pattern. It can't be a coincidence."

"Ari." Laura's voice was reproving. "I know it's strange, but how can it be connected?"

"With all that's been happening? It's too coincidental."

Laura was quiet for a moment. "I think you're right. Someone must have had reason to want her dead. She was a threat to someone."

"Whoever did that website?"

"Whoever killed Edith."

"But what did Sarah do, besides know about that pattern? She doesn't—didn't—even live here anymore. It just doesn't seem right."

"You're in denial, dear."

Ari sighed. "I suppose I am. I just don't want this to be happening."

"So what are we going to do about it?"

"We? What do you mean?"

"Haven't you been talking about it with Josh?"

"I don't know why you think that, Laura."

"Now, Ari. You've been seeing him a lot. Don't tell me you haven't been discussing Edith's murder."

"Laura, I—oh. There's another call coming in. I'll call you." Hastily she switched calls. "Hello?"

"Have you heard?" Josh's voice said.

"About Sarah? Yes. Is it official?"

"Yes. Her daughter identified her."

"Oh, poor Leslie! I'll have to call her," she said, and paused. "Maybe not. It's got to be connected, hasn't it?"

"I'd like to tell you it's not, but something's going on."

"How was she killed?" Ari asked, alerted by something in his voice. "It wasn't a mugging, was it?"

"We don't know yet."

"In other words, you can't tell me."

"I'm not supposed to."

"Why don't you let me guess?

"Ari—"

"She was hit on the head, and that's why it looks like a mugging."

"Yes," he said after a minute, reluctantly.

"With something like a cane."

"Maybe."

"You don't know yet?"

"No."

"Where was she killed?"

"Ari, I'm not supposed to be telling you anything."

"Yes, but . . ."

"Okay." He sighed. "In her daughter's driveway, on the other side of her car from her house."

"How could someone have done it in plain sight?" she asked. "I know it's dreary out, but someone must have seen something."

"No one we've found so far. The neighbors on one side were watching football, and the house on the other side is for sale."

"And there are only woods across the street. Josh, whoever did this is pretty reckless."

"Yeah. Look, Ari." His voice was hushed. "I want you out of this. Now."

"Hell, no."

"For God's sake, Ari. It's looking as if she was killed for what she knew."

"But what did she know?"

"If we knew that, we'd have the murderer."

Ari felt a sudden chill as she wondered who Sarah had talked to this weekend. "But it's so thin," she protested.

"As I said, people have killed for less."

"Less? When whoever it is charges so little for a pattern? And she has to pay for that site," she continued. "I do for mine."

"Paul's been doing some checking." His voice was low enough that she guessed there were people nearby. "Do you have any idea how much money websites like that can make?"

"No. How much?"

"Plenty, especially if she advertised."

"How would she advertise?"

"On other knitting sites. She has advertising on her own, too."

"I didn't know that. So it works both ways?"

"Yes. There are a couple of other things. She keeps track of visitors. It runs in the thousands."

She gasped. "That many? For how long?"

"Over a year. Just think. If only ten percent of the people buy, even at her prices, she's making good money."

"I had no idea." She paused. "So she'd have a lot to lose if someone found her out."

"Yeah."

"Do you think Edith did?"

"No proof, but I'd bet she did. Paul's having a field day with this, by the way. He's never had the chance to do anything with Internet crime."

"I thought you couldn't do anything about it."

"No, not yet, but if it's linked to murder, we've got the foundations for a case—wait." The line went briefly dead, and then Josh came back. "Gotta go. There's a meeting in the chief's office."

"Okay."

"Butt out of it, Ari. I'm not kidding."

"I know," she said, and hung up.

Troubled, Ari drifted across to her drafting table, where a pastel patchwork sweater for spring was taking shape. Taking a marker, she bent over it, and then sat staring into space, absently twirling her hair. Josh had to be wrong, she thought. The murders had to be connected, but why to her? The website could be a McGuffin, a kind of red herring that Alfred Hitchcock had delighted in using. It seemed important, but in the end had nothing to do with the mystery. Still . . .

Ari's gaze went to the computer, sitting silent across the room. With sudden decision she turned it on and then logged on to the Internet. Armed with the information she'd gotten from Josh, she quickly found the general knitting sites, the ones that taught knitting or offered simple patterns. Idly she clicked through, stopping occasionally to study a site more closely. Many sites had advertisements flashing at the top. On the current one was a yarn catalog; she'd also seen ads for craft stores and a big Internet bookstore. She was about to see what the yarn company had, when the ad changed. To her surprise, it was for the site that sold her pirated patterns. Curious, she clicked on the link and waited to see the site.

And it didn't appear.

Ari stared at the screen, reading the error message that told her she'd gotten the address wrong, although she knew she hadn't. Bringing up the *Vogue Knitting* site, she clicked on the link for her patterns there, and again waited.

And again, all she got was an error message.

She searched for her sweater patterns, as she had before, clicked on the link, and got the same result. It happened again when she keyed in the address for the site. She sat back, confused. The site simply wasn't there.

More than a little alarmed, Ari logged off and called the police station. "Bouchard," a distracted voice said.

"Just who I wanted to talk to," Ari said, and identified herself.

"Me?" Paul said. "You sure? Josh is in a meeting."

"I'm sure. What's the web address for the site that's selling my patterns?"

"Wait a minute."

Ari heard paper rustling, presumably her printout of the website. After a moment Paul came back on the line and rattled off the address. It was the same one she'd used. "I can't find it, Paul."

"What do you mean?"

"I've been trying the address and the different links, and it's simply not there."

"It has to be. Hold on." This time she heard computer keys clicking. "Hey," he said after a minute. "That's weird."

"What?"

"Damned if you're not right. It's not there."

"What could have happened to it?"

Silence hummed through the line. "A hidden link," Paul said finally.

"What's that?"

"She's changed the address. The only way someone could get to the new one would be to know it directly."

"Why would she do that?"

"To make it difficult to trace her."

A chill went through Ari. That this had happened so close to Sarah's death was too coincidental. The murderer was behind it. "Could you still do it, though?"

"Oh, sure, with some work. We'd need a warrant first, but we've got someone working on it—wait a minute. Josh wants to talk to you."

There was some mumbling on the other end, as if Paul had put his hand over the receiver, and then Josh's voice came on. "Ari? Paul just told me about the website."

"Strange, isn't it? What happened in the meeting?"

Josh drew breath in through his teeth, by the sound of it, and then let it out. "We're going to trace her through the Internet," he said in a low voice. "Also, the postal inspectors are going to watch the Boston P.O. box."

"Good."

"It might not mean anything. Whoever this is, isn't necessarily our murderer."

"You don't believe that."

"No." Again his breath whistled out. "If she's not, it's damned coincidental."

"I know. After what Sarah told me—oh, darn."

"What?"

"A memory trying to get through. I've got a few of those."

"Such as?"

"If I knew, I'd've remembered them, wouldn't I? I've just got this feeling they're important."

"All the more reason for you to lie low. She's ruthless, Ari. Look who she's gone after. She probably set the Camachos up—"

"You think so?"

"Yeah, though I can't prove it. She went after you, and probably Mrs. Mailloux, too."

Ari closed her eyes. "It's a nightmare."

"Yeah. She's local, Ari. I know that's hard for you to believe, but it's true."

"Yes," Ari said in a small voice, at last accepting the truth of that. The evidence was too overwhelming to ignore. "What do I do, then? If she's already suspicious of me, how do I act?"

"As normal as possible. Shocked at what's happened, stunned, confused."

"I can do that," she said, not without irony.

"Yeah. It wouldn't hurt if you said that you hope the police figure it out soon."

"Meaning I have nothing to do with the investigation?"

"Yeah. We'll have to hope she believes it."

Ari shuddered. It could be almost anyone she knew. Anyone. It terrified her. "All right," she said finally. "I'll watch it."

✂

In the late afternoon, the front door opened, and feet pounded down the hallway. "Mommy!" Megan cried, and ran toward her.

"Hey." Ari, who'd just gotten up from the sofa,

nearly staggered off her feet with the force of Megan's embrace. "I guess you missed me, kiddo."

"Oh, Mommy," Megan said, and started to cry.

"Hey. What's this?"

"I thought—I thought you wouldn't be here."

"Oh, honey, of course I am. Where would I be?"

"We heard about the murder on the way home," Ted said, his voice quiet and grim.

Ari looked swiftly up. "Oh, no. Did you think—"

"No. They said who it was."

Ari looked down at Megan, who still clutched her tightly. "Then what is it, honey?"

"I thought—I thought you'd be in jail."

"What?" Ari exclaimed. "Why would you think that?"

"Jacob Pina—he said that's where you were going, and—"

"I knew it," Ari said. "I knew he said something to you. But, honey, he's wrong."

Megan pulled back, her face red. "But we heard—"

"I know, honey." Ari pushed her hair back. "But I have nothing to do with it." Not directly, at least. "Is that what's been bothering you?"

"Yes."

I could kill that kid. "No, Megan. It won't happen."

"But you went to the hospital," she said in a small voice.

"And that's not happening again, either."

"You promise?"

"Viking honor," Ari said, putting her fingers to her

head, and Megan giggled. "It's really going to be all right, Megan. Really." She pulled back. "You okay?"

Megan was wiping her face with her fingers. "Yes."

"Good." Ari rose, though Megan still leaned against her. "Did everything go okay, Ted?"

"Fine, until this." He looked baffled. "She had a nightmare last night, though."

"I'm not surprised."

"What are you doing, Ari? This has got to stop."

"But what can I do?" she said helplessly. "I didn't ask for any of it to happen."

"Yeah, but . . ."

After a moment, she nodded. With everything that had been happening, she'd spared barely a thought to the effect on her daughter. Yes, she knew she'd been feeling the strain; yes, she knew that the attack on her had upset Megan. What she hadn't realized was how badly Megan had been affected. Guilt spread through her. She'd been too wrapped up in other things to notice. "Honey, how long have you felt this way?"

Megan gulped. "Since Mrs. Perry died."

"That long?" Ari exclaimed.

"That's when Jacob started saying it."

"So what do we do about this, Ari?" Ted said.

"She's seeing the school counselor." Ari paused. "But maybe she needs more, Ted."

"A shrink? I don't think so."

"All of us," she said, the idea firming in her mind. "You, me, Megan. Family counseling."

"I don't need that," he said sharply.

"Ted, we're all in this. I can't be the only cause."

Again she paused. "The divorce," she said, and felt Megan wiggle against her.

"That's not it."

"It's part of it," she argued. "Ted, we need to do this."

"Yeah, maybe," he said finally. "I'll think about it."

"Do that. I'll find out who we should see."

"Yeah. This can't go on, Ari."

"I know," she said, pushing a strand of hair away from her face. In the past weeks she'd thought about the impact Edith's death had had on herself, on Diane, even on her shop. What she hadn't bargained on was how it affected Megan. *Idiot. Shortsighted, stupid idiot.* Ted was right. Josh had been right, before he'd roped her into the case again. She needed to stop investigating. The only problem was, she couldn't. She was too far into it.

Tuesday dawned raw and gray, with a damp northeast wind that chilled people to the bone. Last night's wind-whipped rain had stripped many trees of their leaves, which now lay in sodden piles in gutters or on sidewalks. The long spell of beautiful weather was over. Winter was coming.

Her spirits as low as the day, Ari opened her shop, reluctant to do so for the first time she could remember. The rainbow of colors arranged on the walls and in bins failed to soothe her. Evil had touched Ariadne's Web, and Ariadne's life. Nothing would ever be the same again.

The weather kept people away—in droves, though those few customers who did come in stocked up on pricey Norwegian and Icelandic wools. The time for wearing heavy sweaters was nearing, not to mention mittens and scarves and hats. Although the cash register filled respectably, it was a slow and boring morning. Ari would almost have welcomed the distraction of doing quarterly taxes. Almost.

"Do you mind if I knock off early?" Summer said as she came out of the back room. "You don't seem to need me today."

Ari looked over from the bin she was stocking with yarn. "I can't pay you for the hours you don't work."

Summer grimaced. "I know, and I could use the money. It's just that I've got an exam coming up tomorrow and I need to study."

"Anything I can help you with?"

"Medieval history."

This time Ari grimaced. "I'm not familiar with much before 1776. Oh, go on." She waved her hand in dismissal. "It's no use both of us being bored."

"Thanks." Summer put her hand in her jeans pocket. "Where are my keys?"

Again Ari looked up, sharply this time. A missing key was a sore spot with her. "Where did you have them last?"

"If I knew that, they wouldn't be lost."

"Smart aleck. You should carry a pocketbook."

"I do," Summer called from the back room. "I still lost my keys."

"That's right." Ari stared at her as she came back

out, this time wearing a bright yellow slicker. "That was the weekend I took Megan down Cape Cod. You had to call my mother to lock up."

"But I did find them. Kaitlyn helped," she added.

"Where?"

"Under the sales counter."

"Where you put them?"

"I guess. I lose things all the time, you know."

"You're too young for senior moments," Ari said, still preoccupied.

"Senior in college. Oh, good." From her jacket pocket she triumphantly produced a key ring. "Here they are."

"We've been too careless with keys," Ari said, not smiling in return. "I lost mine this summer, Kaitlyn lost hers—though, thank God, she doesn't have one for the shop—and you lost yours. There's too much at stake now for us to keep doing that, and God knows there were too many floating around before Edith was killed."

"My God."

Summer's tone made Ari tense. "What is it?"

"When I lost them this summer, anyone could have seen them under the sales counter, and—"

"Anyone could have taken them, made a copy, and returned them," Ari said, finishing the sentence for her. "Summer, do you remember anyone coming in twice that day?"

"No." Summer's face was white. "Someone could have. I think it wasn't a very nice day, and people were looking for things to do. But I don't remember, Ari."

"Not Edith Perry?"

"No. I think I'd remember that, or Mr. Perry, too." She stared at Ari. "Could it have happened that way?"

"Maybe."

"Then I'm responsible."

Ari shook her head. "No. Edith had a key, and she probably got in that way."

"I could have given her the chance. I'm sorry, Ari," Summer said again.

Ari turned away, sighing. At another time she might have let Summer off the hook, but not this time. Summer was a good employee, and she was the kind of person who would beat herself up about this, but she had been careless with her keys. "Just don't let it happen again, or I'll have to take the key away from you."

"But I won't be able to close up when you're not here," Summer protested.

"We'll work something out. I can't have this happening again."

"I know," Summer said, subdued, and looked out the window. "Oh, man, look at that. It's pouring."

Ari sighed again. "Yes, it's a real nor'easter. No one will come out in this weather."

"Now you can read the book you've got in the office."

Ari's smile was a little shamefaced. The thought of picking up her book had occurred to her already. "I've got a new design I should be working on."

"Isn't the author Laurie King?"

"Yes, her Mary Russell series." She made a face at Summer. "Brat."

"Oh, go ahead. All you've done lately is worry."

"With reason."

"You need a break, and I need to study." Summer took a deep breath, straightened her shoulders, and pulled her hood firmly onto her head. "Yuck," she said, and went out.

Left alone, Ari stopped smiling, with the last few moments replaying themselves in her mind. The thought that Summer had misplaced her keys again was troubling. Of course there had been few enough people in today that Ari had been able to watch them all. Since that hadn't been true in the past, though, anyone could have taken Summer's keys, even a customer. It could be the answer to the question of how someone could have gotten in to attack her.

The bells over the door rang, making Ari look up from her book. "Mrs. Taylor," she said in surprise. "What are you doing out on a day like today?"

"I had a doctor's appointment and thought I'd stop in." Ruth massaged her fingers. "This weather does me no good, but I couldn't cancel."

"No, of course not. Would you like tea? I was just thinking about making some."

"Yes. What do you have today?"

"Earl Grey," Ari called from the back room. "Loose. I bought it at High Tea."

Ruth climbed stiffly onto one of the stools behind the sales counter. "Expensive," she commented.

"Yes, but good." Ari busied herself measuring tea leaves into the pot she'd just warmed with hot water. "Especially in this weather, with the wind off the water."

"I'm glad I put in my replacement windows this summer."

"How are they working out?" Ari asked, interested. The windows in her house rattled and let drafts in, but she had yet to look into replacing them.

"I love them. The house is so much warmer, and those old sash windows always stuck in the summer."

Ari paused in the act of pouring the tea. Discarding old windows meant that old parts had been discarded as well. Everyone in town had known of the project. The historical commission had given Ruth a hard time, insisting she put in wooden windows rather than the vinyl ones she wanted. And the old paint could match the murder weapon's, whereas it hadn't matched the Camachos'. It could have been planted in their shed, too, she thought.

"My house gets so drafty in winter, and it's a hassle putting up the old storm windows," Ari said, to cover her sudden abstraction.

"Ted never was very handy, was he?" Ruth wrapped her hands around the mug Ari handed her. "Ah. This does my old bones good. That's new," she commented, indicating a bulky fisherman sweater draped with careless flair on the counter.

"Moira brought it in last week." Ari referred to one of the women who knit samples for her, in this case Aran and Guernsey sweaters, and accessories. "The stitches are from Galway. She's planning a series from each county in Ireland."

"Are the stitches that specific?"

"Supposedly." Ari took a sip of her tea. "Ruth, did

you know Edith was buying patterns on the Internet?"

"No. From your website? How is that working, by the way?"

"Slowly." It wouldn't hurt to give Ruth some information, Ari thought. With Ruth's curiosity, she'd be searching for the pirated patterns. Maybe she'd find them. "No, she got them somewhere else. Someone's been selling my designs online."

Ruth gazed at her with avid eyes, apparently thrilled at this tidbit of gossip. "Who is it?"

"I've no idea."

"Are the police trying to find out?"

Ari shrugged. She had no intention of compromising a police investigation. "I think they have other things on their minds."

Ruth's face grew serious. "Poor Sarah. To be mugged in Freeport, of all places. Are you going to the funeral?"

"Yes." Ari sipped her tea, vaguely troubled, again with that feeling that there was something she'd missed. Several somethings, actually, things she'd heard or seen that she suspected were important.

"At least she wasn't killed in your shop," Ruth went on.

Ari caught her breath at the mischief, and the hint of malice, in Ruth's eyes. Of course she'd suspect that the two murders were connected. "That's just silly."

"Oh, of course. Still, you must admit it's strange. Two murders here, of all places, and so close together. Now if they had happened on the waterfront, it would be much more understandable."

With a spurt of her own malice, Ari almost shot back that both victims had been elderly women, like Ruth herself. "I doubt there'll be any more."

"I do hope not." Ruth clambered down to the floor. "I don't know why you have such high stools," she complained.

"They keep me awake on quiet days."

"Nonsense, you hide in your office and read. Dear, dear, look at that." Ruth glanced out the windows as she tied a plastic rain bonnet firmly in place over her tightly permed curls. "I do hope you're right about the murders," she went on. "He seems to be going after old ladies."

"Oh, I don't think you have to worry," Ari said hastily.

"Of course not. Well." She popped open her umbrella. "Out into the storm," she said, and went out.

Ari breathed a sigh of relief as she went back to the counter and picked up the mug of now-tepid tea. Ruth was not easy to deal with at the best of times. Underneath she was kind, but her tendency to gossip made many people avoid her. It was one reason Edith Perry had disliked her. In spite of her well-known and controversial actions, Edith hadn't liked having her business talked about. It was no secret that there'd been no love lost between them.

Idly, Ari doodled a floral design, and then climbed down from the stool. In spite of the book waiting for her in the office, she had work to do. The idea of Ruth as a murderer, as she and Josh had once discussed, really was improbable. So she had motive, especially since Edith had complained so much about Ruth's grandchildren. So she might know how to make a web page from classes at the senior center, and she'd had easy access to old windows this summer. She probably even had a cane, but so what? Her age made her an unlikely murderer. So did her arthritis, even if it wasn't severe. Most important, though, was that Ruth, for all her gossip, was neither vicious nor secretive. Her thoughts and feelings were usually easy to figure out. Ari would certainly have known if Ruth disliked her, thus making her a target as much as the victims had been. Because there was the question that had always been a stumbling block in this case. Why had the murder taken place in her shop?

Bemused, and more than a little confused, Ari knelt to stock yarn in the floor bins. It was a soothing, almost mindless activity, leaving her mind free to wander. Ruth Taylor, murderer, she thought with a little smile. There was a picture in her mind of the short, plump woman swinging a cane above her head, looking as ludicrous and deadly as a cream puff. Or even more absurd, her grandson's hockey stick.

Ari rocked back on her heels, lips parted, eyes staring. The vague thoughts and memories she'd struggled with suddenly came into focus. A hockey stick. Someone who had access to a key. Even the choice of yarn as a murder weapon. "Good God," she said, her voice resounding in the stillness of the shop, and scrambled to her feet.

Stumbling into her office, she grabbed for the telephone and sent it crashing to the floor in her haste.

She was swearing more than she ever had as she hauled it up from the floor and punched in the numbers, her fingers so clumsy that at first she reached a stranger's answering machine. Finally, she got through to the police station.

"Bouchard," a harried voice said on the other end.

"Paul. Is Josh there?"

"No. He's in Boston. Listen, Ari—"

"Boston! Did they get her?"

"Things are moving," he said cautiously.

"Are they going to arrest her? Who is she?" she asked, wondering if her deduction would be proved true so easily.

A squeaking noise over the line told her he'd leaned back in his chair. "Can't tell you that, Ari."

"But—"

"I've got to go, Ari. There's a fire in North Freeport they think is arson."

"Arson! Paul, what's happening to this town?"

"Yeah, it's bad. Listen, I'll have Josh call you when he comes in," he said, and hung up the phone.

Ari stared at the buzzing receiver in her hand. She knew who the murderer was. If he'd waited just a few moments she would have told him all that she knew, the who, why, and how of Edith's murder. Now she had no one to tell.

Incensed, she slammed back in her chair and punched in some numbers on the phone. "Josh Pierce," a hushed voice said a moment later, on his cell phone.

"Josh, it's Ari. I think—"

"I can't talk," he said, sounding tense.

"But—"

"Things are happening. I'll call you back."

Again Ari stared at the receiver as the dial tone buzzed at her, and then put it down. Here she was with such important news, and she couldn't reach anyone. Oh, there were other people she could call, the chief of police or the D.A. They didn't know she'd been investigating, though, and if they found out, Josh would be in trouble. Beyond that, she wasn't sure she wanted to call anyone. This case had been hers and Josh's from the beginning. She felt proprietary about it.

Ari frowned as she crossed her arms over her chest. Her case, she thought, and wondered for the first time exactly why she'd gotten involved in it. Oh, she'd had good and noble reasons, and for a time she'd convinced herself of them. Now, though, now she wondered. Ari the wild, she thought, remembering her younger days. No longer crazy after all these years. But that wildness apparently still was in her. Why else would she have stood against a murderer as she had? Why else was she still doing it, after all that had happened?

To hell with it. Before she could stop herself, she reached for the phone and punched in a familiar number. "Di?" she said. "Want to help me catch a murderer?"

CHAPTER 18

"I'm bored," Diane complained from the back room of Ariadne's Web.

"So am I." Ari was sitting at the sales counter. Outside the rain still poured down, which meant that business had continued slow. "I don't think she's coming."

"Your phone call was awfully vague. Telling her about that website."

"Yes, but as if I'd just discovered it," Ari said, "when she made it hard to find. That's the lure. I wish I hadn't had to leave it on the answering machine."

"I know. We won't know when she's coming. Or if. Anyway, it's a pretty small reason."

"Small things seem to have gotten to her before."

"Not this time, I don't think. Ari, what if she's waiting for you outside? She's been pretty impulsive about attacking people if she thinks she's threatened."

"I know." Ari sighed. "So I'll call the police again."

"It's about time."

"You think I'm nuts for not calling them sooner, don't you?"

"I think it's a hell of a time for you to find your inner teenager again. This is like Lucy and Ethel playing detective. I can hear Joe now." Her voice took on a thick accent. "Diane, you've got some 'splainin' to do."

"How come you get to be Lucy?"

"I can't be a Mertz. I'm a good Portuguese girl."

"Ricardo's Cuban."

"Hispanic. Closer than Mertz." She paused. "What is that, anyway? German?"

"I guess."

"Closer to Norwegian."

"Bite your tongue."

"I'm tired," Diane whined. "I have to go to the bathroom. Joe's expecting me to call."

"Honey, I'm home," Ari said in a creditable attempt at the same thick accent.

"I wish he was."

"Well, if this works he will be."

"If."

"Oh, heck, I guess you're right." Ari stretched. "Let's call it a day. . . ." Her voice trailed off as the door to the shop opened. "Showtime."

"What?" Susan Silveira said from the door, where she was furling her umbrella.

"Susan?" Ari said, confused. "What are you doing here?"

"I got your phone call. You sounded upset."

"Yes, but it's okay. It's something Kaitlyn could help me with, but it's not that important."

Susan came farther into the shop. "I know about websites, too. Are you sure it's something I can't help you with?"

Ari sighed. All the trouble she'd taken to set up this trap, and the wrong person had walked into it. "I'm sure. It's just something I found when I was looking at other people's work." Ari didn't move from behind the counter. "Someone's been stealing my patterns."

"Imagine that." Susan moved into the center of the room. For the first time, Ari noticed the stick she was holding, hidden behind the folds of her umbrella. It was long and thin and rounded, with a crook at the end. It almost resembled a cane, but it wasn't.

"Why do you have Kaitlyn's field hockey stick with you?" she asked, puzzled, and then suddenly she knew what it meant. It had taken her a long time to realize why the idea of hockey made her so uneasy, that the equipment for field hockey gave Kaitlyn a perfect weapon. Kaitlyn, she'd thought, with her skill at designing websites, had probably been the one selling Ari's patterns online. Kaitlyn had known that Ari would be looking at knitting sites online and had attacked her to keep her from finding out anything. Kaitlyn had had access to keys, and to the yarn. Kaitlyn had found out that Edith was downloading those patterns, and had been threatened as a result. It was Kaitlyn who had lured Edith here, to her death, or so Ari had thought. "Susan? What are you doing?"

"Oh, get off it, Ari." Susan's smile was chilling. "You know why I'm here. No, don't go for that phone."

Ari stayed still. "Don't do anything stupid," she said, so steadily she surprised herself. "They're close to figuring this out."

"Not as long as they've got your friend Joe in jail."

"And the other attacks?"

Susan prowled around the counter. "Isn't it awful how Freeport's going to the dogs? Muggings, in this town."

"They know the weapon's the same," Ari said, though of course there was no conclusive proof of that.

"So? How can they prove it?" Susan said in a weird echo of Ari's thoughts.

"Then you admit it?" Ari said, a heavy feeling in her stomach. Until now, she hadn't really believed she was right.

"Why not? You already figured out that Kaitlyn stole your patterns. I told her to hide that website. If you found it, you didn't do it this morning. Now, get out from behind that counter."

"And let you hit me? I don't think so."

"It's a long stick," Susan said, and smashed it down on the sales counter.

That got Ari up. She sprinted for the center counter, barely dodging the stick as it slashed down again. "Jeez, Susan!"

"You knew what you were doing." Susan stalked her on the other side of the counter, stick held high. She was an athlete, Ari remembered, an avid golfer. "You knew I'd come."

"I thought Kaitlyn would come. Susan, anyone looking in will see you!"

"No one will look in on a day like today, and if they do they'll think I'm a customer."

"Get real. Someone has probably seen you with that hockey stick." Ari dodged around the corner of the counter as Susan moved toward her again.

"The police would be here by now."

Had Diane called 911 yet? Ari wondered. Because this had been a really, really dumb idea. "Look, don't do this, Susan. Don't make things worse than they already are."

"Why not? You know too much."

Again Ari dodged around the counter, and her eyes lit on something. Diane's yarn. This time it was honey tan, rather than the purple heather, but maybe . . . "No, really. Why did you do all this? I think I know, but—"

"Okay, Miss Smarty-pants Detective. Just what do you know? And talk fast. I'm meeting someone later to look at a house."

The casualness of that was chilling. The significance suddenly glared out at her. "You were Edith's real estate agent."

"So?"

"She had a key to the shop. Did you have one, too?"

"Of course I did. I showed this building, after all."

Ari sucked in her breath. "You had one the last time, too, didn't you?"

Susan smiled. "Bill was kind enough to give me one. He didn't know I had a copy made, of course."

When Ari saw her landlord, she was going to kill him. "You came in here ahead of time and got the yarn, didn't you?" she said, circling to the end of the counter, near the back room. "But why did you kill Edith, Susan?"

"Don't you know?" Susan's face darkened. "I was her agent, but she fired me."

"What?"

"Do you realize how much I would have made in commission on that Drift Road development? And she just cut me out. She wanted to sell it on her own and save my fee. My God, and she had all the money in the world."

Ari wasn't quite sure why Susan was telling her all this, when her reason for coming here was obvious. The longer Ari could keep her talking, though, the better. "It's about money, then?"

"Of course it's about money. Do you know how broke we are? No, of course you don't. Kaitlyn had to leave RISD—do you know what that meant to me?"

"I can guess."

"No, you can't. You've had all the opportunities in the world and you wasted them, while my Kaitlyn, with all her talent, is getting nowhere. So she was selling your patterns. She needed the money, and then Edith spoiled that, too."

"That argument in the library," Ari said, suddenly figuring it out. "Edith found the site, didn't she?"

"Yes. Stand still!"

Ari dodged around the counter, just as Susan brought the stick down again. So far she'd been lucky not to get hit, but that couldn't last. "And she was going to tell."

"She was going to expose Kaitlyn. I couldn't let that happen." Susan lowered the stick slightly. "You're a mother. You understand that I had to protect her."

Ari shivered compulsively. "By killing Edith? Surely there had to be another way—"

"What? Confessing? Letting Kaitlyn get into trouble? Oh, no. Not my little girl."

"But to kill her? Susan, why here?"

"I told her you had some new designs you hadn't published yet, and I could get them for her, if she came to the shop." Her smile was malicious. "Getting at you was a side benefit."

"What do you mean?"

"You wouldn't let Kaitlyn design anything for this precious shop of yours."

My good God. Susan was crazy. Certifiable. "But she has."

"Not then. What are you doing with that yarn?" Susan demanded.

"I'm nervous." Ari stole a quick glance down at the yarn, now loose in her fingers, and then jumped as Susan raised the stick higher. "Susan, stop it!"

"You know too much. You have to go."

"Susan, you'll be found out."

"I haven't been, so far."

"Where did you get the window stop?" Ari asked, to keep her talking, to buy time.

"The window stop? Oh. For the garrote, you mean.

The landlord in the house we moved into did some work and left junk behind."

"And you left the rest of the wood at the Camachos."

"I wasn't going to—what was that?"

"What?" Ari said, though she'd heard it, too, a tiny gasp from the back room. Until this moment Diane hadn't known the significance of the window stop.

"I heard something. Are we alone in here?" she demanded.

"Don't you think I'd've called for help by now?" Ari shot back.

Susan eyed her distrustfully. "Will you stop moving?"

"Don't be stupid. I don't intend to be a target for you." She shook her head. "Kaitlyn's in trouble, too."

"Not if I can help it!" Susan swung the stick down viciously, apparently done with talking. It slammed into the counter and she danced back, her hand involuntarily going to her shoulder. So she was hurt. *Good*, Ari thought.

Susan was an athlete, though, and could deal with pain. Before Ari could get out of range, the stick came crashing down again, perilously close to her own shoulder. "I'm going to get you, no matter what you do."

"What threat was Sarah Mailloux to you?" Ari asked, still working with the yarn, unwinding it from the skein and looping it in her fingers. It might be stupid of her, but she had to get Susan to admit to that crime, and then scream for Diane to call 911. "What threat was she to you?"

"She knew where Edith got the patterns. She mentioned it when we played golf together."

"So what?"

"She would have figured it out. Just like you, when you started looking at the Internet."

"You were there when I said I was going to look for designs online. Is that why you attacked me?"

"Kaitlyn was afraid you'd find the site."

"My God, Susan, does Kaitlyn know about this?"

"No! She has no idea."

Uneasily, Ari wondered if that were true. Kaitlyn had to at least suspect her mother's actions. Kaitlyn, she remembered suddenly, hadn't wanted to play field hockey the other day. Had she realized that her stick had been used as a weapon? "You attacked me for nothing. I didn't find anything."

"You would have, sooner or later."

"Did you mean to kill me?"

"I don't think so." Susan pondered that. "Maybe. I really wanted to throw you off for a while."

She had. "You didn't."

She shrugged. "It was worth a shot. Damn it, stop moving."

"Susan, killing me won't help Kaitlyn."

"It'll protect her from being found out."

"The police already know! They've got her on mail fraud."

"What?" For the first time, Susan looked uncertain. "What are you talking about?"

"They know about the post office box in Boston."

"And that's your fault, too!" Susan cried, and with that abandoned her careful stalking. She raced forward, stick held high.

Ari barely reacted in time, sprinting away. "Call 911!" she yelled, hoping she hadn't left it too late, hoping her idea would work. The yarn she held was a fragile weapon against a hockey stick, but it was all she had. Hoping against hope, she tossed the tangled loops onto the floor.

Susan's face contorted in anger. "There *is* someone else here!"

"Yes," Ari gasped as Susan rushed her, and, with a prayer that her plan would succeed, that her timing was right, yanked on the end of the yarn she held with all her might, just as Susan stepped into the loops. Susan's arms windmilled for balance as she stumbled forward, her other foot tangling in the yarn. With the reflexes of an athlete, though, she recovered. *Shit,* Ari thought, and pulled on the loops again. This time Susan lurched forward. Ari's foot shot out, hard, and caught Susan on the ankle. It was enough. Susan fell heavily, her stick clattering to the floor.

As quickly as that, it was over. Ari sprinted toward the door, gulping in great breaths of air. On the floor, Susan, cursing the air blue, struggled to get up. "Diane? Di?" Ari called.

"Jeez, Ari!" Diane ran out from the back room. "You cut that close, didn't you?"

"Did you get it?"

"Yeah, it's all on tape. Every word." Something gleamed in her eyes. "My yarn?"

"Appropriate. Don't get up, Susan. We both played sports," she warned, and turned at the sound of car doors slamming outside. "Thank God. The cavalry's here."

"God knows what they'll think of this." Diane looked down at Susan, who was sitting with her head in her hands. "Lucy, you got some 'splainin' to do."

"I could kill you myself." Josh's fingers gripped Ari's arm as he marched her toward her office. The murk of the day had faded to darkness, punctuated by flashes of light from the police cruisers parked outside. "What the *hell* did you think you were doing?"

"You weren't there, and I had to do something," Ari said, knowing her defense was weak.

"So you decided to play Nancy Drew?"

"No, Lucy."

"What?"

"Nothing. I know it was stupid, Josh. Really stupid." She turned to him. "I guess I wasn't thinking."

"You weren't. We'd've gotten her, Ari, without you pulling such a stunt."

"It worked."

"You nearly got killed."

"I also got her to confess."

Josh pulled at his ear. "Her lawyer's already making noises about the confession being inadmissible."

"What? Why?"

"Because it was taped without her consent."

"Oh, come on! What about my testimony, and Diane's? No one forced Susan to say what she did. I didn't force her to come after me, either."

"You knew she would."

"No, I thought it would be Kaitlyn."

"Setting a trap with you as bait? Damn it, that was stupid."

"Yes, it was," Ari admitted. "But I never thought it would be Susan."

Josh wheeled toward her. "You should have left it to us. Ari, I thought you had faith in me."

That made her blink. "I do," she protested.

"It was only a matter of time. Kaitlyn did rent that P.O. box."

"But that only links her to the website, not to the murders, and it doesn't implicate her mother."

"We would have gotten a search warrant for her house. Believe me, we wouldn't have missed that field hockey stick."

Ari digested that for a moment. Of course they wouldn't. She really had been stupid. "Do you think you'll get anything from it?"

"Maybe. She washed it, but where it's wood my guess is we'll find some blood in it."

Ari shuddered again. "Then she'll be linked to the killings."

"Yeah. Solid physical evidence. We've got her, Ari."

"Good," Ari said, and fell still, looking at him.

Josh returned the look, and for a moment they stood facing each other, at loose ends now that the intensity of catching a murderer was behind them. "Well," Josh said finally. "You'll finally be getting back to normal."

Ari tossed a quick, distracted glance around her office. "Whatever normal is. Everything's upside down."

"Yeah. Listen, Ari—"

"Detective?" someone called from the salesroom. "Can you come here?"

"Yeah," Josh called, and then turned back to her. "I've got to go. You okay?"

"Oh, yes, fine." She pulled her Scandinavian cardigan close about her. Somehow, though, she doubted she'd be warm for a long, long time. "Will you let me know what happens?"

"If I can. It's in the D.A.'s hands now, though. Or the feds. They're fighting over jurisdiction."

"Oh. I didn't think of that."

"Yeah." He stood there awkwardly, and the air was filled with unspoken promises. "Well," he said finally, looking away. "See you around, I guess."

"Yes. See you," Ari said, curiously deflated, and watched him walk away.

So it had ended where it began, she thought, standing in the office doorway and looking out at her shop. It felt eerily familiar to see police at work at what was again a crime scene, though she knew that wouldn't last. Soon Ariadne's Web would be hers alone again, and life would return to normal. Not unchanged, though. Not even the most optimistic person would say that. What a waste it had been. Though in some ways Edith Perry's death had benefited people, she still didn't deserve to die as she had. Nor had Sarah, who had never hurt a soul. Even she herself had been in danger, and her life had been touched in other ways. Her friends had been in trouble. Her daughter still was in trouble, clinging to her, afraid, insecure. That alone was something she'd never forgive Susan for. That was something she'd never forgive herself for.

The biggest life wasted, though, was Kaitlyn's. In spite of everything, Ari mourned for her. Kaitlyn would probably never have been a top-flight designer, but she still could have had a good career. Instead she had chosen a different way, and her life might as well be over.

"Excuse me," one of the policemen said, and she moved to the side to let him get on with his work. She sighed. As much as she wanted to keep watch over her shop, she was only in the way. High time she left, and put this strange, unexpected part of her life behind her.

The rain had stopped, Ari saw, as she stopped in the shop doorway to button up her cardigan. There'd be frost in the morning, bringing in more customers. Maybe she had played at being Nancy Drew, she thought, but in her real life she was a designer, a knitter, a shop owner. Dyed in the wool, that was what she was, and what she intended to stay.

As God is my witness, I'll never be involved in a murder again, she thought, and went out into the night.

PATTERNS FROM ARIADNE'S WEB

I am not a knitting designer, but below I've provided three projects that I think you will enjoy. For pictures of these projects, as well as other ideas, please visit my website at www.geocities.com/marypkruger.

PADDED COAT HANGERS

Rug yarn, one skein
Size 10 ½ needles
Wooden coat hanger, without bar across bottom

Cast on 9 stitches. Work in garter stitch (knit each row) for 35 rows, or until piece is long enough to fit on the coat hanger. Center the piece at the hook; put hook through the middle. Fold piece so that it covers the coat hanger. Using a large tapestry needle and an overcast stitch, sew the short and long edges together.

Note: Adjust number of stitches cast on and number of rows to accommodate the tension of your knitting.

FAKE FUR SCARF 1

2 balls eyelash yarn, such as Moda Dea Flip, or
    Lion Brand Fun Fur
Size 13 needles

Cast on 12 stitches. Work in garter stitch (knit each row) until scarf is desired length. Adjust number of stitches cast on for desired width.

FAKE FUR SCARF 2

1 skein thin worsted weight yarn
2 balls eyelash yarn, as above
Size 15 needles

Holding both yarns together, cast on 12 stitches, or number for desired width. Work in garter stitch (knit each row) until scarf is desired length.

Hint: As you work this scarf, stop every few rows to tease out the eyelashes with the point of your needle. Otherwise, they will be knitted into the worsted yarn. Use a relatively thin worsted yarn, or the scarf will knit too tightly and will be too bulky.

Pocket Books
proudly presents

KNIT FAST, DIE YOUNG

Mary Kruger

Now available in paperback
from Pocket Books

Turn the page for a preview of
Knit Fast, Die Young . . .

CHAPTER 1

"It's a small world, eh?" Diane asked Ari, looking across Barn B, the main barn where the Freeport Wool and Yarn Festival was being held. It was a cold, wet morning and the area near Ari and Diane's booths had been pretty quiet for over an hour. "Jeez."

"What?" Ari asked, following her gaze.

"Look who just walked in."

"Wow." Ari stared at the woman who stood just inside the open barn door, eyeing the booths around her with a small frown. "Felicia Barr? What the heck is she doing here?" Ari asked.

"I didn't think she ever left Manhattan." Diane and Ari watched as Felicia began to make her way around the barn, her nose wrinkling as if she smelled something distasteful. Unlike most of the other women at the festival who wore handmade sweaters, Felicia wore a fine-gauge turtleneck under a matching coat. From this distance, both appeared to be cashmere. Her tailored slacks looked equally expensive, and so did her high-heeled leather boots. All were black, as suited someone from Manhattan, except for the paisley shawl tossed gracefully about her shoulders.

"Are those designer boots?" Diane asked, sounding awed.

"You're asking me?"

"You're the former New Yorker."

"Yes, but I'm no fashionista. And I hate black. Wow, look at her," Ari added.

Felicia's presence had an impact far out of proportion to her appearance. Vendors had come to attention all around the barn, some scrambling to display their stock more attractively. *It will probably be in vain,* Ari thought. Felicia owned and edited a small knitting magazine, *Knit It Up!*, which, like Felicia herself, had more influence than seemed warranted. If she liked someone's work, she said so, but if she didn't the consequences could be disastrous. Her word carried a lot of weight.

"Brace yourself," Ari said. "She'll find something about your yarn to pick on."

Diane looked at Ari curiously. "You knew her in New York, didn't you?"

"We met years ago."

"I never heard you talk about her. Actually I've never heard you say much at all about New York."

"Oh, come on. I sent you emails all the time."

"Full of all the things you were doing there and sounding happy." Diane studied her. "I don't think you were."

Ari shrugged. Immersed as she was in her life here

in Freeport, she rarely talked about the brief time she'd lived in the city after graduating from college. She'd been ambitious then, certain she'd make a huge splash in the design world. "I missed Freeport. I decided I could sell my designs just as easily from here. And of course I met Ted." That wasn't the whole story, but it would do for now.

"Oh, yeah, Ted. He was a real catch." Diane's voice was sardonic, but her face, as she continued to study Ari, was thoughtful. "Did she ever criticize you?"

"Who, Felicia? Yes." Ari looked down at her project, wondering for a second what Felicia would say. It didn't matter, she told herself. She was as successful as she wanted to be; Ariadne's Web had turned a profit earlier than she had expected, and her designs, which she marketed herself, were popular. She had nothing to fear from Felicia. At least, she didn't think so.

"Who's that woman following her?" Diane asked.

"I think it's Debbie Patrino, her assistant."

"The one who does all the work?"

"So people say. If she does, she's smart enough not to brag about it. Not like Beth Marley, Felicia's last assistant," Ari said. "It got her fired."

Debbie trailed in Felicia's wake, and while her gaze was sharp, there was a half smile on her face. Like her employer she wore all black, but there the resemblance ended. Debbie was tall, with flame colored hair that spilled over her shoulders. She was also much younger than Felicia. "I've heard Debbie doesn't take much from anyone," Ari added. She watched Felicia continue her progress around the barn, leaving in her wake many angry and disgruntled vendors. "I wonder whose reputation she's going to slay this time."

"You think she will?" Diane asked. "This is a small festival."

"I don't think it will matter. Brace yourself."

Felicia walked up to Diane's table. Reaching down, she pulled out a skein of rich teal blue yarn Diane had spun and frowned. "Chemical dyes," she said disdainfully.

"Yup," Diane answered cheerfully. She never had been one to let people push her around. "I find the natural ones too much work." Diane's gaze went to Felicia's expertly highlighted hair, styled in a French twist. "Chemicals can work miracles."

Ari let out a sound that was something between a snort and a laugh. It drew Felicia's attention to her. "What sort of work do you do?" Felicia demanded.

Ari only smiled. In spite of her experiences in New York, she had never been truly intimidated by Felicia. "Hello, Felicia," she said.

Felicia looked at her more closely and finally recognized her. "Ariadne Jorgensen? I'd heard you live in the sticks now."

"I like it here."

"New York scared you," Felicia said flatly. "You ran away."

"Oh, give it a rest, Felicia," Ari said. "I'm happy here. I like being my own boss. You should come by my shop. I think even you'd like it."

"I've seen some of your designs. They're not bad," Felicia said grudgingly.

"High praise, Felicia," Ari said.

"Hmpf." In spite of her apparent annoyance, a smile lurked in Felicia's eyes. "It's more than can be said than most of what's here."

"Oh, come on. That's not true."

"There's not an original design in the bunch."

"Then why did you come here?" Diane asked.

Felicia looked Diane up and down, frostiness in her manner again. "Do I know you?"

"No," Diane said, still cheerful.

That seemed to put Felicia off-balance, if only temporarily. "I suppose I must inspect the rest of the booths."

"Are you doing an article on the festival?"

"Maybe," Felicia said vaguely, and with a brief wave, walked away.

"Whew!" Diane said. "What a bitch."

Ari watched Felicia stop at the table covered with yarn from llamas. "She's really not that bad, you know."

"Could have fooled me."

"No, really. You have to stand up to her. When you do, she backs off. You saw that. Most people let her boss them around."

"How to lose friends and influence enemies," Diane muttered.

"Maybe— Oh, my God."

"What?"

"At the door." She indicated the woman who had just entered the barn. "It's Beth Marley."

"Felicia's former assistant?"

"Yes. This should be interesting."

"You've got to be kidding me. *She* worked for Felicia?"

"I know." Ari studied Beth, who could not have been more of a contrast to the elegant Felicia. Small and plump, she had evidently tried to emulate her former boss, but without any success. Her driving coat was well-cut, but even from here the cloth didn't look as fine as Felicia's and the length was not flattering to Beth's figure. Beth also wore boots, but under jeans rather than expensive slacks. The entire effect was undercut by the pink crocheted beret pulled down low on her forehead, instead of at a jaunty angle. "Hard to believe they worked together, isn't it?"

"I can see why Felicia fired her," Diane said dryly.

"Mm. I'm sure her appearance didn't help matters." Ari sat back. "Beth's never been able to find work with a decent magazine since Felicia let her go."

Diane looked at Ari. "Where's she working then?"

"For *Knit Knacks*. In New Jersey, no less."

"I'll bet that's where she got the pattern for the hat."

Knit Knacks was not known for original, or particularly stylish, designs.

"She must hate Felicia's guts," Diane suggested.

Ari leaned forward, riveted at the scene unfolding in front of her. Across the length of the barn, Felicia and Beth had spotted each other.

Diane followed her gaze. "Trouble?"

"I think so."

"Jeez," Diane said as the two women slowly, warily approached each other. "High noon."

"Or a duel. Needles at ten paces."

"Well." Felicia's voice, as high and commanding as ever, echoed through the barn. "Look what the cat dragged in." If people hadn't noticed the coming confrontation before, they had now.

"Not particularly original, Felicia." Beth stood her ground, her voice unexpectedly deep for someone her size. "But I suppose that's to be expected."

"You should talk." Felicia looked Beth up and down. "Where did you get that appalling hat? Oh, let me guess. You made it."

"I did." Beth seemed to stand a little taller. Whatever else she was, she wasn't a coward.

"And proud of it? Dear, dear." There was a slight smile on Felicia's face. "How the mighty have fallen."

"Not yet."

"What is that supposed to mean?"

"Your day will come, Felicia. When you fall you'll have a long way to go." Her smile was almost evil. "I can't wait."

"Oh, my God," Ari, watching in fascination, gasped.

"Was that a threat?" Diane whispered.

"I don't know."

"Wow. I never thought a wool festival could be so exciting."

"Talk about falling," Felicia was saying. "*Contributing* editor. Your reputation preceded you."

"I do a lot for that magazine," Beth said defensively, because her current position was lower than her previous one.

Again Felicia glanced at Beth's hat. "It shows."

"At least we don't steal people's designs," Beth shot back.

The crowd gasped. Felicia gave Beth a long, hard look. "Let's go, Debbie. I don't care for the odor in here," she said, and, to everyone's surprise, stalked out into the rain. Debbie scurried quickly behind her.

"Wow," Diane said. "Is what Beth said true?"

"I doubt it," Ari said. "Felicia can be harsh, but I've never heard of her stealing anything. She seems to have some integrity."

"I thought she praised people if they bought advertising, and criticized them if they didn't."

"I don't know. She was just complimentary to me, and I never advertised with her. I'm not sure she deserved that accusation." Beth was now strutting around the barn, though Ari thought much of her attitude was bravado. "Her articles about advertisers are a little more tactful, though, even if she doesn't like their work."

"Well, that woke everyone up." The atmosphere in the barn was much more lively than it had been earlier in the morning. "Speaking of which, I could really go for a cup of coffee now."

"Go, then."

"Out in the rain? I don't think so."

"Oh, all right." Ari stretched and rose. "I could stand to get out of here for a little while. What size coffee?"

"As large as possible."

"Okay. See you in a minute."

Ari walked across the barn, tugging up the hood of her parka as she went. The rain, windswept and strong, hit her full in the face as she stepped out, making her briefly close her eyes. She could just make out the shape of Barn A, where coffee and refreshments were being sold. The parking lot to her left was a blur. Her wool slacks got immediately soaked from the water running down off her parka, and the mud pulled at her feet

It was a relief to reach Barn A, its warmth hitting her in the face. She looked around with interest at the demonstrators and vendors who were crowded into the small space. The wares here tended to be notions such as hand-turned wooden knitting needles, or brightly colored rovings. Reluctant to go back out in the rain, Ari browsed among the tables, stopping here and there to talk to people. She'd half expected to see Felicia here but there was no sign of her. *She probably left,* Ari thought, moving over to the snack bar at last. *But how had she managed in the mud on her high heels?*

Finally, with two coffee cups firmly wedged into a cardboard holder, Ari walked out of Barn A and paused under the eaves in dismay. The rain had intensified and it showed no signs of letting up. She was already soaked. *Better to get it over with,* she decided.

Head down, Ari hurried as best she could toward Barn B, without spilling the coffee. She couldn't see anyone else outside. There could be a huge flock of sheep twenty feet in front of her, and she wouldn't know. Maybe that was why she stepped into a puddle so deep that the water sloshed over her ankles into her boots, making her curse. That did it. She was going home.

As she paused to examine her boots, she noticed another pair of boots approaching. They were expensive Italian boots and it took her a moment to realize that they could belong to only one person. Ari looked up to see that she wasn't alone in the rain, after all. Felicia was coming toward her, her gait uneven. The black wool slacks which had been so pristine in Barn B were now soaked; her boots were mud-bespattered. "Felicia?" Ari said, startled.

"Mud," Felicia gasped, and stumbled. Instinctively Ari put out a hand to steady her, going off-balance herself when Felicia grasped her arm.

The coffee flew everywhere, splashing Ari's parka and hands. "Ouch!" she exclaimed, and let go of Felicia. Without Ari's support, Felicia lurched forward, and before Ari could move, the woman collapsed against her.

"Felicia," Ari said, startled. "What in the world?"

"I—tried to get—the mud—"

"What?"

"Help," Felicia said, and sagged. Ari grabbed at Felicia's arms, too late. Felicia slipped and crumpled to the ground, pulling Ari off-balance again. But that wasn't what made her stumble back. There was, she realized with horror, a knitting needle sticking out of Felicia's back.

MYSTERY SOLVED!

THESE BESTSELLERS FROM POCKET BOOKS ARE WHAT TO READ NEXT.

G'DAY TO DIE
A PASSPORT TO PERIL MYSTERY
MADDY HUNTER

Someone's about to get bushwhacked when Emily Andrews discovers deadly mayhem down under!

MALPRACTICE IN MAGGODY
AN ARLY HANKS MYSTERY
JOAN HESS

Where do A-listers go when they hit rock bottom? The latest rehab center in Maggody, Arkansas, of course! But not everyone who checks in checks out...

NO WAY HOME PATRICIA MACDONALD

Nothing bad ever happens in Felton, Tennessee. Until a pretty teenager disappears one day. No one saw her killer. And no one knows the truth...

THE DEAD YARD ADRIAN MCKINTY

Mercenary bad boy Michael Forsythe knows that when faced with murder, deceit, and desire, it's kill or be killed. And he's not about to die.

Available wherever books are sold
or at **www.simonsays.com**

 POCKET BOOKS
A Division of Simon & Schuster
A CBS COMPANY

 POCKET STAR BOOKS
A Division of Simon & Schuster
A CBS COMPANY

15607

POCKET BOOKS
BRINGS YOU THE BEST
IN MYSTERY AND SUSPENSE...

CASE CLOSED.

BLOODLINES *AN IRENE KELLY NOVEL* JAN BURKE
Buried secrets, old friends, and new dangers make for a deadly
case with fatal consequences for journalist Irene Kelly.

MERCY FALLS WILLIAM KENT KRUEGER
Murder, greed, sex, and jealousy hide around every corner—and
a deadly secret waits beneath the turbulent surface of Mercy Falls.

AT HELL'S GATE ETHAN BLACK
In the relentless search for justice, a NYPD detective faces a man
powerful enough to destroy everyone and everything he holds dear...

CSI: CRIME SCENE INVESTIGATION:
SNAKE EYES MAX ALLAN COLLINS
An original novel based on the critically acclaimed hit CBS series!

ALICE IN JEOPARDY ED McBAIN
A beautiful widow faces the ultimate nightmare—a man has
kidnapped her children, and will stop at nothing to collect the ransom.

Available wherever books are sold
or at **www.simonsays.com**.

POCKET BOOKS
A Division of Simon & Schuster
A CBS COMPANY

POCKET
STAR BOOKS
A Division of Simon & Schuster
A CBS COMPANY

15064